LAURINDA RUBY

Lily's Cure

An emotional young adult novel

Preface

There is no greater agony than bearing an untold story inside you.

—Maya Angelou

While this story is a work of fiction, it bears the untold story inside of me.

When I turned sixteen, my mother was diagnosed with a rare cancer. The experts told her she had six months to live. So, by doing some quick math, it was clear to me that she would not live to see me graduate from high school. She would never meet my husband, or her grandchildren. Needless to say, she wouldn't be around long enough to see me grow up. Much like the protagonist of my story, I felt average and hopeless.

Watching your parents scream in pain and knowing you can't do a thing to help is, well, a helpless feeling. Every surgery, we knew, could have been her last. They removed her organs one after another until, eventually, her cancer went into remission. She wasn't cancer-free, but the tumors were inactive. All seemed well, for the most part.

One evening while I was at work, I received a phone call from a number I didn't recognize. The stranger on the other end of the phone said my father had passed away unexpectedly. He was only fifty-two years old when he died of a heart attack in his sleep. I was crushed. All the years I'd spent worrying that I would lose my mom to cancer, and it had never happened. Then, in one minute, one phone call, my world had been turned upside down.

As I wrote this story, I began to realize it was not a random work of fiction I had created in my mind. The tragedies I had lived through had seeped into the pages I'd written. The story had slowly begun to mold itself into a scrapbook of my most painful memories. Some of the words were easy to write, and some came with tears. Every word I wrote was like a weight lifted off my heart.

Acknowledgement

I want to thank my friends and family for their unbelievable support.

Chapter 1: The Park

With the breeze, it felt more like January, despite being mid-March. It didn't help that Carl Miller Park was surrounded by a thousand pine trees, making the temperature ten degrees cooler than anywhere else. Georgia's climate was known to have mood swings, so it wasn't too surprising to Colin. The day before it had reached the eighties. Now, Colin could see puffs of smoke coming from his mouth as he exhaled. He sat on a park bench with his arms crossed over his broad chest.

His mom looked at him. "Are you cold?"

"Yes, it's forty degrees outside. Why did we have to do something outside in the middle of March? Couldn't we have taken Lily to a bowling alley or the mall maybe?"

"I think you'll survive." She nudged him. "So, tell me, what's my oldest child been up to these days?"

"Oh, you know, staying inside where it's warm."

"Seriously. I wanna know."

"Nothing new."

"I'm going to need more than that. You dating anyone?"

"Kind of."

"What's her name? How'd you meet her? Details. I need details."

"Olivia. She waitresses at my job."

"What's she look like? Is she nice?"

"She's hideous and mean."

"Stop it. A mom needs to know these things."

"She's very pretty—dark hair, brown eyes."

"Nice?"

"Very nice."

"Was that so hard?" She winked at him. "I'm worried about your sister."

Her words came out so quietly, Colin wondered if she was talking to herself.

"Why?"

When she didn't answer, Colin glanced at his mom. She squinted as the breeze blew through her blonde hair. He waited for her to continue her thought, which she finally did.

"She's been kind of clumsy lately, and yesterday while she was talking, her words slurred."

He wrapped his arm around his mom's shoulders. She was a taller-than-average woman, but compared to him, she felt small. "Mom, you're probably worrying for no reason. She's probably just having a growth spurt. And my speech slurs all the time when I'm tired."

"Well, I'm taking her to the doctor on Monday, just in case." Her gaze hadn't broken away from Lily yet. Something about the way she was looking at her, as if Lily were dying or something, made Colin feel uneasy. Her eyes finally broke away from the playground, and she looked at him with a smile that made the uneasy feeling vanish. "They'll probably say she's fine, but it'll give me peace of mind." She patted his knee and stood up. "I'm going to go check on her. Don't freeze to death while I'm gone."

As his mom walked away, he thought about what she'd said

2

some more. Surely, Lily was fine. Moms worry too much. His gaze shifted to Lily, helping one of the smaller kids go down the slide. He wouldn't have been caught dead playing at the park when he was Lily's age, much less hanging out with his mom, but Lily loved it. She hung out with her friends from school sometimes too, like Natasha or Anna. Most of the time though, she preferred hanging out with their mom. Probably the reason why Mom was always worrying about her. They spent too much time together.

Colin slipped his hoodie over his silky blond hair to block the cool breeze. He could see his mom watching Lily from the edge of the castle-shaped playground. Lily laughed as she slid down the slide like a seal. Lily's laughter was contagious, so Colin laughed too. Another kid who looked half Lily's age, but was the same height as Lily, followed behind her. Then another tween slid down as Lily and the five-year-old ran to the top again, and the cycle repeated.

Colin surveyed the park. Moms, a few dads, played with their children. It wasn't the way he'd envisioned spending his day off, needless to say, but it wasn't so bad. Lily skipped back up the playground to the top of the curvy green slide. His mom held her phone camera up to her doppelgänger and told Lily to hold still for the picture. Lily smiled from ear to ear, showing off her perfect dimples. Her thin blonde hair whipped around her little pink, wind-burned face. Then she slid down again.

Colin closed his dried-out eyes for a moment to block the wind. He heard his mom's voice. It wasn't the words his mom was saying that made his heart stop. It was the tone in which she was saying them.

"Hey, Colin. Come here quick."

He opened his eyes again. His mom was looking back at him.

3

Why did she look so worried? Lily was on her knees. Did she fall? His mom held Lily's hair back while something red dripped out of her nose. Lily looked up at Colin with the most pitiful look he'd ever seen. Every fiber of Colin's body wanted to swoop his sister into his arms and take away her pain. Instead, he stood and watched. Why couldn't he move?

There was so much blood. A sharp pain stabbed his stomach as a grunt came from Lily, followed by a cough and another glob of red. His mom rubbed her daughter's back gently.

"What's wrong with her, Mom?"

"I don't know. She was getting off the slide. Then she just fell and hit her head against the ground."

His mom must have noticed her son's deer-in-the-headlights expression. "Colin, can you call for an ambulance?"

In what seemed like an eternity but was probably only a few minutes later, blood-red lights flashed quickly and rhythmically like his heartbeat as the ambulance whipped into the park's parking lot, almost running over someone's dog. Colin's mom's face was white as she watched people in uniforms spill out of the red and white vehicle. It seemed like everyone else at the park was watching along with her.

The man loading Lily into the back of the ambulance looked at Colin and his mom.

"We only have room for one more person."

"I'll go in the ambulance. Colin, you meet me there, okay?"

Moments later, adrenaline coursed through Colin's veins as he ran a red light in pursuit of the ambulance. These guys weren't messing around. They hadn't even waited for Colin to get in his car before screeching out of the parking lot.

Within eight minutes, they were at the Heart of Georgia Children's Hospital. His mom was pacing around the waiting room when Colin ran through the sliding doors.

"Mom, where's Lily?"

"They took her back. We'll know what's going on soon. Can you stay until your dad gets here?"

"Of course. Mom, you should sit down. You look flushed."

"I can't sit still. If I do pass out, at least I'm at the right place."

She began pacing again. Colin sat in one of the hard plastic seats. His mom called his dad again. It went straight to voicemail. Her text message was short:

Tom, it's Margaret. Come to HGCH.

Colin tried to comfort his mother as they waited to hear from the doctors. He told her that Dad would be there soon. Lily would be okay. He couldn't know if anything he said was true, any more than he could have helped Lily ten minutes prior. It comforted him to say these things, either way.

The phone rang. His mom yanked her finger across the touch screen to put it on speakerphone.

"I'm so sorry, honey. I'm en route now. What happened?"

"She fell and hit her head at the park."

"Do they know what's wrong yet?"

"Not yet."

"I'll be there in a minute."

The woman over the intercom announced something incoherent.

"Dr. Vinn ... rep-t ... r-m ... seven."

Somebody should fix that, Colin thought. Hopefully the care the hospital would give his sister would be better than the care they gave their building.

His dad hadn't exaggerated. A minute later, he was walking through the sliding glass doors. His mom ran into his dad's arms, her head pressed into his chest, smearing her black

5

mascara into his cream-colored button-up. He embraced her and apologized again.

"Sweetie, sit down."

Colin said, "She won't sit. I already tried."

"Thank you for being there for your mom and sister today."

"I didn't do anything, Dad."

"The important thing is, you were there." He paused. "Do you remember why I became an officer a long time ago?"

Colin nodded.

His dad continued. "When my mom got shot by that thug, I was only fifteen. I just watched her die. Stood by and didn't do a thing."

"You were fifteen. I'm twenty-one."

His dad started to reply when an announcement came over the intercom.

"Code bl ... ue ... co ... de blue."

That wasn't for Lily, was it? His mom stopped pacing.

"Did they say 'code blue'? Is that bad?"

"Try not to worry, honey. The doctor will give us an update soon."

His mom looked exhausted as she sat in the chair beside him and then put her head in her hands. A few worried-looking nurses ran through swinging doors. Thankfully his mom didn't seem to notice them. What were they running for? Was Lily okay?

Before he or his mom could panic further, the doctor came back through the swinging doors. His mom jumped to her feet.

"You can all come back now."

Lily smiled at them as they walked into a small room where she was lying on a bed twice her size. Doctors had been running tests on her for over an hour. The doctor, a fit-looking man in his forties, addressed their parents with a solemn tone.

"We have some concerns about the test results."

Colin looked up at his dad.

His mom interrupted the doctor before he could continue. "Is there any way we could discuss this privately?"

"Of course."

Colin waited by Lily's bedside so she wouldn't be alone. It was ten minutes before their parents came back to the room. Somehow, Lily had managed to fall asleep. Colin pulled the thin blanket over her shoulders. How could she sleep at a time like this?

The door creaked open.

"Dad—what's going on?" Colin asked in almost a whisper.

His dad walked to the hallway. Colin followed. Nurses walked around in a hurry. Patients passed by in wheelchairs.

"They think Lily needs to go to a pediatric neurologist." He must have noticed the confused expression on Colin's face. "Like a brain doctor."

"A brain doctor. What for? Lily's healthy."

"We won't know what's going on until we go to the neurologist. She's going to be okay."

"How do you know she's going to be okay?"

"I have to believe she will be or I'll drive myself crazy worrying."

Colin looked around for a five-foot-five woman with blonde hair and gray-blue eyes who was bound to be pacing or demanding that someone give her daughter an extra blanket.

"Where's Mom?"

"I suggested that she go home and wait for us. She didn't want to, of course, but I told her Lily shouldn't see her crying—it'll only make her more scared than she already is. Are you going to be able to go back in that room and act like everything's okay?"

Colin nodded. It was the least he could do.

Chapter 2: Procedure

L ily looked at her mother as the heavy-handed nurse wiped the inside of her elbow with a moist cotton swab, cringing as the needle penetrated her skin. Her mother had warned her not to look. She tried not to, but she couldn't help herself from taking a peek at the tube filling up with blood from her arm. She looked away again, this time feeling nauseous. Lily's breath was short and quick. The round-faced nurse frowned at her, making her look like an angry bowling ball.

"The more you move, the worse this is for you. I'm almost done. Just try to relax."

"My stomach feels kind of funny."

Lily felt a quick pinch.

"All done. Follow me," the nurse demanded.

Lily followed the nurse until they came to the entrance of the bathroom and then stopped. The round-faced nurse handed Lily a small clear cup that looked like a thimble compared to her hand.

"I need your urine sample. Go pee in that and give it back to me. If you don't need to go yet, I can give you some water."

"How am I supposed to give you my pee?" The nurse glanced down at the cup, then back at Lily. "You want me to pee in this?"

The nurse smiled for the first time and nodded slowly.

* * *

Lily whispered as they followed the nurse to another room. "Mom, she made me pee in a cup!"

Her mother laughed and held her finger to her mouth as if to say, *Shhh*. They followed the nurse into a small room with a large bed that was propped up more like a recliner than anything. She placed a folded blue cloth on the bed.

"Change into this. The doctor will be in in a minute."

After the nurse had closed the door, her mom picked up a gardening magazine from the pile of literature on the counter to give Lily privacy while she changed. Lily frowned as she put on the thin, uncomfortable gown. The vent above her head blew cold air down her back. She craned her neck to try to get a look at her backside.

"Why doesn't the back close all the way?"

Her mom looked up from her magazine. "It's not supposed to. That's normal."

Lily tried to pull the strings on the back tighter around her tiny waist. Maybe the nurse gave her the wrong size. She could still feel the cold air brushing steadily against her back. What could be normal about having her backside hanging out for a stranger to see (even if the stranger was a doctor)?

Her mom closed the pages of the magazine when someone knocked on the door before opening. A tan black-haired woman wearing a white coat walked in. She looked younger than any doctor Lily had ever seen. Maybe she was another nurse.

"Hello, my name is Dr. Lakshmi Ahuja. I'll be the resident neurologist seeing you. And you are Lily, correct?" Lily nodded. "Good. Let's just do a few fun tests, okay?"

She clicked the back of the small flashlight in her hand. "Just follow the light with your eyes. Good. Now open your mouth for me. Good. Now I'm going to check inside your ears. Good."

A moment later, she pulled out a triangle-shaped rock and began thumping Lily's knees.

Lily laughed. "Why did my leg fly up when you did that?"

"That's your body's reflex. Like when something comes close to your eyes and you flinch. Like this." The doctor pretended to flinch as she waved her hand in front of her own face. Lily smiled. Dr. Ahuja told Lily to push her arm up while she pushed against it. Then she did the same thing with her legs.

"You're a strong girl."

Lily looked at her mom and smiled. Her mom laughed.

"Can you try to stand on one foot for me, Lily?"

Lily tried, but she couldn't seem to keep her balance.

"That's good enough, thank you. You can sit down again."

Lily tucked her blue gown under her as she sat.

Dr. Ahuja smiled at her. "How old are you, Lily?"

"I turned twelve two days ago," she said with an even bigger smile.

"Well, good, because if you were eleven, I might think that the next test was too scary for you, but since you're twelve ... you won't be afraid at all."

Lily frowned. "What's the next test?"

"It's called an MRI. It stands for magnetic resonance imaging." She paused. "Have you ever played with magnets, Lily?"

"Yes."

"Well, this machine is like a giant magnet, and it allows us to see inside your body. Pretty neat, isn't it?"

Lily nodded hesitantly. "Does it hurt?"

Dr. Ahuja laughed. "Oh, not at all! It's a little loud, but since you're twelve, you won't be frightened at all."

Her mom said, "I've had an MRI before. She's right, Lily. It doesn't hurt at all."

Lily took a deep breath. Dr. Ahuja was right: she wasn't eleven anymore. She had to start acting like a twelve-year-old and be brave.

"Okay."

Chapter 3: The Call

"Ow!" Margaret looked at the small line of blood around her fingernail bed. She had chewed through three nails already as she waited for the nurse to come back to the phone.

"Ma'am, are you still on the line?"

"Yes—yes, I'm here."

"Dr. Ahuja would like for you to come in in person to discuss Lily's results."

"Yes, but like I said, I don't want to wait until Monday to find out what's going on with my daughter."

"Ma'am, I understand, but—"

"Really, you understand?"

"Excuse me, ma'am?"

"Is your daughter sick?"

"No, ma'am."

"Then how could you possibly understand?" She took a deep breath. "I don't mean to be rude, but this will be a lot easier for both of us if you just put Dr. Ahuja on the phone."

"I'll tell the doctor to give you a call."

"When?"

"Ma'am?"

"When will she call me? I don't want to wait by the phone all day. I'd like to be given a time when I can expect her call."

"Ma'am, I can't—" She sighed. "It'll be sometime this morning."

"Can you be more specific?" The line was silent. "Hello?"

The nurse had already hung up.

She rolled her eyes. "Unbelievable."

Margaret got up and poured some more coffee. Caffeine was probably the last thing her nerves needed, but she had to do something. Just sitting there staring at the phone was enough to drive any mother crazy. Every minute in which she wondered if her daughter was okay or not was agonizing. She brought the steaming cup of coffee up to her lips. When the hot liquid touched them, she winced and pulled the cup away so fast that the black coffee spilled out of the other side of the cup and hit her hand.

"For cripes sake!" she yelled.

The steam moved away as she blew puffs of air over the surface of the liquid. The phone made a crisp bell sound that traveled through every caffeinated nerve in her body.

"Aagh!" The coffee had spilled down her favorite white blouse as she jumped to check her phone. It was a false alarm—just a regularly scheduled update.

She'd started to take her blouse off to throw it in the wash (she'd learned over the years to wash white clothes immediately) when she heard a knock at the door. Who on God's green earth could that be?

The short, plump woman who lived next door waved psychotically at Margaret as she pulled back the curtains to peep. Margaret sighed and put on a smile. She'd perfected the art of putting on and taking off her smile, as if it were a mask she could hang up at the end of a long day.

14

"Howdy, neighbor!"

The red-haired woman smiled, and Margaret could see an inch of gums above her rabbit-like teeth.

"Hi, Robin. How are you?"

"Well—" Robin eyed her blouse. "Oh my! It looks like I caught you at a bad time."

"Actually, yeah—"

"Well, I won't be long. I was just wondering if you had some milk to spare."

"I can go look," Margaret said as she turned to check. Before she knew it, Robin was standing in her living room, looking at a picture on top of the black-walnut TV stand. Margaret looked at her phone. It looked the same as the TV stand—black and lifeless. The doctor would call soon, she hoped.

"What kind of milk did you need, Robin?"

Robin seemed distracted by her own snooping. "Oh, whatever kind. Doesn't matter. I just appreciate you doing this. What would I do if I didn't have a nice neighbor like you?"

Buy your own milk? Margaret thought to herself.

Robin walked toward Margaret with her small, stubby hand outstretched and holding a picture of the family that was as big as her head. "Y'all are too cute. You have the most gorgeous children." Margaret started to thank her. "No, I am serious, Margie. You've got some good genes. If my husband and I looked like y'all, we would've had ten babies by now." She cackled, showing her gums again. "You look like a bunch of dolls—like Barbie and Ken. You know what, if I weren't mistaken, I'd say you and Tom were siblings."

"Well, we're not." Margaret faked a laugh and handed her a glass of milk. "Here. Is that enough?"

"That'll be just fine, sugar. Oh! That reminds me. Do you have

15

any sugar?"

Margaret looked at her phone again. "Yeah."

She walked to one of the white cabinets she'd cleaned that morning while she was on hold with the hospital and pulled out an unopened bag of sugar. "Take it. I never use it."

"Oh, I couldn't!"

"Take it. I insist."

Robin's gums showed again as she smiled. "You are even more beautiful on the inside than the outside. Tell me, how's Lily doing?"

"She's going to be okay."

"Oh, good. Well ..." It seemed she was out of things to say but desperately wanted to think of something else. "I guess I'd better get going."

"All right, Robin. Goodbye."

Margaret's phone started to ring before the door had closed all the way. She leaped to the table and grabbed her phone. A moment later, Margaret was listening carefully to Dr. Ahuja as she told her the results of the MRI. She was still trying to catch her breath. It sounded like a bunch of medical gibberish.

"I'm sorry, Doctor. Diffuse intrinsic—what?"

"A diffuse intrinsic pontine glioma. It's an aggressive type of brain stem glioma. Unfortunately, we cannot biopsy the tumor, because of its location, but most of the time these tumors are malignant and will spread eventually."

"What exactly does all of that mean? Her tumor is malignant, so she has cancer, right?"

"The tumor is most likely malignant."

Margaret covered her mouth with her hand to stop herself from yelling. "Dr. Ahuja, let me ask it in a different way. Does she have cancer or not?"

"Based on the location of the tumor, and not based on a biopsy, Lily's tumor is most likely cancerous, Mrs. Durnin. So, most likely, Lily has cancer."

It rolled off her tongue as if she were just saying, *It's foggy outside today, and oh, by the way, your daughter has cancer.*

"Why couldn't you have just said she had cancer, then? Not everyone has attended medical school and understands words like 'diffuse intrinsic'—whatever you called it."

"Pontine glioma. Ma'am, I'm very sorry. This is why I prefer to see my patients in person. Is there any way that we could continue this conversation in my office? I'm afraid that I'm not explaining this very well over the—"

"No, it's not you—I shouldn't be taking this out on you. I'm just ... having a hard time wrapping my head around this." She paused. "Is it curable?"

"Unfortunately, it's not, but it is treatable."

Dr. Ahuja said she was going to refer Lily to Dr. Stephanie Long, whom she considered to be the best pediatric oncologist in Georgia. They'd discuss Lily's treatment options with her. The phone call ended.

Margaret couldn't breathe. How could her daughter, her *daughter*, have cancer? Maybe the doctor was wrong. That sort of thing happened sometimes. They could've mixed up the lab results. Doctors made mistakes too. It had to have been a mix-up.

She stopped pacing when she heard the back door open. Had Robin stopped knocking altogether and started letting herself in? She quickly wiped the tears from her eyes when she saw the blonde ponytail bouncing into the room. Its owner skipped into the kitchen. Margaret glanced at the watch on her wrist. How could it be four p.m. already?

Lily stopped skipping. "Mom, are you okay?"

"Huh? Oh, yeah."

"Were you crying?"

"I'm fine, sweetie. How was school?"

Lily shrugged. "It was okay."

"You know I love you, right?"

Lily tilted her head. "Yes ..."

"Good." Lily looked at her like she thought she was crazy. "Do you have any homework?"

"Yeah, but just a little."

"Okay, go do your homework before you watch TV. I need to lie down for a little while."

"Can I have a juice pouch?"

"Sure, honey."

Margaret closed her bedroom door. No sooner had the door latched than the tears began pouring from her eyes. She ignored the buzzing cell phone in her pocket and buried her face into a pillow. Her shoulders shook as she cried harder than she ever had. How did people survive the pain of knowing their child might die? How did they manage to stay strong while everything inside them felt like it was breaking?

She sat up and checked her phone: one missed call. It was from Thomas. She didn't know what she was going to tell him, but she had to tell him something. Thomas's phone went straight to voice mail. All her text said was:

Call me.

She looked at her watch again; it was 4:47 p.m. She needed to start making dinner, but first ...

Margaret got her old laptop out and set her phone down beside it in case Thomas called back. Her laptop was slower than molasses, but it did the job, eventually. She could hear the TV come on in the living room, so she knew she had at least thirty minutes before Lily would come looking for her.

Margaret thought about Dr. Ahuja's words during their phone conversation while she waited for the laptop to turn on. She thought about what the doctor had said about Lily's type of cancer not being curable ...

Maybe Dr. Ahuja was wrong. Margaret looked at the note she'd written in black Sharpie. It was smeared from her tears but still legible. The keys on her keyboard clicked as she typed in *diffuse intrinsic pontine glioma*.

The results loaded five minutes later. She looked at the images of red and blue blobs on a drawing of a brain. She read several articles until she had no doubts that Lily's tumor was aggressive. Her attention was drawn to one of the articles as she scrolled down the page. She typed, *What is the survival rate of DIPG?* Her finger hovered over the mouse. With one simple click, she could know the answer to the question that was eating away at her the most: What was Lily's chance of surviving? Obviously, she might not like what she saw, but if she didn't she would always wonder. There would be no going back once she knew. Did she really want to count down the days of her daughter's life?

She held her breath and clicked. Tears came back to her eyes. There was no unseeing it now. She wiped her eyes with the back of her stained white blouse. She wasn't going to give up that easily. The keyboard made clicking sounds as she tapped the letters: *cure for DIPG cancer*.

Margaret skimmed over the results on the screen until she noticed the words she'd been looking for. She double clicked. The article was an interview with a man named Dr. Lloyd. She mumbled as she read aloud to herself ...

INTERVIEWER: The world has become obsessed with the de-

19

bate over the recent lawsuit involving your medical research and the animal rights activist organization SEVA. Before I address the lawsuits, may I ask, what exactly are you researching?

DR. LLOYD: The cure for cancer, and we aren't researching it; we have it.

INTERVIEWER: That's a bold statement. What type of cancer would it treat?

DR. LLOYD: The cure will eliminate all cancers.

INTERVIEWER: An even bolder statement. Do you think cancer-treatment industries would lose a lot of revenue if that were to happen?

DR. LLOYD: Frankly, that isn't our concern. The current treatment options kill not only the cancer cells but also the healthy ones. Chemo is essentially no more than a glorified poison. After the patient has been stripped down to nothing, they begin to build them back up for weeks and repeat the process again. As a doctor, I vowed to do no harm. If we have the ability to cure instead of merely treat our patients, it's our responsibility to do so.

INTERVIEWER: That's a strong statement, Doctor. You said you vowed to do no harm. Some would say that testing on rats is inhumane, and is doing harm. Some would say, why not test on humans instead of animals?

DR. LLOYD: Rats are highly predisposed to cancer, and their anatomy is very similar to that of humans, which makes them the easiest subjects to use—even easier than humans. And, frankly, I don't believe the way we run our trials is inhumane. We give them the highest level of care, and we cure their cancer, allowing them to live longer than they would have. What's inhumane about that?

INTERVIEWER: If it's as ethical as you make it out to be,

why do you think you're being sued by so many different organizations?

DR. LLOYD: If I knew that, I would be God.

INTERVIEWER: All right. You said that the cure already exists. So why isn't the cure available to patients with cancer right now?

DR. LLOYD: The tests showed that the cure was effective 80 percent of the time when we applied it to the subjects—

INTERVIEWER: And by "subjects," you mean ...

DR. LLOYD: Yes, I mean rats. The cure worked 80 percent of the time when we applied it to rats with three different types of cancers—pancreatic, brain, and mammary. But until we can begin clinical trials, we can't be approved by the FDA.

INTERVIEWER: When do you think that will happen, Dr. Lloyd?

DR. LLOYD: Your guess is as good as mine.

Margaret slowly closed the laptop. It felt as if she were closing her daughter's casket. Tears rolled down her cheeks. Lily only had a 1 percent chance of surviving for the next five years. It would take way more than five years for a medicine to be approved by the FDA. By then it would already be too late. Without that cure, she'd only have five more years with her daughter, if she was lucky. She sighed and checked her phone again. Where was Thomas when she needed him?

Footsteps were approaching her room. She knew they were Lily's. She pulled her lips forcefully into a smile and opened the door. Lily was standing in front of her with her fist in the air as if she was about to knock.

"I'm hungry, Mom."

"Lily ..." Margaret closed her eyes so she wouldn't see the big blue eyes staring back at her. "I need to talk to you about something."

Chapter 4: Honey, I'm Home

She ignored her tired-looking husband, sitting on their king-size bed with his head buried in his hands, and continued pacing around their bedroom. She couldn't stand to look at him when she was this angry. He hadn't been home for more than thirty minutes, and they were already having one of the worst arguments they'd had in their twenty-plus years of marriage.

"Tom, I know you were in DC working, but the least you could've done was return my phone call."

He set the beer bottle down on the antique dresser. "Margie, I just found out our daughter has cancer. Give me a break. And how could you talk to our daughter about this before talking to me?"

"Oh, don't try to shift the blame here." She slapped a coaster on the antique dresser. "Use a coaster. You would've known two days ago if you'd answered your phone." Margaret stopped pacing and faced him, noticing for the first time that her husband looked like he'd aged five years. It only gave her more conviction to say what came next. "You need to quit your job."

"Sorry, what?" He coughed from almost choking on his beer.

"I'm serious, Thomas. Maybe your being gone for days at a time worked for us before, but now you need to be here in case something happens. Besides, look at you! You look exhausted."

"Gee, thanks." He covered his face with his hand as if it were a shield. "I became a cyber-security investigator because you said being a police officer was too dangerous—"

Margaret interrupted him. "Yeah, well, things change."

"Really? Things change? Oh, I didn't realize that things change." He paused. "What would make you happy? Huh?"

Margaret stood still and looked at him. "If you were here more. That would make me happy."

"Maybe I should work with our son at that dinky Italian restaurant. Then I'd be home *and* poor."

"Yes, Thomas. That's exactly what I meant. You should work at an Italian restaurant. Stop being dramatic."

Thomas rubbed the bridge of his nose. "This is giving me a headache. We shouldn't be arguing. We should be figuring out what our plan is for Lily." He looked at her. She continued pacing around the room. "Of course I'd like to be home more, but we need the money."

"One day you'll look back and wish you had spent more time with your daughter and less time worrying about the stupid bills."

"Well, somebody's got to worry about the stupid bills. Now that you're not going to be working as much at the school, I'll need to work more." He sighed. "Maybe I can ask my boss for more local jobs."

Margaret sat beside him on the bed. "I'm falling apart, Tom. What are we going to do?"

He put his arm around her. "Maybe Dr. Ahuja's wrong. She's not an oncologist. Let's see what Dr. Long says before we panic."

Chapter 5: First Round

Colin looked around the room as they walked: it was filled with balloon wallpaper and bright colors. Kids who looked as young as four years old sat in recliners, tubes coming out of their bodies. Some still had hair, and others wore beanies and scarves where their hair had once been. He was startled by his mom's voice.

"Stop staring, Colin," she whispered.

"Sorry, I'm just surprised—these kids are so young."

"Yeah ... they are."

He glanced at his mother. She looked as sad and tired as she sounded. The nurse they were following stopped walking and told Lily to sit in the large blue recliner. Her feet dangled and swung from a recliner that was too big for her, like Goldilocks in Papa Bear's chair. Lily made a face as she drank the "miracle" concoction the nurse had given her. It would help her to not feel as nauseous from the chemo.

Lily gagged. "It tastes like dog poop."

Colin laughed. "How do you know what dog poop tastes like?"

"I've smelled it, and this tastes like how dog poop smells."

"That's not how it works, Lily."

"How do you know?"

"Well, you love the smell of coffee, but you hate the way it tastes."

Lily shrugged. He knew she hated to admit when she was wrong. "I know this drink is supposed to help me not throw up, but I think it's going to make me throw up instead."

"Just plug your nose and drink it really fast."

Lily plugged her nose and drank faster. A second later she gasped for air and contorted her face until her mouth was next to her ear and her eyebrows had become one fuzzy blonde line. Colin laughed. "Attagirl."

By now the nurse had returned with a rolling cart and a pole with bags of clear fluid hanging from it. She wrapped a plastic band above Lily's elbow and tied it tight. Colin stuck his tongue out at Lily to distract her from the needle that was about to go in her arm. She flinched as the nurse slid the needle in, then stuck her tongue out at Colin. His mother turned and looked at him.

"Colin, I'll be right back. I want to ask the nurse a few questions."

She walked with the nurse until they were too far to overhear their conversation. Lily watched with a worried look on her face. Colin's voice seemed to break into her thoughts.

"What's Natasha and Anna been up to? I haven't seen them in forever."

"Natasha and Anna?" She blinked like she had never heard their names before.

"Your best friends?"

"Oh. Sorry. I was distracted. They started middle school in a different district, so they hang out with their new friends now."

"Have you tried hanging out with their new friends too?"

Lily sighed. "That's not how it works, Colin. Everyone knows that once you go to a new school, you move on. Nobody keeps their childhood friends."

"Uh, hello? I did. Rob's been my friend since elementary school."

"You stayed in the same school district."

"Fair enough. I just think you should at least try."

Lily shrugged.

"Do you want to play a game? We're going to be here for a while."

Lily dug through her pink backpack and pulled out a book. "We could read this."

Colin opened the book she'd brought from home: *The Wandering Girl.* He turned to the page she had bookmarked and began reading about the girl who wandered through a jungle island alone after a shipwreck killed her entire family. It wasn't half bad, for teen-girl fiction. His mother came back and sat on the other side of Lily in an empty recliner. Colin pretended not to notice how worried his mom looked and continued reading about the wandering girl being stalked by a jaguar in the most suspenseful voice he could manage.

"She heard something coming from above her, like the sound of a cracking branch. She knew it could only be one thing … the jaguar, and there was no longer any escaping it. Just as she looked up—" Colin grabbed Lily's hand.

"Aaah!" Lily yelped loud enough to cause her chemo-comrades to glance over at her. His mom gave him and Lily a stern warning look. "Sorry, Mom. Lily's a bad influence on me."

"Whatever!" Lily protested.

His mom managed a weak laugh and went back to looking worried.

Colin continued reading in a hushed voice once again.

An hour later, the nurse returned to take the IV out of Lily's arm. Colin stuck the worm-shaped bookmark into the book and closed it.

"I need to get going, Mom. My shift at Al's starts in an hour."

"Thanks for coming, sweetie."

"No problem." He glanced at his little sister. "Bye, booger."

"Bye, butt—"

"Lily." Margaret shook her head. "Colin, can I talk to you privately before you go?"

Lily oohed.

Colin ruffled his fingers through her hair to mess it up. Suddenly he remembered the other children who didn't have hair to ruffle, and his stomach tightened. He kissed the top of Lily's head and said goodbye, then followed his mom around the corner. She rubbed the back of her hand over the bags under her gray-blue eyes and looked at him.

"The oncologist, Dr. Long, said that Lily needs to do one round of chemo every week for right now. Then, hopefully, if all goes well, Lily will only need chemo every other week. Do you think you could try to come again next week? I think it helped Lily to have you here."

"Sure." He paused. "Hey, Mom?"

She lifted her eyebrows as if to say, *I'm listening.*

"Why isn't Dad here?"

"He's working."

"I know, but couldn't he take one morning off? It's only one day a week. You look really tired—no offense. I mean ..." She smiled as he fumbled. "Like, you look—"

"Colin, I know what you mean, but I don't feel like discussing this right now." She raised herself up on her toes and kissed his cheek. "But I love you, and I appreciate you coming with us today."

"No problem." He hesitated. "Mom, what did you ask the nurse?"

"I asked her how long we had before Lily would lose her hair."

Chapter 6: Hair

Margaret pulled another clump of hair from the brush and threw it in the small trash can. She stopped brushing and looked at her daughter through the vanity mirror. Her heart hid itself somewhere deep inside her chest. What was left of the once-beautiful girl with bright-blue eyes and long blonde hair, now a pale, gray, sickly child with little tufts of hair clinging for dear life to her scalp?

"Lily, we need to talk about something."

"Okay. What?"

Margaret spun the stool around so Lily could look into her eyes.

"You remember when Dr. Long said that the chemo treatments would make your hair fall out?"

"Yeah?" Lily looked confused.

"Honey, I didn't want to worry you before it was necessary, but it's been five weeks, and I think it's time—"

Lily shook her head as if to say, *No, please don't say it.*

"We need to shave your hair off, sweetie. Don't panic. Look at me, honey. It'll grow back, I promise."

"No! Mom, please don't make me. I don't want to be bald! I don't mind it being thin; I really don't."

"Look at this, Lily. It's not just thin." Margaret held up the trash can full of blonde hair for Lily to see. "It's time to shave it off. We can buy you a wig, or a beanie. Whatever you want."

"No!"

Thomas walked into the room. "What's going on here? Why are you yelling at your mother, Lily?"

"It's nothing, Thomas," Margaret said.

"Mom said I have to shave my hair off!"

Thomas glanced at Margaret. "Lily, if Mom thinks you should shave your hair, then she's right."

"Nobody will know you're wearing a wig, sweetie. They look so real nowadays. It'll look just like your own hair."

Lily looked at Thomas with puppy-dog eyes. "Why can't I just keep the hair? Maybe mine won't fall out. Dad, tell her."

Thomas glanced at Margaret. Before he could respond, she knelt down and showed Lily the brush. Lily's eyes were already filling with tears as she looked at the brush full of blonde hair.

"Please don't make me go to the salon."

"Honey, I don't want to hurt you. I don't know how to—"

"Please, please, please. People will laugh," Lily sobbed.

"Laugh? I dare someone to even look at you funny."

Thomas said carefully, "Margaret."

She glared at him. His expression pleaded with her to forgive him for what he was about to say.

"Let's do it here. Don't make her go to a salon."

* * *

Her hands trembled. She pressed the razor gently against Lily's scalp and warned her to hold still. The brittle pieces of hair floated to the ground. Lily strained her neck to see her own reflection. She wiggled in her seat anxiously. Margaret lifted the razor away from Lily's scalp.

"Stop moving so I don't cut you."

"Mom, my neck hurts from you pushing it forward. Are you almost done?"

She made one more stroke and lifted the razor up. "All done. Before you look, I want to tell you that with or without hair, you're beautiful."

Lily jumped up from the stool. She froze when she saw her reflection. Her eyes filled with tears as she ran her fingers over her scalp. Margaret held her daughter's tiny, shaking body in her arms and could no longer hold back the tears. As she fell on her knees, the pieces of fallen hair stirred around her. With her daughter in her arms, she sobbed, not just about the hair but about everything: the cancer, the pain Lily was enduring, the fear of losing her daughter.

Margaret wiped Lily's eyes dry. Then her own. She told her that everything would be okay, even though it felt like a lie. She pulled Lily away from her so she could look into her daughter's eyes and then smiled.

"You look very modern, you know."

Lily looked at the mirror. "No. I look like ET."

"Well, I think you look beautiful. Not many girls could pull off a look like this. We can still get a wig, if you want one."

Lily looked in the mirror like she was deciding.

Margaret touched her daughter's shoulder. "Hey, sweetie, you are so brave, and I'm not just talking about this." She rubbed her daughter's smooth head. "I'm talking about the way you've handled all of this. I'm so amazed by you every day." Her lips thinned as they crept into a smile. "You know what I think we should do?"

"Stay far away from anywhere public?"

Margaret laughed. "No. Let's go get ice cream, popcorn, chips, gummy bears, the whole nine yards, since you're not feeling nauseous anymore. What do you think? Girls' night?"

Lily frowned and pointed at her shiny head. "People would see me, Mom."

"No, they wouldn't. We could use the magic cloaking device. That always worked when you were younger."

"I'm not five anymore. There's no such thing as a magic cloaking device."

"Really, you are? Oh my gosh, you must be the Lily from the future who's all grown up."

Lily huffed. "Mom, I'm being serious. I'm too old for cloaking devices and candy."

"You'll never be too old for candy. Trust me."

"Can we just stay home? Please."

Margaret stood up and reached her hand out toward Lily. "We can, but we have to order pizza. Deal?"

Lily smiled and took her hand.

* * *

The doorbell rang half an hour later. Margaret hopped up to answer the door.

"That's the pizza, I'm betting. Keep looking for a movie you want to watch."

A minute later, a gangly teenage boy was following Margaret to the kitchen table, doing his best to balance a stack of pizza boxes. As Margaret had anticipated, the box at the top of the stack started to slide. She leaped forward and caught it just in time.

She smiled at him. "Just leave those right here."

32

He placed the boxes on the table where she pointed and then turned to leave.

"Thank you"—she glanced at his name tag—"Tim. Here's your tip."

Margaret counted out nine ones and reached out her hand. She looked up to see why he wasn't taking the money and noticed he had frozen midstep and was staring at something in the living room with his mouth wide open. Suddenly, he dashed out the door before Margaret could give him his tip. She shook her head.

"What a strange kid."

She glanced at Lily. The tears were already streaming down Lily's pale face.

"Honey—"

"Did you see the way he looked at me?"

"Oh, he probably wasn't looking at you." She realized that he was as soon as she said the words. "He was probably just startled by you sitting on the couch so quietly. I've told you to stop sneaking up on people like that."

Lily didn't laugh at her attempted joke.

"He looked at me like I'm a freak."

"No, he didn't. You just took him by surprise by being so quiet. He seemed like a jumpy kid anyway."

"Sure."

"Hey, I'll be right back. He forgot to get his tip. Keep looking for that movie, sweetie."

Margaret could hear the engine cranking up as she stepped outside. He hadn't pulled out of the driveway yet, to her relief. She waved at him and ran toward the, car with a giant slice of pizza illuminated by neon lights on top. If he tried to bolt, she'd already memorized his name and tag, which wasn't hard to do, since he'd gotten one of those personalized plates: TIMINATER.

After a quick phone call to the Pizzeria Extreme, his boss would be able to handle him. Her steps sped up as the car continued to slowly roll backward.

She was in a jog when the car finally stopped. Margaret slowed to a walk. She rested her arm on the roof of the car while she tried to catch her breath. (Monday she would start exercising again, she told herself.)

"Hi, Tim. You forgot your tip."

"Oh, uh, thanks."

"So, here it is. Next time you see a girl without hair, don't look like you just swallowed your tongue."

"Oh, I, uh—"

"And if you don't want me to call your boss, I'd really appreciate it if you could come back in for just a second and apologize to my daughter. You could say that you were surprised to see that two girls could eat so much pizza by themselves. It doesn't really matter what you say. It's taken me all day to convince her that nobody would stare at her if they saw her without hair. Now she's in there crying, because I was wrong. So, could you please go apologize to her?"

He nodded cautiously.

She smiled. "And also, do you have any breadsticks I could add to my order so it doesn't look like I set this up?"

A moment later, Lily looked surprised as they walked through the door together. Margaret smiled at Lily.

"He forgot something."

Margaret glanced at Tim.

"I have your breadsticks." He glanced back at Margaret nervously. "And I wanted to apologize for looking surprised earlier—it wasn't because of your ... uh ... I mean, it wasn't that you surprised me. I just thought there would be more people

34

here to eat so much food." He scratched the Pizzeria Extreme hat on his head. "So, I'll leave you to enjoy your three large pizzas."

It wasn't the most subtle setup, but it seemed like it worked. Lily was smiling as he dashed through the door again. Margaret couldn't help but feel a little guilty for scaring him, but maybe he'd learned a lesson. Margaret walked over to the couch with a box in each hand.

"Thanks, Mom."

Margaret tried to sound naive. "For what?"

Lily laughed. "For whatever you said to him outside."

"I have no idea what you're talking about." Margaret pulled at a slice of pizza until the cheese ripped. "Okay, so what are we going to watch?"

"I was thinking about this one." Lily pointed at the screen. "It's mystery, romance, and comedy all in one."

"All right, then. What are you waiting for? Press play."

Lily peeled a floppy slice away from the pizza and leaned against her mom's arm. Margaret smiled. "Are you trying to pin my arm down so you can eat more pizza than me?"

Lily shrugged and bit into her slice. "Maybe."

"And here I was thinking my daughter wanted to cuddle with me because she loved me."

Lily laughed. They both got quiet as the ominous music started in the opening scene. Lily put down her slice of pizza. Margaret glanced at her.

"Your stomach feeling okay? "

"Not really."

"I'm sorry. Pizza was a bad idea. I don't know what I was thinking."

"It's okay, Mom."

"Your dad can finish it off when he gets back. I'll go make you some soup."

Margaret put down her slice of pizza and kissed her daughter's forehead. Lily smiled and turned back to the movie.

Chapter 7: A Gift

Her mother smiled as she handed her the lightweight rectangular box. Lily held her ear to it and gave it a good shake. It didn't sound like much.

"What is it?"

"Open it."

Lily pulled on the big red bow until it had unraveled completely. Carefully, she pulled the lid off. Her heart jumped inside her chest. She reached inside the box and touched it.

"Well? What do you think?"

Lily stared at the blonde hair inside the box. It was perfect. She lifted it up slowly.

"You don't have to be so careful. You can brush it, wash it, and treat it just like your real hair."

She brushed her fingers through it slowly. It felt just like her own, before the chemo.

"Can I wear it now?"

"Of course."

Her mother pulled the wig down until it was snug against Lily's head. Lily stared at her reflection for a minute without saying anything.

"Come on. I'm dying to know what you're thinking. We can always go get another one if you don't like it."

"No, it's perfect. I love it!"

"I thought you were beautiful even when you were bald, you know."

Lily's eyes filled with tears. "Thank you, Mom."

Her mom smiled. "Want to wear it somewhere?"

"Like, where?"

"Anywhere! This is your 'hair day.' Now that you've been a hermit for a week, where did you miss going the most?"

Lily thought about it. "Okay, but don't laugh. It's going to sound weird."

"I promise not to laugh."

"The grocery store."

Margaret laughed.

"You promised you wouldn't laugh!"

"You're right. That's weird, but only because you hate the grocery store."

"I know, but before, I was able to hate going. When I wasn't able to go, I couldn't hate going anymore."

"Maybe I should figure out a way to make your hands not work, too, so you'll want to do the dishes."

"Ha ha," she said sarcastically.

"To the grocery store we go, then."

* * *

Lily smiled as the aroma of floor cleaner and semi-fresh produce met her at the door—even if it did make her stomach turn. It was good to be back. An old lady smiled as they passed by. Lily touched her wig.

"Why did that lady smile at me so weird? Is it that obvious?"

"It looks like your real hair." Her mom stopped walking.

"She smiled because she saw a beautiful young woman running around the grocery store as if it was the best thing in the entire world. You're a good kid, and good kids are rare."

"Are you just saying that?"

"Never. Trust me—if you look bad, it makes me look bad, remember?"

Lily nodded and placed both feet on the bottom rail of the cart. Her mom pushed the cart around the store.

Her mom laughed. "Now people are going to look at you because your mom's letting you ride the buggy like a rebel."

Lily closed her eyes as the cart moved forward. The small amount of breeze she could feel rustling through her wig made her imagine she had her own long hair again.

"I have the coolest mom in the world."

Chapter 8: The Envelope

Thomas ripped open the envelope addressed from the hospital. What was the point of having insurance if it hardly covered Lily's treatment? He sighed and rubbed the bridge of his nose. At least now that Colin was living on his own, their costs had gone down a little bit, but still. Margaret placed the salad bowl on the table. Beer spilled on the table as he slammed his fist into it. Margaret stopped humming and stared at the paper in Thomas's hand.

"What's wrong?" she asked as she wiped the table.

"Another bill from the hospital. Didn't they say they wouldn't send a bill if we paid up front?"

"I can't remember. Maybe so." Margaret smiled. "But soon, Lily may not have to get treatments as often. Dr. Long said she was very happy with how the treatments were going on our last checkup."

He took a swig of his beer. "Yeah? I bet she is."

"What's that supposed to mean? You bet she is?"

"I'm just saying, she makes a lot of money off those treatments. I'd be happy if I were her too."

"Thomas, not this argument again. Please. The treatment is working. That's all that matters."

"I'm glad the treatment is working. I really am. But we

can't afford these treatments with only one income coming in, Margaret. I know—"

"Listen, I don't care if the bill is a million dollars! This is the cost of saving our daughter you're complaining about."

"That wasn't what I was saying, and you know it. I was saying ... never mind."

"No. Tell me. What were you about to say?"

"It's killing me to watch our daughter go through this. That doesn't change the fact that we have to have money to pay for her treatments, and that wig you bought her. I bet that wasn't cheap. Why did she need a wig, anyway? Her hair will grow—"

"Actually, the wig was free, but that's not important. Do you hear yourself? Why did she need a wig?" Her voice was growing louder. "She needed a wig because she's a girl and she had no hair."

Thomas raised his hands like he was pleading the Fifth. "Fine. You say she needs a wig. She needs a wig. All of this costs money, though. This isn't Monopoly—"

"I know this isn't a game, Thomas."

"Well, then, you also know that we need real money. I know I promised that I would travel less. But—"

"But?"

"But, either I need to take on more jobs, and that means traveling more, or you need to start teaching at the middle school again."

Margaret threw her apron on the counter and stormed off toward their bedroom. A moment later, he heard the door slam. Thomas ripped the bill in half. The garbage lid spun as he threw the shredded bill inside and then walked to the fridge. He placed the lid against the countertop and smacked down hard. His chest expanded as he took a deep breath as the golden liquid slid

41

onto his tongue. He picked up the phone and dialed the bank. Maybe the bank would give them an extension. After all, he and Margaret had paid their mortgage on time since Colin was a baby. He looked around the corner to make sure Lily wasn't coming.

"Hello, I would like to speak to Todd Craig," he said quietly so Lily wouldn't hear.

The receptionist said she would go fetch Mr. Craig. Thomas waited. He took another swig of his beer. What kind of last name was Craig? The baritone voice came on the line.

"Hi, Mr. Craig. It's Thomas Durnin ... Yes, I got the letters. That's what I was calling about ... I understand, but listen, we've been in a tight spot lately. Our daughter is getting chemo, and ... Uh huh. Yeah. I understand that we aren't the only customers to call like this ... I know this is a business, but I would think that a business would make exceptions for loyal customers like us ... Okay ... Yes. We will find a way to make the payment this week. Could you at least waive the late fee? Thank you, Mr. Craig ... Uh huh, goodbye."

Thomas could hear a door opening. He looked around the corner to make sure it wasn't Lily again. It was Margaret, walking back to the kitchen wearing her mad face: eyebrows pinched, mouth turned down, eyes focused straight ahead. She'd mastered it over the years. He watched as she bent over and opened the oven to check something.

A moment later, she was sliding the dish onto the stove top. It smelled amazing. Not that he was hungry enough to eat. His phone started to ring. Thomas answered.

"I almost didn't believe it when I saw the caller ID. A phone call from my only son. What'd I do to deserve such an honor? ... Slow down. What? Why would she think that? ... We weren't fighting. We were just having a discussion. I've just been stressed lately, and so has your mother ... When did she call you? ... Okay, thanks. I'll take care of it."

Margaret plopped the steaming vegetables on the table and pulled the oven mitts off her hands. She looked at him. "Well? What'd Colin want?"

"He just got a text from Lily." Thomas let out a long breath. "Our daughter thinks we're getting divorced."

She didn't reply. It was probably his imagination, but she didn't seem as surprised as he was. The expression on her face seemed more like she was thinking: I've wondered the same thing. But it was probably in his head. Margaret was just stressed like he was. Their marriage was fine.

Margaret went back to preparing dinner, but her expression remained.

Thomas went to Lily's room. He knew she was pretending to be asleep, since she wasn't snoring.

"Lily?"

She continued to pretend.

"Lily, I know you aren't sleeping."

"How?"

Thomas smiled at her from the door. "Colin just called. I'm sorry about all the fighting lately. Your mom and I aren't getting divorced. It's normal for adults to argue sometimes. You shouldn't be worrying about stuff like that."

"You guys are always fighting, though. I want things to go back to the way they were."

"They will, sweetie. I promise. Now, let's go get something to eat. That sound good?"

Lily grinned and nodded.

"Want a lift?"

"I'm too old for that."

43

"You're never too old for—" He paused as if he was thinking seriously. "Well, maybe when you're thirty. Then you'll be a little too old, but for now, hop on."

He lifted Lily onto his back. She laughed like she was five again. He'd given her hundreds of piggyback rides over the years. She'd been getting too heavy for him to carry over the past year, before the chemo. Now, she hardly weighed anything.

He neighed for added effect as they approached the kitchen table. She really was too old for it, but it was tradition. He stopped neighing and stared at the pink bucket next to Lily's plate. Margaret must've put it there while he was gone. Thomas looked at Margaret as he set Lily down in her chair.

"Lily, this bucket's here in case you get sick, like you did the last couple of times."

"I didn't mean to—"

"No, honey, you're not in trouble. I just want to have it here in case you need it."

Thomas walked to the fridge and pulled out another beer, despite Margaret's judgmental look. The first sip soothed his upset stomach as he walked back to the table.

Lily had already started on her meatloaf when Margaret scooped a pile of vegetables onto Thomas's plate.

"We need to talk about the possibility of Lily homeschooling while we're all here." She looked at Lily. "Lily, eat slower so you don't get sick. Like I was saying, I don't want Lily to fall behind in school while she's getting treatment. I know it's about to be summer break, but we're already behind, so I think we should start now. Then, when school starts back in August, she'll be caught up." She paused and looked at him. "Thomas? What do you think?"

Thomas nodded and took another sip of his beer. This

44

wasn't the lighthearted dinner conversation he'd hoped for. "You're probably right, Margaret, but let's talk about this later, privately—"

Lily gagged before he could finish sticking his foot in his mouth. Margaret placed the bucket up to Lily's mouth just in time. Thomas fought back the urge to join his daughter, while Margaret rubbed their daughter's back.

His throat felt tight as the warmth rose to his eyes. "I'll be right back."

"Where are you going?" Margaret asked.

"The bathroom."

He walked to the bathroom and shut the door. He turned the faucet on. The sound of water running helped him block out the sound of Lily throwing up in the other room. He cupped his hands under the faucet and splashed the cold water onto his face a few times. He felt around for the nozzle, and, after finding it, turned it off. Lily was still gagging in the other room. It sounded like she was crying, when she could catch her breath. He stared at his bloodshot eyes in the mirror as he patted his face dry.

"What are you doing, Tom?" he mumbled to himself. "You need to get a grip, be there for your family, and start acting like a man. Margie needs you. Your daughter needs you."

Chapter 9: Heartburn

D r. Long stepped behind Lily and placed something cold against her back.

"Deep breaths for me." She slid the cold object farther down Lily's back. "Good. One more time."

Dr. Long moved around to where Lily could see her and then smiled. Lily's mom stood in the corner of the room, chewing on her fingernail.

"Dr. Long, are we going to find out what the test results are today?" her mom asked.

"Would you like for me to discuss this with you here or privately?"

Her mother glanced at her as if to ask, *Which do you prefer?* Lily gave her a pleading look as if to say, *Please stay.* Her mother nodded and said, "I would like to discuss it here."

Dr. Long nodded and smiled. "The chemotherapy is working."

Lily glanced at her mom, who followed up: "What does that mean? Is her cancer gone?"

"Well, for now we'll keep monitoring it. The tumor is still there, but there's been no sign of growth in the last eight weeks. It appears that the treatment is working for now. I'm going to suggest that she still get chemotherapy in monthly intervals. As I've mentioned before, this type of cancer can be very aggressive, so I'll need to keep a close eye on her."

Her mom jumped up and wrapped her arms around Dr. Long. Lily watched as tears came to her mother's eyes. Her mom then sat down in the plastic chair and grabbed at her chest.

"Is it heartburn again, Mom?" Lily asked.

Her mom laughed. "No, sweetie. It's just that I'm so happy right now, my heart's jumping out of my chest."

She walked over to Lily and pulled her into her arms. Lily laid her head against her mom's chest. Her heart was racing, just like she said.

Dr. Long walked toward the door. "I'll give you two some privacy to talk. No rush."

Her mom turned toward Dr. Long. "Is it safe for her to go to public school when the school year starts in August? We were planning on doing the whole homeschooling thing, but I'm sure Lily would prefer her teacher to be someone she doesn't have to live with." She patted Lily's knee.

"Public schools are one of the worst places for germs, but as long as she' s mindful to wash her hands and use basic precautions, I don't see anything wrong with that." Dr. Long paused. "And Lily, I almost forgot to tell you. I like the new hairdo."

Lily smiled.

After her mom hugged her again, they went downstairs to check out at the front desk. Lily skipped as they walked to the car. She slid into the passenger seat and looked at her mom, who was still beaming.

"Can we call Colin and tell him?" Lily asked.

"Yes. Put him on speakerphone."

Before Lily could dial her brother's number, she felt the car turn left out of the parking lot. She looked at her mom curiously.

"Where are we going?"

"Shopping."

"What for?"

Her mom smiled. "You need clothes for school."

"School doesn't start until August twentieth. We have two more months to go shopping."

Margaret winked. "Honey, it's never too early to go shopping ... unless you don't want to go?"

"No, I want to go." She looked down at her lap. "Can we afford it?"

"Honey, you shouldn't be worried about that."

"I heard you and Dad the other night before dinner."

"Well, that's for me and your father to worry about. One day you'll have your own bills to worry about, but for now, just try to enjoy being a kid."

Lily smiled and went back to calling her brother.

Chapter 10: Bros

"Yeah, I'm off today. I'll head your way soon … Love you too. Bye."

Colin hung up the phone and noticed that Rob was staring at him. "What?"

"I don't want to seem nosy, but it sounded like that was Lily on the phone. How's she doing?"

Colin laughed. "It's okay if you're nosy—you're basically family. My mom and sister were calling to say that Lily's cancer is doing better, or not doing worse, or something like that. The chemo's working. They want me to go over there for dinner to celebrate the good news."

Rob shook Colin's shoulder. "Man, that's amazing."

"Yeah, thanks. It's been really stressful. Maybe everything will be okay after all."

"Yeah, maybe." Rob shifted side to side without picking up his feet. "Hey, don't get mad at me—"

"Are you about to ask me about Olivia again?"

"She asked about you yesterday. She said she's worried about you, and I wasn't sure what to tell her. I mean, Lily's doing better now, and you still haven't called, so, I didn't want to hurt her feelings. Are you just not into her, or—"

"Why'd she ask you? I was there yesterday. She could've just asked me about me."

Rob laughed. "Really?"

"Really, what?"

"You never called her back. It's been how long since she called you—I don't know, eight or nine weeks? It doesn't seem like you want to talk to her."

"Why does it matter so much to you? And why are you two even discussing our relationship?"

Rob scoffed. "What relationship? You went on four dates and then never called her back. That's only considered a relationship if you're a fruit fly."

"You know what? I don't have time for this." Colin paused and shook his head. "I just found out that my little sister's doing better, and I need to go see her and give her a hug. Whatever's going on between you and Olivia, I don't care. Hope you two have a happy life together. In fact, you two would make a real cute couple."

Colin grabbed his keys and opened the door.

"Colin, stop. We' re just worried about you—"

Colin shut the door to their apartment before Rob could finish.

* * *

Lily twirled like a drunk ballerina in the middle of the living room.

"What do you think, Colin?"

His mom set the last plate on the table. "Lily, don't spin like that. You'll make yourself sick."

Lily stopped and looked at Colin.

He smiled. "I like the bell-bottoms—very retro."

"Mom picked them out for me," Lily said.

His mom nodded. "It took some convincing for her to try them on, but when she did, she loved them." She looked at the ballerina wannabe. "Lily, come eat your food before it gets cold. You can try on more clothes after dinner."

His dad exhaled sharply. It was the first sound he'd made since they'd sat down.

"You okay, Tom?" his mom asked.

"You bought a lot of clothes today."

"Yeah." His mother glanced at Lily quickly and smiled. "She needed them for school. We found some really good discounts, and half of it was from the American Cancer Society Discovery Shops. The people that volunteer there are so nice."

His dad didn't respond. The room became silent suddenly. The only sound came from their forks clanking against their plates. Colin piled more broccoli onto his plate to avoid eye contact. No wonder Lily thought their parents were getting divorced.

"How much did you spend?" his dad finally asked.

His mom looked surprised by his question. "Let's talk about this later, Tom."

"I'd rather know now."

"Tom, let's enjoy dinner with our kids. We can talk about it later."

His dad set down the bottle in his hand and stood. "I'll be back in a little bit."

"Where are you going?"

"Out."

"Tom, out where? You can't drive—you've been drinking."

Lily's eyes darted between their two parents as their dad walked to the back door and opened it.

"I just need some air."

The door closed before his mom could ask any more questions.

She stood up and followed him outside. Colin glanced at Lily, who was still staring at the door.

"Lily, do you like your food? You haven't eaten much."

She looked at him anxiously. "Why's Dad upset?"

"I don't know. Don't worry about it, though."

"They fight all the time."

"All couples do."

"That's not true. Mom and Dad didn't use to fight."

Colin frowned. She made a good point.

"I think dinner's over. Do you want to show me your other outfits?"

She jumped up and ran to her room. She seemed to have totally forgotten that she'd been worried about their parents a moment ago. Colin could hear the tires screech outside. A moment later, his mom walked through the door. A wave of heat blew in from outside as she shut the door. He knew better than to ask any questions.

"Your father will be back soon. Where's Lily?"

"Trying on more clothes."

"I told her to wait—"

"Mom, I asked her to. I thought it'd be a good distraction for her, because she was worried about you and Dad. To be honest, I'm worried too. What's going on, Mom?"

She sighed. "I don't want you or Lily to worry. Your father and I will be fine."

His mom picked up the plates, still piled with untouched food. For a moment she stopped and balanced the plates in one hand and held her heart with the other.

"What's wrong, Mom? Is your heart hurting?"

"Hmph," she scoffed without answering his question. "So much for a nice family dinner."

Colin tried to think of something to say as his mom scraped the warm food into containers.

"Hey, Mom. Let's have a good time. We're supposed to be celebrating tonight. Maybe we can get the old digital camera and let Lily model for us or pretend to be a ballerina or something."

She smiled. "That's a wonderful idea. I'll go get my camera and lip gloss. How did I get two such amazing children?"

A moment later his mom returned with the items in her hand. Lily came out of her room with a new dress on, and she began jumping up and down when she spotted the camera and lip gloss in her mother's hands. Like a professional model, Lily stuck her hand on her hip and began strutting down the imaginary runway—a.k.a. their hallway.

It sounded like a car had pulled up in the driveway. Maybe it was his dad. Colin tried not to look worried as he snapped another picture of Lily. They all turned to look as the door opened. His dad closed the door behind himself and then stood like a deer in headlights. He looked surprised to see the fashion show happening.

His mom said, "We're doing a fashion show. I don't want to argue—"

"I'm not here to argue. I'm sorry." He hung his head lower. "I would love to watch the fashion show."

Colin smiled at Lily and spun his finger in a circle as if to say, *Do a twirl.* Lily twirled, making her dress fly up like she was Marilyn Monroe. His dad belly laughed suddenly.

"She'll have to wear a pair of shorts with that dress so the boys at her school don't get a peep show."

Colin chuckled. Suddenly, Lily and his mom joined in until everyone was laughing together for the first time in weeks.

Chapter 11: Great Expectations

Margaret brought another box of tissues to Lily's bed. Lily sniffled, either from crying or the runny nose. After months of making sure Lily had the summer of her life (other than the chemo treatments), Margaret now listened to Lily as she complained that it wasn't fair. Why'd she have to get sick now? she asked. Why couldn't she have gotten sick during the summer break instead?

"I know you're disappointed, but you had fun this summer, right?"

Lily sniffled. "Yes."

"What was your favorite part?"

"When we went to that party at the hospital. That was pretty cool."

"Yeah, you made a few friends, huh?"

Lily shrugged. "Not really. Everyone was younger than me."

"Well, I think you should try to make some friends at the hospital, just in case you have to spend some time there."

"Why would I have to spend time there?"

"If you get sick or something."

"I don't know. I have friends at school."

"Yeah, but you're about to go to middle school, and you'll have to make new friends."

Lily buried her head into her pillow. "And I'm already behind on trying to make friends." Lily blew her nose into a tissue and looked at Margaret. "Can I please go to school tomorrow? I'm feeling better."

Margaret pressed the back of her hand against Lily's forehead. It was still hot.

"Honey, we knew this could happen, remember? Dr. Long said your immune system would be weak from the treatments."

"Yeah, but I wanted to start school with everyone else." Lily sniffled. "Now, I'll be the new kid."

Margaret laughed. "I'm not sure if being a few weeks late to school makes you the new kid. It just makes you the newer kid."

"Everyone will already have their groups."

"You'll find a group too."

Lily blew her nose into the tissue. "They won't need another person in their group. I'll be the outcast. Why'd I have to get sick now?"

"Okay, that's enough. You're not going to be an outcast unless you make yourself one. Nobody will want to be around the mopey girl. Stop throwing yourself a pity party. Starting school a few weeks late isn't the end of the world. Got it?"

She sniffled. "Yes, ma'am."

"Good. Now get some rest." Margaret leaned over and kissed her daughter's forehead. "I love you."

* * *

Margaret walked to her bedroom. She pulled back the covers and slid next to Thomas, who was sitting on the edge of the bed. She couldn't see his face, but something about him looked tense. He didn't look at her as she curled up behind him.

55

"She's finally asleep. I'm so exhausted." She yawned as she spoke. "Are you going to get in bed, babe?"

He turned and looked at her instead of answering.

"Why are you looking at me like that?" she asked.

"I need to tell you something."

She didn't say anything as she waited for him to tell her what she'd been anticipating for weeks. He'd been acting strange ever since they'd found out their daughter had cancer. He'd been home less often, out late more, less affectionate. All the signs had been there, but she hadn't wanted to see them. She needed him here—with her and Lily. After twenty-three years of marriage, they'd gotten through a lot. Whatever he was about to say, they could get through it too.

"Are you having an affair?"

"What? No! No, oh my gosh, Margie ... I'd never do that to you. I needed to tell you that I have a drinking problem."

Her mouth fell open as she tried to wrap her head around his words. "A drinking problem? Tom, are you saying you're an alcoholic? That's ridiculous."

"No, it's not ridiculous. Margie, I'm serious. I need to get help."

"Drinking a few beers when you get home doesn't make you an alcoholic, honey." She rubbed his arm. "I mean, I would like it if you drank less, and if you were home more."

"I told you that I'd try to be home more, and I have been trying." He paused. "But after work, I stop by the bar—"

"You what?"

"Margie, listen. I'm not proud of this, but—"

She stood up and paced around the room.

"Margie, I found a rehab close by—only ten minutes away, actually. It's in Fulton County, too, so—"

Her face contorted. "I'm sorry, you want to go to rehab?"

She put her hands over her face and laughed.

"What's funny about that?" he asked. "Please stop laughing and tell me what you're thinking. You're acting crazy."

"I'm acting crazy? Maybe I should go check myself into an asylum. Then Lily won't have either of her parents, because we'll both be getting treated for diseases we don't have." She laughed again. "No, I'm sorry. You're right, Tom. You should go to rehab, and I'll stay here and take care of our sick daughter by myself."

Tom stood up and walked to the closet.

"What are you doing?" she asked.

"Packing."

"You're not seriously about to leave, are you?"

He unzipped his duffel bag and looked at his wife. "I can't do this on my own. I am an alcoholic, Margie. I need help. Believe me, don't believe; it doesn't make a difference."

"You're not on your own—you never were. If you'd just told me what was going on, I could've helped."

He shook his head. "Margie, you're not listening to me. I need professional help."

"I am listening, but have you thought this through? What about your job? What about Lily? What about our marriage?"

"I have thought it through, and I've already spoken with Jay. He said my job will be there when I get back."

Margaret didn't know whether to nod or shake her head. Had he lost his mind? The conversation had caught her off guard.

"So you've just decided all of this without even talking to me first?" she finally asked.

"I wanted to tell you. I just didn't know how. I'm not good at talking about what's on my mind. I tried to tell you last month."

57

"You did not! When did you try to tell me?"

"When you were cooking, and I said I needed help."

Her mouth fell open. "You said you needed help? Thomas, I thought you meant with finding your keys or something, not going to rehab."

"I don't know, but I was trying. The rehab offers counseling, and I was hoping it would help me communicate better."

"It offers counseling? And you think that's going to help you communicate better in one month? Okay, since you seem to have thought of everything without me, I'm assuming that you thought about how we were going to afford this. Are you still going to get paid?"

"No."

Her eyes felt like they were going to pop out of her head as she glared at him. "I'm a substitute teacher, Tom. I don't get paid year round, and you know that. Without your income, we don't have any money coming in. How are we supposed to pay for anything?"

"Use our savings if you have to."

"Our savings are for emergencies!"

"This is an emergency. If I don't get help soon, I won't have a job at all."

She sat on the edge of their bed and rested her head in her hands. "What am I supposed to tell our daughter?"

"Tell her I went on a business trip."

"Hmph." She smirked and shook her head. "Un-freakin'-believable. So you want me to lie to her?"

He sighed. "Tell her what you want then, Margie."

"How long will you be gone?"

"It'll only be a month."

"Only a month." She did the strange laugh she'd been doing

a lot lately. "Only a month, you say."

He turned to leave.

"Tom, I'm so mad right now I can't even see straight, but I have to ask: Why didn't you tell me before tonight? We're supposed to be partners. Do you love me at all anymore?"

"Of course I do. I'm doing this because I love you." He looked down. "I was too ashamed to tell you."

Chapter 12: New Girl

Everyone except Lily took their seats as the bell rang. It was impossible for Lily to tell if what she was feeling was nausea or just the butterflies in her stomach. She couldn't remember ever feeling so nervous on her first day of school before, but this time it was different. She'd gone to the same school since she was eight years old. All of her old friends had gone to Parson's for seventh grade (not that any of them had checked on her since she'd been diagnosed with cancer), while Lily had to go to Coweta Middle School. The faces were new and unfamiliar, unlike elementary school. She was the new kid for the first time in her life.

Lily adjusted her beanie carefully to avoid moving the wig underneath. Her eyes scanned the room a third time. Every eye was looking back at her. No one smiled. No one frowned. What were they thinking about? Did they know she was wearing a wig?

Mr. Green cleared his throat. "Class, this is Lily Durnin. Since she's a couple of weeks behind, would someone volunteer to help her get caught up on what we've already discussed?"

A brunette girl in the back of the class raised her hand. She waved at Lily and smiled. Lily smiled back as she adjusted her beanie slightly.

The teacher added, "We don't allow beanies or hats of any kind in the classroom, Ms. Durnin. I understand you weren't aware before now, but please remove it."

Lily blushed and removed the beanie with one hand while securing the wig with the other. The wig moved slightly. She scanned the room again. Their expressions hadn't changed. Maybe nobody had noticed. Lily walked to the back of the class and took a seat beside the brunette girl.

Mr. Green told the class to take out their workbooks and turn to page seventeen.

"I'm Makayla," the girl whispered.

"Hi."

Mr. Green interrupted their conversation. "Lily, no talking during class. Thank you."

She'd been there less than five minutes and had already been reprimanded twice. She slid down into the hard seat as the teacher started talking about mitochondria ...

Suddenly, Mr. Green was beside her. "Ms. Durnin, am I boring you?"

She lifted her head. A string of drool followed. Had she fallen asleep?

"No. I'm sorry."

"I don't allow sleeping during my class, Ms. Durnin."

"I'm sorry," she said again.

"Please see me after class."

The bell rang. Books closed shut. Mr. Green reminded the class of their assignment. Lily collected the notes from her new friend, Makayla. Kids ran through the hallway laughing and yelling. A moment later, the classroom was quiet.

Mr. Green sat at his desk, writing something down. Lily swayed from side to side while she waited for him to finish.

"Mr. Green? You wanted to see me?"

"Lily, do you know why I asked to see you after class?"

"No."

"I' m only going to give you a warning today, but if you disrupt my class again, I' ll be forced to give you detention. Do you understand?"

Lily nodded. She sighed as she turned to walk away.

* * *

Lily pushed the door open. The smell of her mom's pot roast greeted her from the kitchen. She could feel her mouth starting to water. She turned to lock the door behind her.

"Lily, is that you?"

"Yes, Mom."

"How was school today?"

Lily plopped on the leather couch. The cushion deflated slowly.

Margaret laughed. "That bad, huh?"

"I almost got detention."

"What have I told you about picking fights?"

"It's not funny."

"Sorry. How did you almost get detention?"

"I didn't mean to."

Lily told her mom about the beanie, talking in class, falling asleep.

Her mother picked up her phone. "Don't worry, I'll handle this. Go to your room, and do your homework."

She went to her room. She could hear her mom's voice coming from the other room. "I don't appreciate you singling my child out in front of the entire class on her first day of school, Mr.

Green. Yes, I understand perfectly well that you have rules. It may surprise you to know that I am a teacher as well. As a teacher, Mr. Green, it's my job to take into account the circumstances of my students before humiliating them in front of their peers. Yes, you humiliated her. That beanie is not a fashion statement. Were you aware that she had cancer? Okay. So then you can understand why she would wear a beanie to keep her head warm. Yes, I know it's September, but your class has air-conditioning, so she still needs something to keep her head warm. So I'm also assuming we're on the same page. Tomorrow, Lily will wear her beanie to school, and I will not find out that she's been given detention, I hope." Lily heard a pause. "Thank you for your apology."

A moment later, her mother walked into her room and smiled. "Dinner's ready."

Lily followed her mom to the dining table.

Her mother looked at her. "What's wrong?"

She covered her hand over her mouth and pointed at the pink bucket on the table.

"I thought pot roast didn't make you sick."

Lily gagged over the bucket.

After the nausea had passed, she went to the bathroom and brushed her teeth with the special toothbrush Dr. Long had given her. By the time she'd come back to the kitchen, her mom had already scraped the roast into a container. She gave Lily a glass of apple juice, only because Lily said the orange juice tasted too bitter after brushing.

Lily looked at her mom. "I'm sorry."

"For what? Honey, you can't help that you get sick. It's the treatment. I know that." She slid the container of pot roast into the freezer. "More for your dad when he gets home."

"Mom, when is Dad getting home?"

"Soon, honey. How about you go finish your homework and get ready for bed."

Chapter 13: Good Nnight

An hour had passed since Margaret had last checked on Lily. She walked into her room to find her brushing out her wig. Lily was being particularly precise about the bangs. Margaret walked to her bed and sat. She moved a stray piece of hair that Lily had missed.

"I thought of another advantage to not having hair."

Lily turned and looked at her doubtfully. "What's that?"

"You don't have to wash it or dry it now. It must be kind of nice."

Lily laughed. "That's the only advantage." She examined her wig again. "I was so scared the other kids would find out I was wearing it today when Mr. Green told me to take off my beanie."

"Hmph." Margaret chuckled. "Wanna know my really embarrassing story from when I was about your age?"

Lily's eyes widened. "Yes!"

Margaret rolled onto her stomach and propped herself up on her elbows. She felt like a teenager again.

"Okay. So, I liked this boy ... and then, when I went to stand up in my brand-new dress my mom had bought me, the hem got caught under my chair and the dress ripped, right where the whole class could see my flowery underwear."

"Are you making this up?"

Margaret laughed. "I wish!"

"Then why haven't you ever told me that story before?" It sounded more like an accusation than a question.

"And let my daughter know what a loser her mom was in school? I had to keep my street cred. You're almost a teenager, and soon you'll realize that your mother isn't cool. I wanted to hang on to that illusion as long as possible."

Lily rolled her eyes. "How could you have been a loser? You were a cheerleader."

"That wasn't until after my entire eighth grade class saw me in my skivvies."

Lily giggled. "What happened to the boy you liked?"

"Nothing. But a few other boys noticed me after that." Margaret winked. "But don't get any ideas, missy."

Lily laughed and crawled under the covers. Margaret stood up and grabbed the bottom of the blanket. She pulled up until the blanket was in the air, then pulled down to make the blanket land evenly over Lily. It had been Lily's favorite way to be tucked in since she was a child. Margaret sat down again next to the two lumps where Lily's feet were and put her hand around them. Lily wiggled her toes playfully.

"You know I love you, right?" Margaret asked.

"Yes."

"More than the entire world."

"I know, Mom," she said, exasperated.

She kissed Lily's forehead.

"You really do rock the bald-and-beautiful look."

"You have to say that because you're my mother."

"I'm sorry, where is that written in the contract?"

"In the fine print."

Margaret laughed. "What do you know about fine print?"

"I'm a seventh grader now."

"Oh, right." She smiled. "Hey, sweetie?"

"Hmm?" Lily said with a yawn.

"Did I ever tell you how I came up with your name?"

"Yes."

"Well, you're about to hear it again." Lily rolled her eyes lazily. "When the nurse handed you to me, I looked at you, all tiny in my arms, and I thought to myself how fragile you were, and your skin was so perfect—so soft and pale and flawless—and then I thought: she's like a little flower, a lily." Margaret remembered the day fondly. "You are still my little flower—my Lily."

Lily nudged her. "Mmmommm. Stop being sappy."

"All right, all right." Margaret put her hands up. "Good night, honey. I love you."

"Love you too."

Margaret walked to the door. "Tomorrow will be better, I promise."

* * *

Lily had barely begun to drift off when the sound of her dad's voice woke her up again. He was home, finally. Lily sat up and threw the blankets off her feet. She ran to the door and had started to open it when she heard her mother's voice, sounding upset. Lily pushed her ear against the door and listened.

"You aren't supposed to be back for two more weeks," her mother said.

"I had to come home—I missed you, sweetie."

"Oh my G—you've been drinking again. I can't believe this. You know I wasn't on board with this whole thing, but I tried to be because you said you needed the help. Is this your way of trying to prove to me that you were right? Well, bravo. I'm convinced that you need help now. Let's go."

"Where?"

"I'm taking you back."

"No. I'll go back tomorrow. I was sober for two weeks, so I earned a few drinks. It's not a big deal."

"A few drinks? It smells like you've drunk the whole bar, Tom. I can't believe you would stop at a bar on the way home. Actually, why are you home?" she asked.

"I missed you so much. Aren't you happy I'm home?"

"Wait, did you drive here or get a taxi?" Lily couldn't hear her mother's voice for a moment. "You drove here? You could've killed someone! What were you thinking?"

"I was thinking I missed you. Come here … give me a kiss."

"Thomas, don't come near me. I mean it." Lily heard a pause. "And answer my question. What happened to getting help? I thought you were going to stay at the—"

"I was getting help!"

"Tom, keep your voice down. You'll wake up Lily. So are you going to go back?"

"I don't know yet … honey, where are you going? Margie, I haven't had a drink in two weeks."

"I'm taking a bath. I need to calm down before I can talk to you. That should give you some time to sober up."

Lily jumped as the door next to hers slammed. She could hear water running in the bathtub a few moments later.

Her dad spoke louder, like he was trying to talk through the door. "Honey, I got a call from the bank today—from the bank. From that guy Craig—his first name is a last name, or his last name's a first name." Lily tried to understand the slurred words. "They said we're going to lose our house if we don't catch up on the payments soon. Margie? Did you hear me? I said—"

The water stopped running. A creaking noise came from the bathroom door.

Her mom was speaking in almost a whisper. "Are you trying to wake our daughter up? We can't talk about this out here."

Lily tried to figure out whose footsteps she was hearing. It was impossible to tell. She lowered her head to the floor and tried to look under the crack. She was too late. The door across the hallway closed shut. Lily couldn't make out the words through the door. It sounded like both of her parents were yelling from their bedroom. She slowly cracked open her door to hear better. It was still too difficult to make out the words they were saying.

After a while, everything was quiet. Lily closed her door and crawled back into her bed. The blankets had gotten cold again. She shivered and curled up into a ball on her side. Everything would be okay. Her dad had told her they weren't getting divorced and that it was normal for married people to fight. I have nothing to worry about, she thought doubtfully. If only she could believe that.

Chapter 14: Sirens

Thomas's head was pounding the next morning. He rolled over to find her still in bed. He squinted at the light coming in through the curtains. He glanced at the clock. The bright-red numbers showed 10:02. If he remembered right, which wasn't likely, it was a weekday, which would mean she was supposed to be at work by now.

He grunted.

"Margaret, wake up."

She was lying still. He rubbed his sore eyes. His brain was swimming.

"You overslept. Wake up. It's ten in the morning."

Thomas shook her shoulder. Her skin was pale and cold. He propped himself up on his elbow and squinted. Was she breathing? He jumped to his knees. He pressed his fingers against her neck. No pulse. His heart competed with his head to see which could pound harder. He placed his ear against her chest. Silence.

Before he knew what he was doing, he swung his leg over her limp body and started compressions. He pushed his hands against her sternum as rhythmically as he could manage. His body felt detached from his brain as it operated on muscle memory. He'd given CPR countless times during his former career as a police officer, but never had it felt this terrifying. She seemed to be getting colder somehow. He stopped and listened. Nothing. Come on, come on, come on!

The door creaked open. Thomas looked up to find Lily standing in the doorway. Why was she still home? Margaret was supposed to have taken her to school. He cursed himself for forgetting. Her mouth fell open as she stared at him. Suddenly, he realized she didn't need to see this.

"Lily, go to your room. Now!"

His head pounded.

Lily stared at him.

"Lily, call 911. Now. Go!"

Lily disappeared. Thomas tried to catch his breath. He stopped doing compressions and listened. Silence.

"Come on, Margaret. Breathe. Come on!" he sobbed.

He pushed his hands harder against her chest. It'd been so long since he'd had to do this. Why wasn't it working? He had to be doing something wrong. Then he felt something pop under his hands as he pressed down. He pressed his ear against her chest again. Silence. He knew what had caused the sound, but he couldn't stop. She had to wake up; she just had to. He listened again. Her body was cold and still.

"Come back, sweetie. I can't lose you."

In the distance, he could hear the sirens getting closer. Lily had called. Thank God. He continued to press rhythmically. They'd be coming through that door any minute to save her. He just needed to keep going a little bit longer. His wrists were aching and his head was swimming, but he couldn't stop now. Not when they were so close.

The sirens continued to scream as they passed by the house. The screaming got quieter. Everything was silent.

71

Chapter 15: Flashing Lights

Colin's tires screamed as he turned into the Spring Water subdivision. When he could see the vehicles with red lights surrounding his parents' little white house, making it look like it'd been painted with blood, he slowed down and caught his breath. What was going on?

Neighbors were watching from their porches. Red Robin, as Lily called her, was talking to a police officer about something. He was scribbling down whatever she was saying on a notepad. That couldn't be good. He looked at his phone, attached to the dashboard, to make sure she was still on the phone.

"Lily, I just pulled up in the driveway. I'm going to hang up now," he said.

The line was silent. Colin hung up and jumped out of the car. EMTs were standing around, casually talking and drinking their cups of joe. One of them complained about the coffee and said they should've gotten something cold to drink. Nobody seemed to be in a hurry. Finally, Colin spotted his dad through the door and ran inside.

"Where's Mom and Lily?"

His dad seemed to be in a daze.

"Dad, where are they?" He paused. "Dad, why aren't you answering me?"

An officer walked up. "Hey, Colin. You probably don't remember me, but I'm De'Jerome Digger. I used to work with your dad. It's been a while since I've seen you. You were only yay high the last time I saw you." He pointed to his knee. "Why don't you come sit down?"

"I can't sit right now, sir. I need to find my sister. Why are all those cops and EMTs outside? Is my mom hurt? Is Lily okay?"

Digger nodded. "I think it'd be better if you sat down."

Digger reached out and grabbed his arm. Colin pulled his arm away and ran down the hall to his parents' room. When he got there, an officer was taking pictures of his parents' bed. Another was zipping up a large bag. Colin's legs started to tremble. Was that—no, it couldn't be. A hand reached out and grabbed his arm. It was Digger.

"You shouldn't be in here, Colin. Come with me."

"No." He pulled away again. "Let go of me. Someone needs to tell me what's going on, right now!"

Digger looked into his eyes. "Your mother passed away this morning. We aren't sure what the exact time of death is yet. The coroner will do the autopsy and let us know." He paused. "Your father called us this morning around eleven. He said he'd been performing CPR for an hour, and he said he thought your sister had already called when the ambulance never came. Well, anyway, they have to confirm his story, but I know your father would've done everything he could to save your mother. That woman was the love of his life."

Colin could hear his heart beating in his head. Digger's words sounded far away. He watched as the officer wrapped his arm around Colin's waist, as if he were watching a movie. Digger's arm helped him stand as they walked away from the room. A moment later, they were in the living room again.

"Here, sit down. I'm sorry about all of this."

"That bag—was that ..." Colin's voice trailed off.

Digger frowned as if to say, *Please don't make me answer that.* Colin felt light-headed suddenly. How was this happening?

Digger stood up. "You just sit here. I need to go check on your sister. She wasn't doing too well earlier."

"Did you say my sister? Lily? Where is she?"

"We found her hiding in the closet when we got here. She wasn't responsive to our questions. The specialist said she was in shock. We let her sit in the cop car with Jerry—you remember Jerry?—anyway, with him and a specialist. They're out there talking to her now."

Colin glanced at his dad, who hadn't moved an inch since Colin had arrived. Why wasn't he out there, comforting Lily?

He looked at Digger. "I want to see her."

"You can, but the specialist made it clear that Lily needs to be surrounded by people who are calm right now. She's been traumatized. And according to Dr. Reece, it's crucial that, for the first few hours, Lily feels safe."

"Who's Dr. Reece?"

"The specialist."

"Right." Colin tried to process everything. Too much was going on at once.

Digger rubbed the short wavy hairs on his head. "Look, Colin, I don't mind taking you out there to see your sister, but you can't get worked up in front of her like you did earlier. Not that I blame you. You just lost your mom, and you're still processing this yourself. Maybe it'd be best—"

"Officer, she needs to see me. She's scared and sitting in the back of a cop car with two people she's never seen."

Digger nodded.

74

Colin followed him and thought about what he'd said a moment before: "You just lost your mom." It was the first time he'd heard it said since he'd arrived. His mom was dead. He tried not to think about it as they approached a cop car with a small blonde girl in the back. It was Lily. She looked like a tiny criminal, sitting in the back of the police car. It made Colin's stomach twist even more than it already was. Lily didn't appear to be talking to the woman who was sitting in the back next to her, or the police officer who sat in the front seat. She just stared ahead at the back of the passenger seat, in a daze.

Digger patted Colin's back. "I'm going to go—"

"Wait, you can't leave. I still have some questions."

"My shift ended an hour ago. I know this is difficult for you ..." He pulled a card out of his pocket. "But if you need me, call that number. There are people that specialize in grief counseling. I could give you a few names, if you want."

Colin looked at the card Digger had handed him.

By the time he looked up, Digger had already walked halfway across the lawn. Colin looked back at Lily, who still appeared to be in a daze. He opened the front passenger door and leaned in. Lily didn't move.

"Lily? It's me. I'm here now. Everything's going to be okay."

The woman stared at Colin. "I'm sorry, who are you?"

"I'm her brother, Colin Durnin. Officer Digger, De'Jerome, said I could come out here."

She didn't seem excited to see Colin, but she agreed to let him talk to Lily. He slid into the passenger seat. The woman watched him without changing her intimidating expression.

"I'm Dr. Reece. I'm just asking your sister a few questions. She hasn't been able to say what she saw this morning. It's very important that we get her to talk about it." She turned toward

Lily again. "Sweetie, now that your brother's here, maybe you can look at him and tell him what you saw."

Colin's throat tightened. It seemed like she was putting a lot of pressure on Lily, and him, without warning. But what did he know about this stuff? Nothing. He looked at Lily, who didn't seem to be listening to the woman. Did this woman know what she was doing?

"This is a safe place, Lily." She added, "You can say anything in this car, and nobody will be upset with you. Did something happen this morning that made you afraid?" She waited for a response. "Did you think your mommy was being hurt?" She paused again. "Was your daddy mad at your mommy this morning? Was he yelling at her ... or at you?"

Colin looked at the doctor. "What is this—"

Dr. Reece held her hand up before he could continue. "If you don't mind, this is a safe place for Lily to talk about what she saw. Are you going to be able to listen and not interrupt again?" She turned to Lily again. "Do you know what CPR is, Lily?" She paused. "CPR is ..."

The doctor continued to tell Lily what CPR was, and she asked if their daddy had given their mommy CPR. Lily looked like she had mentally checked out while the specialist was attempting to extract information. Colin reached out and held his sister's hand. It was cold and still, almost lifeless. He felt the tears fighting to come up as he imagined his mom's hand feeling similarly now. Then he noticed the red light from the ambulance passing over Lily's face rhythmically.

"Dr. Reece, could the lights from the ambulance be putting her into some kind of trance?"

Dr. Reece looked toward the ambulance. "It's unlikely, but—"
While she was still talking, he noticed that the flashing

red lights stopped. He looked back at the white house. The lights from the ambulance had stopped. A few of the men in white uniforms carried out the large bag he'd seen earlier on a stretcher. They made their way down the staircase outside his parents' house successfully. Other men dressed similarly stood around, wiping the sweat from their brows, blowing on their cups to make the hot liquid inside cool faster. They talked and laughed as if nothing in the world was wrong. Colin's stomach turned. He tried not to think about what, or who, was inside the bag. It was too disturbing to think about. If he didn't distract himself quickly, he knew he would need to throw up. Colin looked back at Lily.

"Colin, did you hear me?" Dr. Reece asked.

"Sorry. What'd you say?"

"Is there another relative or place where Lily could stay for a couple of days?"

"Why would she need to stay somewhere else?"

"Step outside with me for a second, please."

Colin stepped out and closed his door. A moment later, the specialist was standing in front of him.

"Your sister just witnessed something that would be traumatic for anyone to see, but especially a twelve-year-old. She hasn't spoken a word since I arrived. It's crucial that she goes somewhere that she'll feel safe, and, frankly, right now, that place isn't here."

"We don't have any close relatives near here. Our only living grandparents are in Michigan."

"What's your relationship with your sister like, Colin?"

He shook his head. "Normal ... good, I guess."

"How old are you, Colin?"

"Twenty-two."

77

"Do you live with your parents, or on your own?"

"With a roommate. Why?"

"And this roommate of yours—does Lily know them, or like them, even?"

"Uh, yeah. She loves Rob."

"Normally, I'd prefer a young girl to stay somewhere with no unrelated young guys around, but since you're her closest relation, I need to ask you if you could take Lily to your house for a few days."

Colin rubbed one of his sideburns. "I don't know. I mean, I have to work."

She frowned. "Colin, look at me. Your sister is going to need support right now. You said you don't have any other relative she could stay with. She needs to feel safe. If you need a note to give to your boss explaining the situation, that's no problem."

He rubbed the back of his neck. "I just need a minute to think. This is all happening really fast. Why can't she just stay with my dad? Wouldn't she feel safe with him right now?"

"Look, I understand how you must be feeling right now. And I'm sorry to be asking so much of you, but my priority is Lily, and I need to know if you can take care of her or not. Your dad's going to be busy for the next few days talking to the authorities. And frankly, I don't think this is the best place for her to be right now. Colin, your sister's going to need to be with someone she loves and trusts twenty-four seven. Do you understand?"

Colin nodded slowly. What'd she mean by "your dad's going to be busy" with the authorities? He looked back at Lily, who was still staring at the seat in front of her.

"I can take her."

Chapter 16: Bad Cop

The officer, named Fred, pushed the notepad to the side and looked at Thomas from across the table. Thomas had never thought he'd be on the other side of this table. Who was this guy kidding? Good cop, bad cop? It was insulting that they'd sent a rookie to question him.

The rookie leaned back and smiled innocently. "I'm going to try to level with you here. You used to be one of us, so you get it. The more you tell me, the faster this will all be over. You're innocent, right? So, what's the silent treatment about?"

"I already told Jerry."

"Tom —can I call you Tom? You know the drill. You tell me the same story you told Jerry, and I see if the story lines up with what you told him."

"Why don't we just wait for the autopsy report to prove my innocence?"

"The autopsy results won't be back for another twenty-four hours. Why don't you just tell me what happened again?"

"I'm good."

"One of your neighbors reported hearing yelling the night before the call."

"Robin?" Tom genuinely laughed for the first time. "You'll need a better witness if you're planning on taking me to court.

She's crazier than a June bug in May."

Fred stood up. He looked flustered. Typical impatient rookie.

"Getting a doughnut, Fred?"

Fred smirked. "You're a real smart—"

"Don't say something you'll regret later."

Fred stormed out of the room. Thomas stared at the two-way mirror. Who was on the other side? Charlie? Toby? They were still a bunch of punks. Ever since he'd left the force, they'd been giving him a hard time. Petty stuff, like pulling him over for going five miles an hour over the speed limit. He was fortunate they'd never gotten him while he was drinking. They would've loved to find him too wasted to drive.

How much longer were they going to make Fred do this stupid routine? It was nothing more than a bunch of circus tricks. In the end, it was all about covering their tracks if something went wrong. If they made a mistake, nobody could say it was their fault.

A few minutes later, Fred came back in the room with a cup in his hand. The steam rose from it, giving off the aroma of the slightly burnt roast. Thomas's stomach growled.

"If you're going to insist on keeping me here any longer, could you at least bring me something to eat?" Thomas tried to look sad. "I'm starving."

Fred scowled. "Fine. I'll be right back."

It was obvious he didn't like being bossed around by a suspect. No cop did, but especially not rookie cops. They were determined to show who was boss, and Freddy dear knew he wasn't the boss. Tom couldn't help but get pleasure out of irritating Fred, even if it did make things harder on himself.

More time passed, and still Fred hadn't returned. Thomas leaned back against the hard plastic back of his chair and put his arms behind his head. He looked smug, and he knew it. What did it matter? They'd probably already made up their minds that he was guilty—in which case, there was nothing he could tell them to convince them otherwise.

* * *

At one p.m., Fred finally walked back in and slid a greasy bag and a to-go cup across the metal table. Thomas recognized the logo on the bag: Chang's Mexican-Asian Cuisine. He frowned. Everyone knew he hated that place. Besides, the food had already gotten cold, which meant Fred had stalled in bringing it in for an hour while they waited for him to sweat. Chang's was a two-minute drive away.

"What's wrong, Tommy? I got you food like you asked."

His stomach growled again. "Nothing. Smells great."

Anything was better than the burning pit in his stomach. He pulled the five-pound burrito out of the bag and dug in. The mixture of sriracha and shredded cheese did miracles for his hangover, even if the smell did make him want to yak.

"Anything else I can do to make this a more pleasant experience for you?" Fred asked.

Thomas swallowed his food. "Not unless you can bring my wife back."

Fred let out a pathetic laugh.

Tom frowned. "Fred, are you married?"

As Tom expected, Fred didn't answer. So Tom continued. "See, I asked because I'm not really in a laughing mood. You wouldn't be either, of course, if you woke up next to your wife to find her dead. And after doing nearly thirty minutes of CPR —"

"Which, by the way, seems like an awfully long time to me—"

"A long time? She's my wife!" He beat his fist on the table in frustration. "Like I was saying, thirty minutes of CPR, and calling the cops yourself, and you find yourself being interrogated." Tom set the burrito down and leaned forward. "Tell me this, Fred, is it a coincidence that I'm being interrogated by one of the only cops in this entire city that doesn't know me? Have you stopped and asked yourself why a man would call the cops if he'd just murdered his own wife? Wouldn't a guilty person at least try to hide the body? Answer me. You're still a cop, unlike me. So I'm sure your mind is sharper when it comes to these things."

Tom knew Fred wouldn't answer, but he paused anyway.

"You asked if you could make things more pleasant for me. Well, for starters you can treat me like a human being who's just lost his wife. Then you can end this silly game you're calling 'protocol' and wait for the autopsy report to come back and verify my story. And you did the third thing already." He held up the burrito. "Who told you I hated Chang's?"

Fred smirked. "You make an interesting point."

"Only one? Hmm, I thought I made several."

"You ask why a man would call the cops if he had something to hide. I asked myself the same question, and I have a few ideas. Maybe you were inebriated the night before and didn't remember doing it. After all, you are a drunk, Tom. Everyone here knows that." He smirked. "Or maybe you found out she was leaving you, but you decided that if she wasn't going to live with you, she wouldn't live at all. When you realized what you'd done, you knew you needed to make it look like an accident, and what better way to look innocent than calling the cops on yourself? Someone would have to be pretty smart, or pretty cocky. But then again, you used to be a cop. You know all the tricks. What would you be thinking if you were in my shoes?"

Thomas smiled.

"What's amusing?"

"Just picturing your face when you get the autopsy report back and realize you wasted your entire day trying to get me to confess to a crime I didn't commit. I wish I could be there to see it when it happens, but picturing it is making me pretty happy too."

The chair squeaked as Fred stood. He hesitated, as if he wanted to say something. Then he left. Finally, Thomas was alone again. He rubbed his wrists, which were still sore from doing compressions on Margaret. He thought about Fred's theory and tried to remember what had happened, but the details were still hazy. He'd drunk too much at the bar. Margaret was upset. They'd fought. What if ... Fred was right?

Chapter 17: Shock

She stared at the worn leather seat in front of her. A strange woman had introduced herself as a specialist. She'd said she was there to help Lily; she wanted to know what had happened. She asked lots of questions like, "What happened? What did you see? How did you feel?" Lily couldn't find the words.

The officer didn't say much while this woman was telling her she was safe. "Everything will be okay," she said. Be okay? How could she say it like she was so sure?

Colin had sat in the car with the woman who'd promised Lily she would be safe and the cop who said nothing. Then Colin talked to the woman outside the car for a while. Then he was gone again. The woman got back in the car and sat beside her.

"You're going to be staying at your brother's house for a few days, Lily," she said.

Lily listened but said nothing. Her body suddenly felt a wave of heat. She squeezed her legs together and wiggled slightly. The woman must've noticed. "Lily, do you need to use the bathroom?" she asked.

Lily wanted to say yes, but she couldn't. The woman asked again. Sweat formed around Lily's forehead.

"Lily, I need you to tell me what's wrong. Are you in pain, do you need to use the bathroom, can you point to where the pain is?" she asked.

The officer turned around suddenly. "Lady, you better do something quick. I'm not cleaning up her mess if she goes."

"Please be quiet. This is a delicate process." She turned back to Lily. "Lily, I can go with you to—"

Lily's legs felt warm, and she smelled a strong smell of ammonia. She stopped wiggling. The woman didn't talk for a few minutes.

The officer opened his door. "Lady, I hope you plan on cleaning that up, because I'm telling you, I'm not cleaning that up."

"Sir, with all due respect, please stop talking."

"What about my car? I've gotta drive around with that smell—"

"Officer, I'm sure this little girl isn't the first person to have had an accident in the back off this car. Maybe you can walk around for a little while and give this young lady and me some privacy while you calm down."

Lily heard a sound. It was Colin's voice. He was back again.

"Sorry about that. I told my boss I needed to take off a couple of days. Is Lily ready to go with me?"

Lily stared at the seat. The door beside her was opening, and Colin's arm was reaching toward her.

"I would advise you not to force her to move. She'll get up when she's ready."

"Fine." He stepped back. "How long does that usually take in these cases?"

"It'll take however long it takes. You need to be patient."

He sniffed. "Did she use the—"

"Colin, walk over here with me, please."

85

Everything was quiet again.

* * *

"It's perfectly normal for children to wet themselves in cases like these. It's their body's fight-or-flight reaction. Lily's body only has one goal right now: to survive."

The cop walked up. "My shift ended an hour ago. How much longer do you think this will take?"

Dr. Reece smiled. "Jerry, if you want to keep your job, I strongly suggest you stop making my job harder."

"Is that a threat?"

"My job is to make sure that young lady is safe. If you continue to derail my progress, you'll be lucky to work as a security guard at the Tanger Outlet."

Colin watched Lily while the two so-called professionals argued. He interrupted Jerry while he was still complaining about his car smelling.

"Dr. Reece, Lily looks uncomfortable."

She sighed. "You're probably right; it's been about ten minutes. Hopefully, she'll move on her own soon, but if not we'll have to move her, or she'll get a rash." She looked at Colin. "Can you pack Lily's things? She'll need clothes, toiletries, blankets, pillows, and anything else that might make her feel comfortable—like her favorite sweater or book." She walked back toward the car. "Lily, your brother's going to get your things. He'll be right back."

The woman turned back to Colin. "Does she have anything that has a special connection with her mother?"

Colin nodded.

"Good, bring that too."

Lily could hear Colin tell the woman he'd be back as if she were listening to the radio. She could hear their voices, but it felt like the voices were coming from somewhere far away, where they couldn't hear her if she tried to talk back. Then Colin's voice was gone, just like her mom's and dad's voices were gone. Everyone around her was leaving her, and she couldn't say anything to stop them. She'd had dreams where she couldn't scream or run. Maybe this was just one of those dreams.

Colin returned with a duffel bag full of Lily's things and her favorite beanie in his other hand.

"I could carry her to my car, if that'd help," he said.

"No, thank you."

"I've carried her a thousand times before. She loves it."

"This time's different."

The woman told Lily that she could get into her brother's car if she wanted to. Lily could take all the time she needed, said the woman. The cop sighed, giving away his impatience. "I don't have all day," he mumbled. It seemed obvious to Lily that he wanted everyone to know he was irritated that he had to wait.

The woman ignored the cop and told Lily they were going to start driving to Colin's house. Lily could stay in the cop car if she wanted to, or she could go to Colin's car. Lily wanted to speak, scream, something, anything. Instead, she sat and said nothing.

Suddenly, the car started to move. Lily started to feel sick as the cop drove. He didn't talk to the woman anymore. The woman didn't say anything to Lily during the drive. After they had driven for a while, the car started to slow down. Then it stopped moving completely.

"We're at your brother's house, Lily," the woman said.

The cop mumbled loud enough for Lily to hear. "My wife's gonna kill me."

The cop said he needed to make a phone call and stepped out of the car. He paced with the phone glued to his ear, like it was a conch shell and he was trying to hear the ocean. A moment later, his voice sounded strange and high pitched as it traveled through the crack in the window. He explained to his wife that he wasn't at the club again, he swore on his son's life, then said sorry for swearing on their son's life, then said he was working still, he wasn't lying, this crazy lady was making him work overtime; then he started to tell her that the woman was a professional, he didn't even know her; no, he couldn't let her speak to the woman, she was working; no, he wasn't at the club. He'd gone full circle. Lily thought about her own parents arguing the night before. Maybe Colin was right—all married couples argue. Lily's thoughts were interrupted as the woman started talking again.

"This is a beautiful picture of your mother. When was this taken, do you know?" she asked.

Lily glanced at the photograph. The picture was from her mother's wedding album. Colin must've given it to her. He knew it was Lily's favorite. Warm liquid filled her eyes. Suddenly, it didn't feel like a dream, or nightmare, anymore. Her tears were real and tickled her cheek as they rolled down. She'd never felt tears in her dreams before. A hand was rubbing her shoulder.

"Crying is good. You'll be okay," the woman said.

Lily waited for the woman to ask another question, but instead she continued to rub Lily's shoulder quietly. The woman was gentle like her mother. For a second, Lily closed her eyes and imagined it was her mother rubbing her shoulder and not the woman beside her whom she had never met. It seemed so real that Lily was tempted to open her eyes and look at her mother's face, but she knew if she opened them the moment would be over. A stranger would be sitting beside her again.

The moment ended anyway when the woman started to speak.

"You're in a safe place now, Lily. The feelings you're experiencing will get easier to understand. I'm sure you're feeling confused right now, but that's okay." She paused. "You know, when I was close to your age, my mother fell asleep, too, and I was afraid just like you are now. Do you know what helped me?"

Lily sniffled. The woman seemed to know that she was listening.

"What helped me was talking about her. For instance, my mom was so funny, and she always smelled like sugar cookies. I bet your mother was funny too. She looks like she had a great laugh in this picture. I bet you can hear her laugh now? Even though she's not here right now, you'll always be able to keep her alive in your memory if you talk about her."

Lily listened. The woman pointed at her heart.

"In there, your mother will always be alive. And nobody can take that from you."

Lily jumped as the cop swung open the driver's door and sat down. The car rocked from side to side, like one of those waterbeds Lily had sat on once, before settling again. He wiped the back of his hand against his forehead and complained about the weather; it was too hot to be standing outside. The woman didn't respond to him.

Lily could feel herself reaching for the photograph. Her body had felt like a statue all morning, and for the first time she felt human again. The woman let go of the photograph so Lily could take it. Lily gently moved her fingers over her mother's blonde hair. A sharp pain traveled from her fingers to her heart: it was just a picture, glossy paper. It wasn't hair; it wasn't really her mother. She felt the photograph fall into her lap.

"What you're feeling, Lily, is called grief. It's your body's way of dealing with loss. This isn't going to be easy, but try not to fight it. The more you think about your mother, the less it'll hurt when you do. It's just going to take time."

Lily quivered. The woman wrapped her arm around her. Lily leaned into the stranger and closed her eyes. It felt so much like her mother's arms.

"Mom ... m-m-mommy," Lily sobbed.

Chapter 18: Butterflies

It was hard to believe it was only four p.m. It felt more like midnight. A lifetime had happened in the last six hours. Dr. Reece came back from Colin's room, Lily's temporary room, and sat facing him from across the foldable table. Dr. Reece set her tote down as if it weighed a hundred pounds. It was filled to the brim with binders and notepads. Colin could see the edge of one of the notepads where the tote had fallen open. One of the scribbled words looked like it said "Lily," which wasn't surprising, since she'd been interviewing Lily all day. Colin tried to tilt his head to see what the other squiggly letters said about Lily. One of the words was "trauma," which wasn't much of a surprise either. Colin screwed his head back on straight as Dr. Reece cleared her throat. He looked at her, expecting her to chastise him for being nosy, but it seemed she hadn't noticed and was actually just clearing her throat. Her eyes were closed as she tugged on the elastic band in her hair. She seemed human for the first time as she rubbed her tired-looking eyes.

The scent of the doctor's shampoo traveled toward Colin as she took her hair out of the tight ponytail she kept it in. It reminded him of the way his mother's hair always smelled when he was a kid. In a matter of seconds, a thousand memories came flooding back: of him playing with his mother as a child, being held by her, breathing in the flowery smell of her daisy-colored hair. The memories were already fading away again as Dr. Reece brushed her fingers through her tangled brown hair. The pain was gone again. He'd noticed that the pain had come in waves all day.

The uptight specialist had disappeared along with her tight ponytail, and a newly transformed woman with long wavy hair stared at him. He didn't like the strange feeling in his stomach as he looked back at her. She had to be old enough to be his mother, and he didn't find her very attractive, but the butterflies were there nonetheless. His emotions had been off all day. That had to be the reason for the queasiness in his stomach.

"Colin, you look pale. Do you feel okay?" she asked.

He shook his head as he jumped up from his foldout chair and sprinted to the bathroom. When he made it to the toilet, his knees hit the tile floor, hard. He'd barely made it in time before the acidic orange contents from his stomach were coming up. It felt as if his emotions were being heaved into the porcelain bowl as he retched up the last morsel of food inside of him from the day before. He hadn't eaten anything all day, and his body seemed to desperately want to rid itself of everything inside him. What his body couldn't know was that he couldn't throw up the one thing he wanted to: the pain of losing her.

After a few minutes, he stopped. His insides felt empty and yet full at the same time. The pain of losing his mother seemed to fill every atom in his body, like somehow he was absorbing her absence.

The nauseous feeling hadn't been butterflies after all.

* * *

He gargled and spat the minty-flavored mouthwash into the porcelain basin again and opened the door. His eyes opened wider as he turned the corner to find Dr. Reece still sitting at the table. After what he'd just gone through in the bathroom, he'd completely forgotten she was there. She looked up from her phone and smiled.

"Feel better?" she asked. "Lily isn't the only one who's experienced trauma today. It would be advisable for you to speak to a grief counselor. I can give you the name of someone I recommend."

Colin nodded. "That's okay. I can't exactly afford a therapist, but thanks. I'll get through this. I'm more worried about my sister right now."

"Okay, that's your decision. Let's talk about what Lily's going to need, before I leave. She managed to get herself into clean clothes, and she'd already fallen asleep when I left the room. She made some good progress earlier, but she's still going to need to see me for the PTSD. Based on what I've seen already, she's going to be fine now that she's gotten through the initial …"

She was still talking as Colin looked around for a notepad or a pen. How was he supposed to remember all this?

"… over the next few days, especially these initial hours, I want you to watch out for things like panic attacks—sweating, difficulty breathing, things like that. Watch her eating habits. Many children who witness a parent die won't eat for days. If she won't eat or drink, we'll need to give her fluids intravenously …"

Colin nodded and tried to listen.

"We can do the sessions at—"

"Should I be writing this down?"

93

Dr. Reece paused. "I don't think that's necessary. All of this is common sense, really. She may act hostile, agitated, or start to isolate herself. If you get worried, just call me. It doesn't matter what time it is. I'll answer. My phone stays on twenty-four seven. Otherwise, I'll just see you both at her session."

"What session?"

"Weren't you listening?" She paused. "I realize that this is a lot to take in. She'll need therapy at least two times a week, for now. Someone needs to be with her twenty-four seven."

"How many weeks are we talking? How am I supposed to be with her that much? I have to work five nights a week."

"Colin, I'm not going to pretend this process will be easy, but your sister needs you. She can't be alone right now, and your dad will be busy for the next couple of days, if everything goes well."

"What do you mean?"

"I'm sorry. Which part wasn't clear?"

"Why wouldn't everything go well?"

"They're just trying to figure out what happened. Once they find out, we'll go from there. Let's just focus on Lily for now." She paused and sighed. "Just so you know, my responsibility is your sister, and your sister only. I don't mean to come across as uncaring. This has been a lot for you to process as well, and I suggest you talk to someone about all of this. Unfortunately, that person cannot be me, because that would be a conflict of interest. However, since my priority is your sister, I'm suggesting strongly that you get the help you need to deal with all of this for your sister's sake as well as your own."

She slid a brochure across the table—"What to Expect After Trauma"—followed by a small card with the name TODD BAR- LEY, GRIEF COUNSELOR. She tapped her red fingernail against the card. "In case you change your mind." She paused and added, "I'll be in contact with you tomorrow morning to find out how Lily's doing." She stood up. "Well, that's all for now. That idiot downstairs—Jerry, I think his name is—probably already left me. How someone like him even keeps a job, I'll never know." She swung the large tote over her shoulder. "Call me if you have questions. Good night."

Chapter 19: Nightmare

Colin was awakened from his deep sleep as someone jiggled their keys in the door lock and opened it. It had to be Rob—or a really nice burglar who used a key. He cringed and pulled the cover over his head as the light came on, hitting his pupils and making them close in on themselves too quickly. Suddenly he heard a gasp come from the other side of the room.

"Dude, you almost gave me a heart attack!" Rob said.

It was the most words Rob had said to him since their fight two months ago.

"Yeah." Colin pulled the blanket down and squinted as his delicate pupils adjusted to the light. "Well, you blinded me, so we're even."

Rob was walking toward the recliner while simultaneously trying to step on the back of his nonslip shoes to take them off. He reminded Colin of a dog trying to remove those little shoes their owners put on their paws . Finally, Rob gave up and sat on the recliner. He shook the shoes off his feet and onto the floor like he always did. Colin had tripped on them at least a dozen times before but had never told Rob, since that would have been the beginning of the "Let's talk about our pet peeves" discussion, which he didn't feel like having. The shoe made a loud noise as it fell onto the floor. Rob repeated with the other shoe.

Colin pushed the air through his teeth. "Shhh," he whispered.

"Dude, have you been drinking or something?" Rob asked. Colin shook his head while Rob laughed. "Why are you sleeping out here? And why are you whispering?"

"I tried to call you earlier. Lily's sleeping in my room. It'll only be a few days."

"Why? What's going on?" He yawned and pulled his socks off, exposing the shriveled raisin-looking feet underneath. "Olivia asked where you were today. I told her I wasn't sure. I thought today was your day to work, but I can't keep up with my own schedule, so—" He cringed as he rubbed the heel of his foot. "My feet are killing me. I need to get new shoes."

Colin decided to say it before he could chicken out. "My mom died."

Rob's tan skin turned gray. "When?"

"This morning ... or last night. Well, I don't exactly know yet. They're doing an autopsy."

"What happened, man?"

Colin propped himself on his elbow and rubbed his eyes. "I don't know. Lily was there, but she hasn't spoken to anyone since this morning. Now my dad's being questioned by the police—"

"What for?"

Colin scowled at Rob. "Keep your voice down. I don't want Lily to wake up."

"Sorry. What on earth would they question your dad for?" he whispered.

"I don't know."

Colin could tell Rob was trying to think of what to say next. "I

97

can't believe this," he finally said.

"Yeah. Me either. It doesn't feel real yet, you know?" Rob nodded like he knew. "I haven't even cried."

"It's a lot to process."

Colin nodded. "So, you don't mind if Lily stays here, do you? That's what I was calling about earlier."

"Of course not, man. I know we haven't been talking a lot lately, but she's always family. You don't have to ask."

The phone buzzed. One new message from Olivia. Colin gulped. He'd been the world's worst boyfriend, if he could even call himself that. Olivia had to be the most patient woman on the earth, but she would have to wait one more day. Colin set his phone down and looked at it. Rob raised one eyebrow. "You good?"

"It was Olivia. I'm just not ready to talk about this yet."

"I get it. Do you want me to tell her when I see her?"

"No, it should come from me. I'll tell her tomorrow. Thanks, though."

"All right. I'm sorry, Colin. This really sucks."

"Yeah ... I don't mean to be—I really need to try to sleep."

"Of course." Rob jumped to his bare feet. "I'll turn the light off so you can sleep. I'll try to be quiet."

* * *

Colin gasped as he was awakened once again. Someone was shaking his shoulder. His eyes shot open. The lights were still off and it was dark, but he could see enough to tell that Rob was staring at him like he'd seen a ghost. The white of Rob's eyes showed through the darkness like two moon crests. "Colin, wake up. Your sister's in the bathroom."

Colin sat up, startled. "What?"

"The lights were off, so I didn't see her at first. When I turned on the light, I swear, man, I almost crapped in my pants—she was curled up on the floor, it sounded like, I don't know, like she was crying—"

Colin threw his blanket off and ran to the bathroom. He'd walked around their apartment enough times in the dark to know his way around blindfolded. He remembered that Rob's shoes were still lying somewhere on the floor and prepared himself to trip over them. His shoulders relaxed as he made it to the hallway without falling or stubbing his toe on anything. Rob must've left the light on in the bathroom because a soft yellow glow escaped under the crack of the door, like a beacon showing him the way to shore.

When he opened the door, Lily was as Rob had described her, except she'd sat up against the tub with her knees tucked tightly to her chest. Her shoulders shook as if she was crying, but there weren't any tears coming from her eyes. She looked the way Colin felt. Colin knelt in front of her. She was trembling.

"Lily?" He spoke softly. "Hey, Lily, what's wrong?"

His voice still sounded stiff and groggy.

She shook her head. "I want Mommy."

"Yeah." He sighed. "I know."

Her face twisted like she was in pain. "I miss ... Mo-m-m," she sobbed.

The sound of her sobs felt like someone had swung a baseball bat right into Colin's ribs, making it hard for him to breathe. Her face was bright red. He worried that she wasn't breathing. "Lily, breathe ... breathe." He grabbed hold of the edge of the bathtub and sat on the cool tiles beside her. He was fully awake now.

"It's going to be all right." She leaned into his chest as he wrapped his arms around her. "You'll feel better when you see Dad."

She pulled back so fast it pried his arms apart. "Don't make me see him."

He looked into her wild-looking eyes. "Who, Dad?"

She leaned into him again and buried her red face against the pit of his arm. Her body shook so hard that Colin worried she would have a seizure. Her choppy breaths tickled his skin through his thin T-shirt, but he stayed still to not disturb her.

"He—" Her voice sounded muffled from under his arm.

She couldn't seem to form the words. Colin wished he could read her mind so she wouldn't have to say it, but he cringed at the thought of what he might find out if he could.

"He what?"

"I think he—he killed Mom."

The blood drained from Colin's face. Lily cringed. "Ow, you're squeezing my arm, Colin." He looked at her. "Oh, sorry." He couldn't believe the words that had just come out of her mouth. Killed? Mom? How? Dad? No.

The doctor had told him to call if something like this happened. He couldn't call her, though. Lily would tell her, and she'd have to tell the police. But how could he not call? Lily needed help. Maybe there was one of those confidentiality things. Therapists weren't allowed to tell the police what their clients said, or something like that. It wasn't like his dad could actually have done what Lily was saying.

He pulled his arms away from her gently. "Lily, I'll be right back."

He pulled the door shut carefully, to avoid startling her. The apartment was pitch black again; Rob must've gone to bed already. This time, his pupils had adjusted to the light of the bathroom, so it seemed the apartment had grown even darker. He cautiously tiptoed to the couch, where he'd left his phone, still trying to catch his breath, which he realized he'd been holding for some reason. He fumbled around in the dark in search of the small object. If he'd been thinking clearly, he would've turned the light on first.

Something cold and metallic was lying in the crack of one of the cushions—it was either a remote or his phone. He grabbed it. Please be the phone, he thought.

The blue LED glow made him squint as he searched for the number he'd saved in his phone earlier. He felt like someone had tightened a belt around his chest and he was struggling to breathe against it as the phone dialed. He pulled on the collar of his thin cotton T-shirt in an attempt to alleviate the feeling of being suffocated, but to no avail.

The phone rang once. Then twice. He glanced at the bathroom door. It was still shut. Only the small line of light still slipped through the crack under the door. His heart skipped a beat as Dr. Reece answered the phone. "Hello?" Her voice sounded raspy, like he'd just woken her up.

"Sorry to call this late. It's Colin. You said I could call if there was an emergency."

"What's the emergency?" She sounded awake now.

He tried to catch his breath. "Are therapists allowed to tell the police what they're told?"

"It depends." She was quiet. "Colin, did Lily tell you something?"

"I can't tell you if there's any chance you'll tell the police."

"You're not protecting anyone by not telling me." The belt was getting tighter. "Colin, are you still there?"

"Yeah."

"I'm coming over."

"No, wait. She's just upset. I don't even know if what she's saying is true."

"What exactly is she saying?"

"I—I shouldn't have called." His heart pounded. "This was a bad idea."

"You did the right thing by calling. I'm coming over now." She sighed over the phone. "I don't have a choice."

She hung up.

Chapter 20: The Witness

After passing Colin as if he weren't there, Dr. Reece grabbed the towel, folded it on the bathroom shelf, and placed it on the floor next to Lily. She was wearing the same thing she'd been wearing the last time he saw her: a navy-blue pantsuit with pointed blue high heels—except now the pantsuit was wrinkled. She held on to the edge of the tub and eased herself onto the towel. Colin stood back and watched anxiously from the doorway as Dr. Reece asked Lily to tell her what she'd told Colin thirty minutes ago. Lily said nothing.

"Were your parents fighting that night, Lily?" Colin suddenly realized it had already been an entire day since his mom had died. "It's okay, Lily. You can tell me if they were fighting. It's normal for couples to fight sometimes."

Lily nodded slowly. Colin felt his throat tighten.

"I'm sure you were scared. Did they yell a lot?"

Lily continued to nod.

"Lily, did your dad hurt your mom?"

Lily stopped nodding and looked at Dr. Reece. Even without saying a word, it seemed to Colin that she was thinking, *Yes*.

"Did he do more than hurt her, Lily?"

Lily looked at her lap, where she was holding her own hand as if imagining that one of the hands were her mother's. She

103

began nodding again.

Colin whispered. "She's just nodding at everything you say. That doesn't mean my dad hurt my mom."

"No, it doesn't. But remember what I said about being patient. Nodding is progress. At least she's responding." He could see her jaw moving as she spoke to him without looking away from Lily. "How about we take you back to your bed now, Lily? You can try and get some sleep again."

Dr. Reece looked at Colin for the first time since she'd arrived. "Can you help her up? Gently."

Lily looked at his outstretched hand as if she was deciding whether or not to let go of her mom's imaginary hand to take his. It was obvious even to him which one she would choose. He avoided looking at Dr. Reece, who wouldn't approve of what he was about to do, and knelt down in front of Lily. She was his little sister, and he knew what was best for her. He promised Lily that he wouldn't drop her before wrapping his arms around her and picking her up like a little child.

As if he'd carried Lily a million times, he navigated through the narrow doorways without as much as Lily's beanie brushing against the frames. Colin could hear Dr. Reece's sharp-sounding steps follow closely behind.

The bed felt like a long way down as he lowered Lily onto it. She curled up under the thick comforter and closed her eyes. He stood quietly and waited for her to fall asleep. The tightness in his chest began to ease as her breaths became slow and steady. He tried to imagine why Lily would think their dad would hurt their mother. Of course their dad couldn't have done something like that. It didn't matter right now. Soon they would all be together as a happy family—well, almost all together.

It had only taken a few minutes for her to begin snoring

quietly. Colin walked lightly across the hardwood floor to the doorway and turned off the light. Dr. Reece followed him into the hallway as he closed the door. Dr. Reece's heels echoed through the apartment as she walked behind him. When they stopped walking, Colin could hear the faint sound of snoring coming from both bedrooms. He wondered how they could still be asleep.

Colin opened the front door for Dr. Reece. She stopped walking, as if she was waiting for something. He felt like he should thank her for coming, but then again, he hadn't exactly wanted her to come. Calling her had been a mistake. She hadn't done anything to help Lily, and now she probably suspected his dad of being guilty. She turned to look at him. Somehow her face looked older and softer at the same time. He suddenly realized she wasn't wearing any makeup.

"You did the right thing by calling."

He looked down at her pointed blue shoes. "I thought she was in shock or something. I hope you don't tell the police about this. I don't think she understood what you were saying. Our dad would never hurt our mom."

Dr. Reece nodded, like she was considering. "The autopsy report will clear your father's reputation if he's innocent."

Colin looked into her dark-brown eyes. They each looked like one big pupil, without an iris. "You won't tell the police, will you?"

"For right now, there's not enough to tell. She didn't actually say anything. Nodding isn't exactly enough to count as a testimonial in a courtroom." She checked her phone. "It's almost three in the morning. I have a session in—wow, four hours." She shook her head. "I'm going to try to get another hour of sleep. Call me if you need anything else. Otherwise, I'll be back at ten tomorrow to talk to Lily."

Colin knew better than to object. Dr. Reece would come whether he wanted her to or not. He nodded and closed the door as she walked away.

Chapter 21: Five A.M.

Thomas stumbled through the doorway. The lights were still on in the house. Great. One of those idiots must've left the lights on after they'd finished snooping around. They were treating him like a criminal, not a suspect. How'd they know about the fight, anyway? That nosy neighbor, Robin, probably told them. Why couldn't that woman keep her nose in her own business? He shook his head. Him—a murderer. He scoffed and swung the door shut behind him. He and Margie had had their disagreements, sure, but what couple didn't?

He leaned against the hallway walls as he stumbled toward their—his—bedroom. From the hallway he could see that the bed was in the same state as it'd been earlier that day. He'd forgotten that he was supposed to get rid of the mattress. There was no way he was going to sleep on that thing. He would just have to sleep on the couch, if he could stand up and get to it.

Something moved as his hand bumped it. It sounded like metal or glass as it hit the floor. He turned back and looked for what had caused the sound. A picture frame lay on the floor, facedown. He leaned against the wall as he tried to pick it up. He felt like he was operating a claw machine game at an arcade that gets close but never grabs the toy. Finally, he had it. The glass protecting the picture had shattered, but the picture underneath was unscathed. Margaret was only twenty in the photograph. They had just found out she was pregnant with their first child, Colin.

The night before came flooding back to him in all its fuzzy details as he stared at the broken picture frame. Margie had been upset that he was home from rehab. Something had fallen and broken. He tried to remember what it was as he looked up at the counter. The vase his wife's deceased mother had given them as a wedding present was missing. His wife loved that vase. No wonder she was so upset. He could be a class-A jerk sometimes.

Tom looked back at the picture in his hands. He could still hear her saying "Tom, could you at least try to look happy?" as the photographer snapped the pictures. He was only twenty-four and terrified. She was so happy to be a mother. Tom began to sob quietly as he shielded his face with his hand. The memories were bittersweet. How could she be gone?

Tom tried to navigate through the foggy memories. What had happened when they'd gone into the bedroom? He'd never seen her that angry before. She'd picked up her phone. He'd thought she was trying to call the police, so he took the phone from her; if the cops knew that, that alone would be enough to send him to jail. She'd fallen on the bed when he'd taken it. She wasn't hurt, though. Was she? The memory was too foggy. He couldn't have hurt her—could he?

He rubbed his bruised wrists.

Digger answered the phone. It sounded like he was sleeping.

"No, honey. Go back to bed. Everything's fine." His voice sounded distant. "Thomas, the sun's not up yet."

"I think I killed her."

Chapter 22: Paintings

C olin's phone buzzed. To his surprise, it was his boss Al this time, instead of Olivia. Rob must've told him what had happened to his mother, which meant everyone at the restaurant would know by now. Colin forwarded the incoming call to voice mail and looked at Dr. Reece, who patiently waited to have his full attention before continuing.

"Sorry, what were you saying?" Colin asked when Dr. Reece didn't say anything.

"Do you need to get that?"

The phone dinged. "No. It's fine."

Dr. Reece continued finally. "Okay, like I was saying, Lily's first session went very well." She pointed at the painting Lily was still working on in the corner of Colin's bedroom. "Paintings can tell us a lot about what's going on in a child's mind. As you can see, Lily's painting is of two girls at a park. Based on the photograph I saw, I believe it's Lily and your mother. Did she enjoy going to the park with her mother?"

Colin nodded. "That was one of Lily's favorite places to go. Our mom took her there every weekend, unless there was a tornado or something. They stopped going when Lily started chemo."

"That helps me a lot, Colin. Thank you." She scribbled something on a notepad. "Did your father ever go to the park with them?"

"Sometimes."

She scribbled something that looked like Chinese characters. "I want to talk to you about Lily's relationship with your father. What's that like?"

An uneasy feeling rose inside Colin—defensiveness maybe?

"It's normal. I guess. He works a lot. She was always closer to Mom. I was always closer to Dad."

"Did your dad ever put his hands on you or Lily growing up?"

"No!"

The feeling was definitely defensiveness. She was stirring the pot, looking for secrets and scandals as if she were looking for noodles, when there were none to be found.

"Colin, I understand that you don't want your father to get in trouble. But Lily's safety comes first. I need you to be completely honest with me. Did your dad ever have a temper?"

"I mean, he got angry, but who doesn't? I wouldn't say he had a temper. I mean, he's yelled at me a few times when I did something really bad, but I'm sure I deserved it."

She scratched the pencil rapidly against the notepad. Colin swallowed.

"Did your dad ever hit your mom?"

"No! He never hit any of us."

"Did he drink a lot?"

Colin stared at his shoes. She'd found the only noodle in the pot there was to be found. How'd she know about the drinking?

"He likes to drink beer occasionally. What's a lot?"

"Have you ever seen your father drunk?"

"I don't know. If he was, I couldn't tell."

"What about drug use?"

This was exhausting.

"He didn't do drugs. He didn't drink a lot. He didn't hit us. He's a normal guy."

"You said he worked a lot. How often was he gone?"

"I don't know. Maybe twice a month."

"For how long?"

"It varied."

"Give me an estimate."

"A week at a time."

"That's a long time to be absent from his family's life. How'd your mom feel about him being gone so much?" she asked.

"She knew he was just trying to pay the bills."

"So they talked a lot about their financial problems in front of you and Lily."

Colin squinted. "Not really. Is there a reason why you would assume they did?"

"Colin, did you know that your parents were having financial problems?"

"No, and I'm not sure I'm comfortable with you telling me about them. Whatever my parents were dealing with was their personal problem."

"My point is that your parents were under a lot of stress. That takes a toll on a marriage."

"With all due respect, you know nothing about my parents. You're assuming a lot about two people you've never even met."

"Is it assuming to believe that two people raising a child with a life-threatening disease would be under a larger than normal amount of stress? I don't think it is. And is it assuming to believe that stress takes a toll on a marriage?"

She shook her head to answer her own questions. Colin longed for Dr. Reece to remove the bow wrapped tightly around her hair again and become the Dr. Reece he'd seen a glimpse of the night before—the one who seemed almost human, the one who said they'd wait for the autopsy report to come back before making any assumptions. He longed to see that Dr. Reece.

Colin rubbed the short blond hair on his neck. "All I know is they were both great parents. How is any of this helping Lily get better?"

"I need to understand her relationship with your father so I can decide what's best for Lily, long term."

"Meaning what?"

"Until the autopsy report comes back this afternoon, we can't be sure that your sister will be able to go back to living with your dad. Depending on your circumstances, you may be able to take care of her, but you'd have to go to court and petition for guardianship. For now, we're taking precautionary steps to find out what'll be best for Lily."

"When the autopsy report comes back, my dad will be innocent, so you're wasting your time."

"Even if it does prove his innocence, I've seen and heard enough to wonder if Lily is safe with him."

How could she say that? Of course Lily was better off with their father. Colin glanced at Lily. She seemed absorbed in her painting. "I'm not sure I understand. Aren't you just supposed to help Lily get better from the trauma of losing our mother?"

"I am helping Lily get better. My job is to decide what's best for Lily going forward."

"How is that your job? I thought you were a therapist?"

"Yes, and I'm hired by the court to decide what's best for Lily. If I don't think she's safe with your father, which I don't right now, then I'll suggest to the court that they find another arrangement for Lily."

It was like she'd knocked the air out of his lungs. He wanted to tell her how stupid she was being, but the words couldn't come out. He sat with his mouth gaping open instead.

"My father isn't a bad man," he said finally.

"So you've said. Your father is aces in your eyes." She looked very serious. "Colin, has your father called you once since yesterday?"

"Yes."

Colin looked into her eyes and lied. Why hadn't his father called?

* * *

Colin opened the front door. Dr. Reece grabbed a different tote than the one she'd had the night before. It had the logo "We Believe the Children Are the Future" on the side of it. The bag looked like it had lost weight since she'd arrived. She was like Mary Poppins, pulling canvases and paintbrushes from her magic tote. She turned and smiled at him. It felt like déjà vu of the night before. This woman was coming and going like the waves, leaving relief and pain behind.

Colin closed the door behind her as she walked out of the apartment and then cursed himself. How could he have been so stupid? Why had he told her all that stuff? They were going to take Lily, and it'd be his fault. As if Lily hadn't been through enough. Now this.

Lily was painting a new picture when Colin walked in the room. The picture looked like their house, with a blond stick-figure family. He squatted beside her and watched. "Is that you, Mom, and Dad?" he asked, pointing to the two taller stick figures.

"No."

"Who is it then?"

"That's me and Mom." She pointed at the last stick figure. "That's you."

"Where's Dad?" She shrugged. "Lily, Dad isn't gone. You'll see him in a couple of days."

"What if I don't want to?" She returned to her painting like she was Picasso making a masterpiece.

"Why wouldn't you?" She leaned so close to her painting that Colin worried she'd get high from the paint fumes. "Lily, why don't you want to see Dad again?"

She turned and looked at him. "It's his fault Mom's dead!" She turned back to her painting. Colin's heart stopped again. Even when he'd played football, he'd never felt his heart race as much as it had over the last two days. "Lily—did you tell Dr. Reece that?"

She shrugged. He started to worry that she'd told Dr. Reece too much, and he remembered what she'd said. Lily hadn't said anything that could be used in court. He exhaled sharply. The sooner the autopsy report came back, the sooner this doubting and questioning would be over. It felt strange to have such a morbid thought. He never would've believed there would be a day when he could want to get his mother's death certificate, but now, there were worse things than his mother being dead—like his father being the one who'd killed her.

Chapter 23: Sunrise

The sunrise seemed brighter and pinker than usual from the passenger seat of Digger's car. They'd sat together, in Tom's driveway, for almost ten minutes without saying as much as a hello. Tom blew on the coffee Digger had brought him and then sipped. He watched Digger as he sifted through the piles of sugar packets in his glove compartment, which he'd collected from a million different restaurants over the years.

"Still collecting, huh?"

Digger answered in the form of a weak laugh. The smell was almost enough to make Tom feel better, but not quite. The scalding drink burned his tongue as he tilted the cup back farther than he meant to, but he didn't care. Digger's attention seemed to be consumed as he doctored his coffee up some more before drinking it. Once he'd gotten it how he wanted it, he settled into his seat and sighed.

"Thanks for the coffee," Tom said.

"Tom, let me take you to the hospital, please."

Tom pulled the lid off his paper cup to let the coffee cool quicker. "I'm fine."

"I found you passed out on the floor with pieces of glass next to your hand. Which part of that is fine?" He paused for a long time. "Tell me the truth. Were you going to try to—"

"Kill myself?" He flipped the visor down. "No. I was trying to look at the photo and lost my balance."

"I want to believe you." Digger sighed. "Tom, do you remember calling me this morning?"

"Yeah. Vaguely."

"I don't even want to repeat what you told me." Digger waited while Tom tested his coffee again. "We've been friends for a long time. So I'm giving you a chance to explain, since you were obviously drunk before, but you know I can't turn a blind eye to something this big."

Thomas nodded and scratched the itchy scruff on his cheek. "I can barely remember anything from that night. I'd had way too much to drink. I remember we fought—then I remember waking up next to her." He could feel her again like she was there. His chest trembled. "She was so cold."

Digger stared at the coffee as he moved the stirrer in circles, as if the truth about what happened that night might appear in the ripples.

"So you don't remember ... doing anything?"

"No."

Digger looked up from his coffee. "Then why do you think you did?"

"She was forty-two, and healthy. We were fighting that night. How else could she have—"

"Look, I've known you now for, what, twenty-three, twenty-four years. I've seen my share of domestic violence in this field. I don't think you're capable of doing something like that."

Tom rubbed his eyes, then his hair, then nose, until he'd touched every part of his face. As the sun rose higher over the horizon, its rays found a way to make it around the visor and beam into his eyes. He grunted as he sat up straighter to get back out of the sun's reach. Digger's voice added to the discomfort he was in. "Tom, you really should go to the doctor. You could have a concussion."

"I don't have a concussion. Just a hangover," Tom snapped.

"Okay." Digger put his hands up innocently. "Can I make one suggestion?"

"What?"

"Assume you're innocent until proven guilty. Wait till the report comes back from the coroner so you don't put that burden on yourself unnecessarily."

"She was so young. She couldn't have—"

"Young, healthy people die unexpectedly too, Tom. You were a cop. You saw it happen."

"Yeah, and I always suspected foul play. Young, healthy people don't just die."

Digger sighed. "Tom, try to put aside your paranoia for a moment. Your daughter is staying with your son right now. If you get convicted, that won't be a temporary arrangement. Lily just lost her mother. She doesn't need to lose her father too."

"It's easier if I assume the worst."

Digger grunted. "Maybe I'm wrong, but why's it sound to me like you want to be found guilty?"

"I've been a terrible father. She's better off with Colin."

"Regardless of what kind of father you've been, you are her father. You're what she needs."

Tom gave up fighting with the sun and closed his eyes. "I used to take children from parents that were just like me." Tom shook his head, with his eyes still shut. "Gosh, I remember this one case. The angry neighbor called and said that the music was too loud next door. Remember?" Digger didn't answer. "Well, when

I got there, everyone was still partying and drinking. They were probably just celebrating something. I wanted to tell everyone to leave and then get on my way, but the girl was playing with one of her dolls in the living room. Her mother ran and picked the girl up, and I could tell she'd had too much to drink. The protocol was to take the child until the parents could sober up and talk to CPS. Of course you know that, but I'll never forget the look on that little girl's face when I pulled her away from her mother's arms—I felt like a monster." He scoffed. "The next day, Margie asked me to quit the police force, and I was upset but also relieved. She said she didn't want me to be killed before our son could know who his father was. Now I can't help but think they would've been better off if I had been."

"Tom, stop talking like that, man, or I'll have to check you into a hospital—and not the kind you check yourself out of." He sighed. "Maybe you are the kind of parent that you took kids from, but you were just doing your job. Now you need to start acting like you've got some sense and be a better father. Let the past go. Move on."

"It's not that easy—"

"Maybe it isn't, but it is that simple. Get yourself help if you need to. Just do what you need to do to be there for your family."

"I'm not sure if I can."

Chapter 24: The Report

A sharp ringing sound woke Thomas up. He looked around and realized he'd fallen asleep on the couch. The clock above the TV showed it was 10:06 in the morning. It'd been three hours since Digger had left. He thought about letting the call go to voice mail, but what if it was the coroner calling with the report? He'd been waiting for the call. He grunted as he sat up and reached for the phone on the coffee table.

"This is Thomas."

"Hello, Thomas. This is Cindy at the Brothers' Mortuary and Cremation calling to let you know that the preliminary autopsy report came back. The coroner put on his initial report that the cause of death was myocardial infarction. He'll send the provisional anatomical diagnosis to you today. You should receive it in the mail within forty-eight hours. The official death certificate will come in about five weeks, after he finishes the full autopsy."

"I'm sorry, what was the cause of death?"

"Myocardial infarction."

He was starting to feel frustrated with the woman. "What I mean was, what caused the heart attack?"

"I'm not legally at liberty to explain that. I can only tell you what the report says."

He sighed and thanked the woman on the phone before hanging up. After waiting for twenty-four hours to find out what had killed his wife, he was still waiting.

How could she have had a heart attack at forty-two? Thinking back on it, they'd always known that heart disease ran in her family, but they'd just assumed that she'd have another twenty years before she'd need to worry. Both of her parents had died when she was in her thirties, almost back to back, both of heart attacks while in their late sixties. Now it all added up. She had been stressed all the time, complaining about heartburn ...

He rubbed his eyes and walked back to the couch. How could he have missed the warning signs?

The phone rang just as he'd started to drift off again. He held the phone over his face so he could see the caller ID. Not now, Fred. He let it go to voice mail. The phone dinged, informing him Fred had left a voice message. He set his phone on the table and closed his eyes again. His phone started ringing again. Annoying weasel. What's wrong with that guy? he thought. Thomas pushed the pillow over his ear. It didn't matter if he annoyed Fred now. The autopsy had proved he was innocent. The phone dinged, informing him of another voice message. Maybe that was the last of him. He lay still for a few minutes, but the urge to sleep was gone now. He sat up and looked at his phone. The corner of his mouth stung as he yawned. He licked his cracked lips. He wondered when he'd last drunk any water. It'd been too long.

There was one new voice mail and one new text message. The text was from Colin. Crap. He'd forgotten to call and tell him what the results were.

Someone knocked at the door. Before he could stand, the door was opening. Who in the world was—

"Hey, Dad. I got worried when I didn't hear from you."

"Colin!" Tom's heart was still pounding. "You almost gave me a heart attack." His choice of words seemed poor to him. "I thought you were Fred."

"Who?"

"The rookie cop that questioned me yesterday."

Colin sat in the recliner. "You never told me what happened, so I—"

"Yeah. I'm sorry. It was a long day and I was tired." Colin frowned. "I'm really sorry."

"What happened?"

"Nothing yet. They're probably still reading the report."

"What report?"

"The autopsy report. I got the call a few minutes ago." He couldn't tell him it'd been an hour ago. "I was about to call and tell you."

Colin didn't look convinced. "Dad?"

"Yeah."

"Before you tell me the autopsy results ... I don't know how to ask this—"

"What is it, Colin?"

"Lily thinks you ... hurt Mom. I don't think you did. It's just that—"

"Why does she think that?"

"That's the thing—I was hoping you would know."

"Huh. I wonder if ..." Thomas frowned as he remembered. "Lily walked in the room while I was giving Margie, your mother, CPR. She must've thought I was hurting her. When I saw her standing there, I told her to call 911. When I looked up again, she was gone. At first I thought she'd called, but when the cops never came, I called them myself."

"What time was that?"

"Why?"

"I'm just ... trying to figure something out."

"I didn't look at a clock, but probably around 10:30."

Colin looked pale. "She called me at 10:33."

"What?"

"She must've panicked and called me instead. That's how I knew to come over. She just kept saying 'Mom' over and over. I made her stay on the phone until I got there." Colin paused. "Is the reason Mom died because the ambulance didn't get there sooner? Was it my fault?"

"No! She'd already been dead for hours." He paused. "I'm sorry. I shouldn't have said that. I was going to tell you—I'm not doing a very good job at this. Your mother died of a heart attack. They said it probably happened around two in the morning. So by the time I tried to save her, it was too late." There was a long silence. "Colin, it wasn't anyone's fault."

"Mom died of a heart attack?"

Thomas nodded. "I found out just before you got here."

"Was she having heart problems?"

"If she was, she never would've said. All she worried about was Lily, and you. She never worried about herself." Colin processed this. "Did you come here alone? Where's Lily?"

"In the car. She didn't want to come in." Colin looked around. "She was right. It's weird being here without Mom."

Thomas exhaled. "Yeah." He stood up carefully and stretched. The dilated blood vessels in his head pounded.

"Dad, you okay?"

"Just need some water."

"I can get some for you."

"No, it's okay. I need to get up. I want to go talk to your sister."

* * *

Thomas held on to the open passenger door and squatted. "Hey, sweetie." Lily looked at him like he was a stranger. "I've missed you." She nodded. "Are you comfortable at Colin's place?" She nodded again. "Good. I'm glad. It won't be much longer till you can come back."

"I don't want to," she said finally.

"Honey, I know it's strange being here without your mom. We'll adjust."

"I don't want to adjust."

Thomas glanced at Colin, who decided to chime in.

"Lily, I don't want to adjust, either, but we'll learn to."

"No. I just want Mom back."

"I want your mom back too," Thomas said. He reached for her hand. She pulled it away. His heart stung.

"Colin, can we go, please?" she asked.

Colin frowned. "Lily—"

"Go ahead. It's gonna take time." Thomas stood carefully. "Can you bring her back tomorrow?"

Colin nodded. "Sure, Dad."

Chapter 25: Stable

The next day, Dr. Reece spoke softly as Lily painted another picture of the park. "Thomas, the reason I wanted you to come to her session today is so I can see how she behaves around you. After a child goes through something traumatic, it's important that they feel safe and loved."

"She is."

Lily turned and looked at him. He realized it had come out louder than he'd meant it to.

Dr. Reece spoke even softer. "But does she feel that way? I'm not saying she isn't safe with you. What I'm saying is that the last time she saw you, she thought you'd hurt her mother—"

"The full report showed that her mother died of natural causes. I didn't hurt my wife."

"Yes. I know that. But she thought you hurt her mother. Do you understand?"

Thomas inhaled slowly.

She leaned closer to him. "Nobody's accusing you of anything, Thomas. My job is to do what's best for Lily."

"So is mine."

Thomas looked at his daughter. Who was he kidding? Margaret had done everything when it came to the kids. He provided, sure, but he didn't know how to do what Margaret had done. She seemed to have some sort of telepathic connection with their children. She always knew what they needed before they ever even asked. How could he know what was best for Lily?

Lily turned and faced them. She'd finished her painting. It wouldn't win first place in any competition, but Thomas smiled and said it looked good anyway. Was that the right thing to do? Were you supposed to lie to your kid about their art? He was overthinking it. He'd been a dad for almost twenty-three years. Lily smiled and started on another canvas.

Dr. Reece's voice interrupted his thoughts. "Thomas, have you considered asking Colin to move back in?"

He rubbed his chin. "No. Why?" The words came out flat.

"You used to have a wife to help you raise Lily. Now, all the responsibility will fall on your shoulders only." Her eyes narrowed. "You travel a lot with your job. Am I correct?"

He nodded. It probably wasn't a good idea to tell this lady about his addiction-related sabbatical from work, assuming she didn't already know.

"So, who will pick Lily up from school?"

"She takes the bus home."

"Who will be home when she gets off the bus?"

"She's twelve. She can stay home alone if I'm not there for at least two hours."

Dr. Reece frowned. "She just lost her mother. This will be a huge adjustment for her, and you. She's not used to living with you, without her mother around, much less coming home to an empty house. What if your job takes you away for days, maybe weeks?"

"She can stay with Colin."

"You can't—you shouldn't—make her feel any more unstable

125

than she already does right now." She spoke slowly, as if he were one of the five-year-olds she was probably used to dealing with. "She'll do better staying in one place full time rather than living between yours and your son's houses."

Thomas sighed. "So what do you suggest I do? I have to work. You said yourself that she feels more comfortable at her brother's. So what's the problem?"

"Yes, which is why I'm suggesting that Colin move back in with you."

"We only have two rooms."

"Mr. Durnin, if I'm not positive that Lily will have a safe environment, I can't send her home with you. Either Colin moves back in with you, or I have to consider suggesting to the judge an alternative option."

She was throwing her weight around. He'd seen it before when dealing with these social workers. She'd dug her heels in and wasn't going to let go easily. Most people fell for this kind of game-playing. If she wanted to play, he'd play.

"Alternative option ... as in foster care? How could that possibly be better for her than living with her own father?"

"A father who isn't home half the time?" Ouch. "You should be able to figure that one out on your own. So what's it going to be?"

Chapter 26: Under the Tree

Tom laid the single gladiolus on top of the small mound of dirt. There hadn't been a funeral or reception. Instead a small box had been placed inside a small hole in their small backyard. Tom thought the best place to bury Margaret's ashes was right under the dogwood tree she had planted when they'd first moved in, over twenty years ago. Margaret had said that she never wanted to be put in a nursing home when she grew old; she wanted to live in her own home—the one she'd raised both her children in—until she died. And now she had.

There was no music. Instead there was silence, except for the gnats and mosquitoes they fanned away. There were no guests. (Being married at nineteen and pregnant by twenty had a way of changing friendships.) Instead, her family of three stood with their hands held in each other's, palms slippery from sweat.

Nobody had been invited to her burial. Most people would've thought that the deceased must not have been loved to only have three people at her burial. Anyone who knew Margaret even a little knew better. Her burial wasn't small because she wouldn't be missed—really she was already missed sorely. The only three people she loved, she had loved with her entire heart. Her whole existence had revolved around being a mother and a wife. Tom thought about all of this as he stared at the single gladiolus on top of his wife's ashes. He wanted to yell, or kick something, but instead he stood quietly next to his children, painfully sober for the first time in a long time. The breeze disappeared, leaving the air more muggy than it already had been. Sweat drops rolled down his face, burning as they fell into his eyes. The physical discomfort was minute compared to the discomfort he felt in his heart. He'd never felt so much pain, but to his surprise, the pain was so great that he couldn't cry. His body felt numb and painful all at once. It was supposed to have been him who went first, not her.

The sky turned from deep bluish gray to purple, then purple to pink, and then pink to red. There was no telling how long they'd been standing outside. Lily was the first to pull her hand away and walk back to the house.

Chapter 27: Policy

After Colin had watched her sulk, become reclusive, and go through all five stages of grief, plus a few extra, Lily now appeared to be happy for the first time in over a month. Colin waited till she was in her room to ask his father how they were going to afford a trip to Disney World.

Their dad had told them he had some big news. Then, wham! There it was. They were going to Disney World for a week. Colin had noticed the beginning of a smile start to form on Lily's lips for the first time in weeks. He tried not to look worried while his dad went on and on about the rides, the shows, the people dressed in costumes. It was the first time he had seen his father completely sober since Colin had moved back in. Maybe this would be the turning point for them.

It wasn't that Colin didn't want to be excited, but something didn't seem right about the timing of the trip. For one thing, they'd just lost their mother. Colin couldn't speak for Lily, but he didn't exactly feel like celebrating or having fun. Something else wasn't adding up, though. His father hadn't worked in almost two months and was constantly stressed over the bills. Now, out of the clear blue sky, he was Mr. Happy-Go-Lucky and wanted to dump five grand into a vacation. How was he going to afford a trip for all three of them to go to Disney?

His dad walked to the fridge and grabbed a beer. It was his first of the day, and it was already four in the afternoon. He seemed to be in a better mood than he'd been over the past few weeks. Colin watched as his dad hummed to himself quietly and took a sip.

"Dad, I don't think rides are the best thing for Lily. Have you asked the doctor about it?"

"Well, she doesn't have to go on rides. We can just watch shows and eat food." He took another sip. "You can get the time off work, right?"

"I don't know, Dad."

"What's wrong?"

"I just took a week off so I could take care of Lily and then move back in with you. Al's not going to be happy if I ask for another week off less than a month later."

His dad raised one eyebrow as if he wasn't convinced. "Doesn't Al have other cooks?"

"Yeah, but I don't know if I should be asking for time off for a vacation right now."

"Do you want me to talk to Al? Tell him how important this is?"

"No."

"I thought you said he was really understanding about all of this."

"He has been. That's why I don't want to ask for time off unless it's important."

"Spending time with your family *is* important. Trust me, I've lost enough time with my family because I put work first."

"I know it's important, but—"

His dad walked past Colin before he could finish his thought. Colin followed him hesitantly to the living room and sat on the other end of the couch. His good mood seemed to be gone. Colin took a deep breath. He'd forgotten what it was like to live with his dad after being out of the house for so long. Now he remembered why he'd been so anxious to move into the crappy apartment with Rob four years ago. "Don't get me wrong, the trip sounds great, but isn't Disney a little on the expensive side? And what about Lily's treatments, and school? She's already three weeks behind. And I thought you were going back to work?" He knew his dad didn't want to make her go back too soon, even though the specialist had said she thought Lily should go back to her normal routine as quickly as possible, but his dad had said he wasn't going to listen to some lady without kids of her own tell him how to raise his.

"You're getting worked up like your mom always did, and over nothing." Heat rose to Colin's face suddenly. His dad added, "I've already thought about all of that. My boss told me to start work after the trip. It's one week, not a whole month. Lily can do her treatment when we get back. I can explain to Lily's school that she needed this time off to grieve. Dr. Reece could probably sign off on that."

"Dr. Reece said Lily needed stability, not a trip to Disney."

His dad shot a look at him. "Watch your tone. Listen, I wasn't around as much as I would've liked when you and Lily were growing up. Now I want to make up for that. What's wrong with wanting to do something nice for my kids?"

Colin looked at the tan carpet. "Dad, how can you afford a trip like this?" He was walking a fine line now. "I know you and Mom were having financial problems."

Thomas almost choked on the beer. "What are you talking about—who told you that? Robin? I swear that woman doesn't know when to shut up."

"Dr. Reece told me. Look, Dad, I appreciate you wanting to spend time with us, but we can spend time with you here. Maybe we could go see a movie or go to the park. Lily loves the park."

"That woman had no business telling you about our private life. She shouldn't have told you that. I can afford the trip—not that it's any of your business."

"Are you sure? I can help spot you if you need it."

"You're forgetting that you're the kid. I'm the parent." Thomas covered his mouth as he burped. "Colin, not that I need to tell you this, because—

"It's none of my business?"

"Exactly. But I'll tell you so you'll stop worrying." His chest rose and fell as he took a deep breath. "A check came in the mail yesterday."

"A check?"

"Your mother had a life insurance policy. To be honest, I had no idea she even had life insurance." He shook his head. "Anyway, I got the check yesterday in the mail. It was enough to pay off what was left of the house payment, and still have a little left over. So when I was thinking about what we needed, I thought we could all use a break." He patted Colin's shoulder. "This trip is the least I can do to thank you for moving back in and for being willing to sleep on this old piece of garbage." His dad patted the futon he was sitting on.

"Yeah, well, it's only temporary."

"Right." The words came out flat and unconvincing.

Colin walked to Lily's room while his dad flipped through channels on the TV. It was obvious he wasn't going to change his dad's mind. It seemed best to give up while he was ahead. Lily was still painting and humming something their mother used to sing, some classical song by Debussy. She was finally starting to seem like herself again. Maybe the trip would be good for her, like his dad had said. Colin could hear his father yell at the TV: "Come on, Minshew, you can throw better than that!" It was the same game his father had DVR'd and had watched twice already. Colin walked back to the living room and joined him.

Chapter 28: Vacation

They made their way through the sea of children dragging their parents around by the hands. Colin threw his twelve-dollar mouse-shaped cup in a garbage can. Like the other kids, Lily tugged at his arm as they walked to the next show. He glanced back at his dad, who had fallen behind when a family of twelve got between them.

"Colin, come on. Hurry!" Lily demanded.

He stopped walking. "Wait for Dad."

"Y'all go ahead!" his dad called out. "I'll catch up."

Lily smiled. "Come on!" Colin walked next to Lily, with her hot hand around his sweaty arm, until he felt Lily's hand yank away from his. When he looked down, Lily was regaining her footing. "Are you okay?"

"I'm fine." She swept the curtains of bangs away from her sticky forehead. That wig had to be making her hotter.

"What happened?"

"I just tripped. Come on!"

Colin looked back at the flat ground as she pulled him forward again and wondered what she could've tripped on. Lily started to clap. "We're here!" He looked ahead again and saw the long line up ahead. There were at least a hundred people ahead of them, but he'd gotten used to that over the past few days. Lines were part of the experience. People usually came by in costume and entertained them while they stood for two hours. It didn't make them less hot, and it didn't stop their feet from swelling, but it did make the two hours feel more like an hour and forty-five minutes. So, that was something to be thankful for. Lily let go of his arm when they made it to the back of the line.

Lily stretched her arm straight out and pointed at a woman dressed like a princess. Right on cue, an actress dressed like Cinderella approached and asked Lily to dance with her, probably mistaking her for one of the younger kids there, since Lily was shorter than half of them. Lily's eyes beamed up at Colin. "Can I?"

Colin laughed. "Go ahead."

Colin looked around as Lily danced with the actress. He could hear Lily laughing as his eyes left her to scan the crowd for a tall man who looked like him, but older and in khaki shorts. Where could their dad have gone that was taking so long? He checked his phone. His dad would've called if he was lost. In unison, the group gasped at something behind him. He realized Lily wasn't laughing anymore. His head turned so fast he felt a muscle pull in his neck. Where was she? His eyes searched for Lily in the same place she'd been before, but she wasn't there. Her voice called out nearby.

"Colin!" she cried.

He could see the tall actress dressed like Cinderella through the crowd. Lily had to be near her. Colin left his place in line to follow his sister's voice behind a wall of people staring, instead of helping. There Lily was, on the ground, holding her scraped knee. She cringed in pain but didn't cry. A young man dressed in a park uniform of navy blue shirt and khaki shorts ran up with a first aid kit in his hand and squatted on the other side of

Lily. Cinderella moved on to another part of the line. The young-looking employee looked up at Colin. "Is this your daughter?" Colin shook his head. "She's my sister." Lily made a funny expression that said, *Eew, I can't believe he thought you were my dad.* Then she winced while the young man sterilized her wound and bandaged it. Colin helped Lily to her feet. Lily tried to downplay her limp. "Lily, you need to sit down." She hobbled on.

"I'm okay. It doesn't hurt."

Colin stepped in front of her and faced her. "What happened back there? Did you trip again?"

Lily frowned. "I got dizzy and fell."

"It's nonnegotiable: you're going to sit for a few minutes. I think you need to eat something."

He spotted some shade under a large maple tree and helped her walk toward it. She stopped hobbling and full-on limped once the gig was up. He glanced around again. What was taking their dad so long? She balanced on one leg as she hopped up on the four-foot-high wall under the tree. Colin pushed up under her arms to assist her. She hardly weighed anything. "When did you start feeling dizzy?"

"Earlier, I guess."

"Maybe you're overheated or something. I'll go get you some water. Wait here."

Colin kept a close eye on Lily as he walked toward a booth shaped like a spaceship. His dad had said people came to places like these just to take kids. (When Lily wasn't around, his dad had called it a pedophile's playground.) Colin glanced down at his billfold and handed the cashier a sweaty twenty-dollar bill. He looked back at his sister. She was still on the brick wall, pouting. The cashier took the bill from Colin's outstretched hand and exchanged it for two cold bottles of water in its place.

Lily looked up at him with her blue eyes as he approached with two large bottles of water a minute later. Her face was bright red. He passed her a bottle of water covered in condensation. She took a sip. "It's too cold ."

He shook his head. "You're welcome." She didn't catch the reminder to say thank you and drank some more. "Close your eyes. I'm gonna pour some of my water over your head."

She looked at him like he was crazy. "Why?"

"To help cool you down."

"You'll mess up my wig, though."

"I wish you would take that thing off. It's making you overheat."

"And let everyone see me bald? No way!"

"Then I'm going to cool you off this way." He held up the water bottle. "Close your eyes."

She closed her eyes as he poured the cold water over her face. It was probably too cold, but it had to be better than letting her overheat. He pushed her sweaty bangs to the side and poured the rest on her hot forehead. Once he'd finished, she rubbed the water from her eyes and pushed her bangs back to their normal spot. She looked past him with a strange expression. Colin followed her gaze to their dad, who was waving his arm, showing the sweat stains in the armpit of his button-down polo shirt. He came over and said, "What are y'all doing over here?"

Colin leaned back as the smell of booze hit him. "Lily just needed to cool off. She fell while she was—"

"Lily fell!"

"Dad, can we talk over there ... privately?"

"What for?"

"Dad, please."

Colin walked to where he could still see Lily, but he hoped she wouldn't overhear their conversation. His dad stumbled behind him.

"I think we should go back to the hotel," Colin said.

"It's only four."

"Lily's overheated, and you're—"

His dad cursed. "You're always too worried about Lily, just like your mom. She's fine!"

Colin looked at the family walking by, shamefaced. "Dad, come on. You're making a scene."

"Since when did my son become my boss? I'll leave when I'm good and ready."

His dad pulled his arm away as Colin reached for it, almost causing himself to fall over, but he managed to recover. Colin caught a glimpse of the shiny edge of a metal flask in his dad's back pocket. He scoffed. He'd been sober for a week; so much for that. Of all the days to start drinking again. Colin glanced at Lily, who was still on the wall. By the time he turned, his dad had already walked too far for Colin to go after him. He rubbed the sweat from his forehead and walked back to Lily.

"Dad's been drinking, hasn't he?" she asked.

"Umm, he's just tired, that's all."

"That's how he gets when he drinks."

"Don't worry about Dad. He'll be fine. I need to get you back to the hotel so you can rest."

"But the park doesn't close for five more hours!"

"It's not up for debate." Colin shaded his eyes with his hand and looked for their dad. He was long gone already.

"Are you looking for Dad?" Colin ignored her. "How are you going to find him?"

"Lily, give me a second to think, please."

138

She sighed. "Fine. I'm hot."

It had to be a hundred degrees outside. It couldn't be too hard to find their dad, could it? He couldn't have made it far in this heat. He'd probably be sitting on a bench close by. Still, that was too much walking for Lily, and he couldn't just leave her tied to a tree like some pet dog. Then Colin remembered the wheelchairs available at the entrance of the park. That was still too far for her to walk, though. He looked around for someone dressed like an employee. Within a few minutes, a young woman wearing the uniform—a navy blue polo with khakis—walked by.

"Excuse me, ma'am." The young woman looked at him. "Could you tell me where's the closest place I can get a wheelchair for my sister?"

Lily's eyes popped open.

The young woman smiled. "Sure, walk straight ahead, and you'll see a first aid sign on the right. They have wheelchairs there."

"Thank you."

Lily waited till the woman walked away to object.

"Wheelchair?"

"You've already tripped twice. It's either the wheelchair or the hotel."

She jutted her jaw out and crossed her arms.

He smirked. "Wheelchair it is."

* * *

The hotel was dark and quiet, except for the sound of snoring. Colin moved his hand along the wall, looking for the light switch. He flipped the light on and walked into the kitchenette to get some water. He was still exhausted and dehydrated from pushing Lily around the park in that old wheelchair for three hours.

His father was still in the same position he had been in when they'd gotten back to the hotel—facedown on the couch, drooling on a pillow. He seemed to be out cold. Colin shook his head and walked to the couch with a glass of water in his hand. His stomach turned from the smell of booze and BO coming from his dad's body. The alcohol must've soaked into his clothing from him sweating all day. Colin set the glass of water down gently on the coffee table and pulled the shoes off his dad's feet. The stench made him gag.

He heard the door to Lily's room unlatch. Colin turned his head to look. She didn't seem to notice him as she staggered to the bathroom. Colin grabbed his glass of water and started to walk back to the room he and his father were supposed to have shared. As he passed the kitchenette, he turned the lights off again and used the wall to guide him through the dark. A moment later, a loud thud came from the bathroom. It sounded like something heavy had fallen. No sound was coming from the bathroom now. He blindly searched for the door handle with his hand. Not even a sliver of light came from under the bathroom door. Lily must not have turned it on.

Finally, Colin found the handle. The bathroom was pitch black. He felt along the wall for a light switch and turned it on. The light flickered on, illuminating the room. Colin's heart stopped when he saw Lily lying on the floor. He ran to her and fell to his knees. She was unconscious but still breathing.

Colin grabbed a rag and wet it. He propped her head onto his leg and dabbed her face with the cold rag. When she came to, she looked around like she was lost. Colin spoke gently to her and told her she'd fallen.

Family vacation had turned into a nightmare.

Chapter 29: Symptoms

Lily growled. "Ugh. This sucks."

"You know Mom hated when you said that word."

"Yeah, well, she's not here," she mumbled.

"Lily—"

The door opened, and Dr. Long walked back in the room.

"It's a good thing you decided to come back early from your trip." She looked inside the file in her hand. "There's no way of knowing if Lily had a mild heatstroke while you were in Florida; however, I am concerned that her tumor might have grown, since the symptoms fit: dizziness, falling, and weakness. I'm afraid that due to Lily missing her last two treatments, her tumor may be more resistant to the treatments this time." Dr. Long looked at Colin. "I know you weren't planning on this, but I would like Lily to stay at the hospital, where we can monitor her closely over the next few days while we give her her treatment." Colin glanced at Lily, and the doctor added, "I know you said your dad isn't feeling well today, but I'll need him to sign some paperwork for Lily. You don't happen to have a fax machine at your house, do you?"

Colin nodded. "My mom always kept it just in case the internet crashed."

She looked surprised. "She was smart. If I fax the paperwork to him, could you ask your father to sign and fax it back to me later today? It's not normally how I do this, but I can make an exception for my favorite patient." She winked at Lily.

* * *

Colin called his dad for the third time since Colin had left the hospital. Maybe he was still asleep. Colin could see his parents' brown house as he turned into the Spring Water subdivision. He couldn't see his dad's pickup truck in the driveway. Nine thirty was early for his dad to be up. These days he'd been sleeping in until ten or eleven each morning. Colin was worried about him, but there wasn't much he could do.

Colin parked his car over the oil stain in the driveway and ran into the house. The door was still unlocked. His dad must've forgotten to lock it. Colin dashed through the house, collecting the items on Lily's list. He still had to drop her things off at the hospital, talk to his dad (wherever he was), and get to work before 11:30. He glanced at the clock. It was already ten.

Colin walked to the couch with his arms full of little things Lily wanted—books, pencils, a sketch pad, her favorite blanket. He stuffed everything into a pink suitcase and zipped it shut. He would have to call his dad later and tell him about the fax. Colin looked around to make sure he hadn't missed anything Lily might need. Then he noticed the note on the coffee table.

Colin, I'm sorry. I wish I could tell you how sorry I am. I left to go get help. My behavior recently hasn't been fair to you or Lily. I'm going to check myself into a rehab. The house is paid for. I've left enough money to pay for Lily's needs for a couple of weeks. I'll be back after that. If there's an emergency, call the rehab's number.

He ripped the note to shreds. How could his father do this?

143

How could he just leave without saying anything? Colin turned and looked at where the strange sound was coming from in the corner of the room. It was the paperwork from Dr. Long being faxed over. The top-left corner of the paper said, HEART OF GEORGIA CHILDREN'S HOSPITAL: ONCOLOGY DIVISION. He'd forgotten about the signature. Colin picked up his phone and tried to call his dad again. He was forwarded to voice mail. Of course.

His mom had always taken Lily to the hospital, so it was unlikely that Dr. Long knew what his father's real signature looked like. Before Colin could change his mind, his hand was dashing across the bottom of the paper: Thomas Durnin. He only needed to do that ten more times.

Chapter 30: Parker

Lily looked around the small hospital room, decorated with teddy bear wallpaper (like the rest of the rooms) and filled with toys. She'd never been to this part of the hospital before. Dr. Long touched her shoulder gently. "Stay in here as long as you like. I'll be right over there if you need me." Her hand left Lily's shoulder. When Lily looked back, Dr. Long was already at the nurses' station. Lily looked around the room for someone close to her age, but most of the kids playing looked to be around five or six years old. The other children wore beanies and scarves around their heads to stay warm. She adjusted her wig. For the first time, she was the only person in the room with hair, fake or not.

The oldest-looking boy, near the back of the small room, stopped playing solitaire and looked at her. "Hi, my name's Parker."

She smiled timidly. "Hi, I'm Lily."

"Wanna play cards with me?"

"Sure, but I don't know any games."

"I'll teach you."

Lily moved carefully over the kids playing with dominoes and LEGOs on the floor in the middle of the room. She sat in the awkwardly small plastic chair across from the boy playing cards.

He looked a little older than the other kids, but only by a few years. Lily watched as he pushed two halves of the deck into a U shape and let the cards slide from his thumbs so they overlapped each other. He looked at Lily with his dark-brown eyes and smiled. "Neat trick, huh? I've had a lot of free time to practice stuff like that. I've been here on and off since I was six."

"How old are you?"

"Eight. How old are you?"

"Twelve."

"You're new here, aren't you?"

"Yeah. I've never stayed here before. Do you miss your family?"

"They come and visit. I try not to think about it, though. If you think about stuff like that all day, you'll get pretty sad."

Lily thought about his answer. "Sorry."

"For what?"

"Making you sad."

He smiled, showing off a gap between the bottom row of his teeth. "You didn't make me sad. You're the first person to play cards with me since I got here." He looked up from his cards and studied her face. "I think I've seen you in the chemo room before."

"Maybe."

She didn't recognize him, but it was hard to distinguish people without hair from one another. Lily tried not to think about how long he'd been in the hospital. She'd been able to live at home for the past year. For the first time in a while, she felt fortunate but somehow sad at the same time. To get her mind off it, she looked at the shuffled deck of cards.

"How'd you do that?"

"I can show you, if you want. But it'll cost you."

Lily laughed. "Cost me what? I don't have any money."

"Chocolate pudding."

"Really? Okay, deal."

"Wow, you are new here. Pudding is like gold. You'll learn, though." He handed her half the deck. "Separate the deck into two." She did. "Now squeeze your thumbs and fingers together to make the cards look like U's."

Lily squeezed on the cards. One flew out of her hand, followed by the rest of the desk.

"Umm ... it was Lily, right?"

"Yeah."

"Okay. Like this, Lily. More like a curve than a U, I guess. Then bring your hands close together so they'll overlap when you let go."

"Maybe I'll just let you deal for us."

"I could, but then I wouldn't get chocolate pudding. Try again."

* * *

A deck of cards lay on the side table, ready to be shuffled. They played for the next hour. She tried the shuffling trick a few more times, and she eventually started to get the hang of it.

Lily had been waiting anxiously all morning for Colin's visit. It'd been weird sleeping at the hospital, away from her own bed and her family. She was trying to do what Parker said and not think about it, but it was harder than she'd expected. When she wasn't playing cards with Parker, all she could do was sit and think. In her whole life, she'd never had so much time to think. The small TV in her room showed nothing but commercials. She'd sat and watched an infomercial about a magic scrub brush that could clean tar off trucks for an hour the night before because she couldn't sleep.

Lily smiled as the door opened, then sighed when it was only a nurse, one she hadn't seen yet. The nurse did her job and left again, unlike the other nurses, who liked to make small talk and try to cheer Lily up with words like "You'll get used to it here" and "Just wait until Meatloaf Monday." They must not have ever stayed in a hospital before. They were nice enough, but Lily was glad this nurse wasn't like them. She could go back to waiting for Colin, uninterrupted.

The door started to open again. Lily sat up straighter. Her shoulder sank down when she saw it was only Dr. Long.

"You don't look happy to see me, Lily," Dr. Long said with a wink. "Were you expecting someone else?"

"I was hoping you were my brother."

"Sorry to disappoint you."

"No. I didn't mean—"

"I'm only kidding. How'd you sleep last night?"

"It was strange—" Her eyes lit up as her brother walked in the room just then. "Colin!"

"Wow, you're excited to see me." He nodded at the doctor. "Hey, Dr. Long."

Dr. Long smiled as Colin made his way across the room and hugged Lily. "Perfect timing, Colin. I needed to talk to you about something. I received the fax from your father yesterday, but I need him to sign some more consent papers for a test that wasn't listed in the paperwork I sent."

"Can you fax it again?" Colin asked.

She squinted. "I suppose, but I also was hoping to talk to him about everything. He didn't answer my call yesterday. Do you think you could ask him to give me a call?"

"When's Dad going to come visit me, Colin?" Lily asked.

Colin looked panicked. "Uh, Dad went on a long business trip. It was unexpected. He said he's sorry that he couldn't say goodbye and he won't be able to call, but he can't wait to see you when he gets back."

Lily's smile disappeared.

"Oh ," the doctor said, sounding surprised. "I must've misunderstood you yesterday. I thought he was at home, not feeling well."

Lily gave Colin a strange look. Colin looked away from her and rubbed his arm.

"He was at home, but he left last night ... after he signed the paperwork."

Dr. Long raised one eyebrow. "Okay, do you know if he has a fax machine where he's staying?"

"Umm, I can ask him."

Dr. Long said she'd be by to check on Lily later and then left. Lily pulled the deck of cards out of the cardboard box. Colin quickly unpacked the things he'd brought in her pink suitcase. Lily watched Colin as if it was the most exciting thing in the world to watch her brother unpack, and for now it really was. He handed her the soft plush blanket her mother had knitted before she was born. Lily wrapped it around her shoulders and inhaled the scent of the blanket through her nose deeply. It felt like her mother was there, hugging her again. She picked up the cards again.

"Colin, look!" she demanded.

Colin looked as the cards cascaded from her fingers, overlapping each other perfectly. "I learned all kinds of card games yesterday."

"Where'd you learn that?"

149

"Parker. He's only eight, but there weren't any kids my age, so I hung out with him."

Colin laughed. "An eight-year-old taught you how to play card games?"

"Yeah, but he can't count very well, so it was pretty easy to beat him once I got the hang of it."

"Well, he's four years younger than you. Maybe you could go easy on him."

Lily shrugged and went back to shuffling the cards. "Hey, Colin?"

"Hmm?"

"It was really strange sleeping here last night. Some of the kids here have had cancer most of their lives. I don't want to stay here another night. Parker told me that some of the kids that come here never leave."

Colin stopped moving around the room and faced her. "Why would he tell you that?"

"He wasn't trying to scare me. He was just being honest."

Colin moved across the room and sat next to her on the hard hospital bed. "I'm sorry you have to stay here. I wish I could take you home, but this is what's best for you. We have to trust Dr. Long. Not trusting her is what got us into this mess to begin with."

"Am I going to end up dying here?"

Colin looked shocked. "What? No!"

"One time, I overheard Dr. Long telling Mom that kids only live a few years with my type of cancer, but she'd make sure I was comfortable. Is that what she's doing? Making sure I'm comfortable? You can tell me. I'm old enough to handle it."

"Oh, Lily, no. No. That's not why you're here. I promise I will bring you home soon. You're not going to die here."

Lily thought for a moment.

"Hey, Colin, where did you say Dad's business trip was?"

"I didn't really get many details. You know how his trips are. He's gone, and then he's back. Anyway, I have to go to work."

"But it's only ten thirty. Can you stay ten more minutes?"

"Sorry. I'll be back tomorrow." He leaned over and hugged her. "Bye, munchkin."

Chapter 31: Guardianship

Colin left her room and headed for the elevators. He could've stayed ten more minutes, but with every minute that passed, he'd grown closer to cracking and telling Lily where their dad really was. He'd never lied to her before. It was sickening to think about how he'd just looked her right in the eyes and said a flat-out lie. First, he'd forged his dad's signature, and now he was lying to his little sister and Dr. Long. This was all his dad's fault for backing him into a corner like this. What was Colin supposed to do? Lily needed treatment, and this was the only way. Still, that was the last time he was ever going to lie to her like that. She'd already lost one parent; she didn't need to feel like she'd lost the other. It was better that she didn't know about the note. What she didn't know couldn't hurt her ... at least he hoped not.

Later that evening at work, Colin hid behind the huge trash bin in case Al came looking for him. He'd already tried calling three rehab places and asking for his dad, but two of them said they didn't have anyone by the name of Thomas Durnin with them, and one said they couldn't give out that kind of information. He was starting to regret ripping up that note. Maybe his dad had already checked out and was on his way home. Colin tried calling his dad's cell just in case, but it went straight to voice mail. He'd already been hiding behind the giant metal bin for ten minutes, but he needed to try one last time.

Colin decided to call one more rehab place before heading back into the kitchen. He listened to the phone dial and ring twice. A woman answered the phone and asked Colin to hold. The back door to the restaurant opened. Olivia stepped out and looked around. She had to be looking for him. The only other cook in the kitchen was Bob, and he couldn't be trusted to boil water. They were probably getting behind on their orders. Colin ducked behind the huge bin. A moment later, the woman came back on the phone. Olivia was still standing in the doorway when he checked. He squatted lower and tried to whisper into the phone so Olivia wouldn't hear him. The woman said she couldn't hear him. He asked if there were any patients there by his dad's name. She told him to hold again. He peaked out around the bin. Olivia was gone. Thank goodness. He sighed and stood up straight, much to the relief of his knees.

"What are you doing behind the garbage bin?"

Colin jumped. "Olivia! Why'd you sneak up like that?"

"I didn't—"

Colin held up his finger before she could finish. His dad answered.

"Hello?" the voice in the phone asked.

"Dad, it's me."

The line was silent. Olivia put her hands on her hips and sighed impatiently.

"I got your note. I'm calling about Lily."

Olivia's eyes widened. Colin heard the back door to the restaurant open. Olivia glanced over and looked back at Colin. "It's Al. I'll go distract him. Hurry up, though," she whispered.

Colin realized his dad was asking him a question.

"What happened? Is she okay?" his dad asked.

"No, she's not okay !"

And how could you leave her? he thought but didn't say. He added, "She said she was feeling dizzy yesterday while you were still sleeping, so I took her to the hospital. Dr. Long said she wanted Lily to stay so she could keep a close eye on her." Colin paused, expecting his dad to interrupt. When he didn't, he continued. "When I got home, I saw your note. Anyway, Dr. Long needs you to sign some paperwork."

"Colin, I can't leave—I can't blow this opportunity again."

"What do you mean 'again'?"

"Nothing. I just meant I can't be talking on the phone again."

"Fine. I can tell Dr. Long you don't have a phone where you are, which isn't a lie. And I can bring the paperwork to you, if that's what you want, or Dr. Long can fax it to you. Whatever. Just give me the fax number."

"They won't let us use the fax machine here, and I can't have visitors. I'm not even supposed to be talking on the phone. They made an exception this time."

"Then they can make another exception."

"That's not how it works. Colin, I know you don't under-stand—"

"I understand that you left when Lily needed you most." Colin exhaled sharply. "What am I supposed to tell Dr. Long?"

"Look, I won't be here long. Just sign for me."

After realizing he wasn't going to get anywhere with his dad, Colin said his goodbyes and hung up. He wanted to throw his phone in the garbage, but what good would that do? He never imagined his dad could be so selfish, and why now, of all times?

Colin kicked the side of the metal bin. The deep metallic sound echoed. The kitchen staff was probably backed up, and he'd be hearing about it from Al if he didn't get back to work soon. He headed back toward the little restaurant and took a deep breath. What was he supposed to tell Dr. Long now?

And what did his dad mean by "again"?

* * *

Colin paced around the living room. Dr. Long had taken his call, even though it was after hours. She sounded like she was at home, because it was much quieter in the background than the hospital ever was. He thought he heard a man in the background; it sounded like Dr. Long's husband, Zach. Colin had met him twice before at the hospital. He could hear Zach ask her who was on the phone. Dr. Long told him she'd be off the phone in a minute.

"I'm sorry to bother you while you're at home, Dr. Long."

"I told you to call me anytime, Colin. You're not bothering me. So what were you wanting to know about the paperwork?"

"Can you fax it over again, and I'll sign for my dad?"

"I'm sorry, unless you are a parent or a temporary guardian, you can't sign the paperwork. I need your father's signature."

"I'm her temporary guardian." It slipped out before he could stop himself from lying again.

"You are?" she asked, sounding skeptical.

Colin held the phone away from his mouth so Dr. Long wouldn't hear him breathing. He hated lying to her. It wasn't technically a lie—maybe it was a stretching of the truth—but his dad had given him permission to sign while he was away on his "business" trip.

"Yeah, I should've told you that yesterday, but I didn't think about it. My dad made me Lily's temporary guardian while he's away on trips like this one."

"Mhmm." She didn't sound convinced. "I can't fax the paperwork over now because I'm at home, but you can sign it in the morning."

"Thanks, and Dr. Long, should I be worried about Lily?"

She sighed. "Worrying won't do any good. Let's just see how she responds to the treatment first."

Colin thanked her again and hung up. He dreaded having to sign those papers in the morning. He'd lied more in the past twenty-four hours than he had in his entire life. There was nothing he could do about it now, though. He closed his eyes and tried to fall asleep.

Chapter 32: Poker Face

Before Colin walked into Lily's hospital room, he could hear laughter from behind the door, which was open slightly. It sounded like Lily and Parker. They'd become best friends over the past five months. It was unusual for him to find Lily alone anymore, not that he minded. If it hadn't been for Parker, staying in the hospital day in and day out would've been more torturous for Lily than it already had been. She seemed to be adjusting to living in the hospital, which made Colin's heart want to snap in half. Still, he knew she hadn't adjusted to the absence of their parents.

Colin opened the door to Lily's room slowly. She was sitting in her usual place on the bed, and Parker had pulled up a chair. Cards and chocolate pudding were sprawled out across the rolling side table. It looked like a juvenile FIFA match.

They didn't seem to notice there was a large man standing in the room, watching them play cards. Lily stared at Parker with a mischievous look in her eyes as she pulled her hand toward her. Colin knew she was about to bluff. She always had a certain look when she tried to lie. He couldn't describe it, but she was doing it now. "I'll raise you three chocolate puddings," she said, sounding confident.

Parker grimaced and said, "I fold."

"I win. Read 'em and weep."

Lily clapped victoriously and then looked over at Colin standing in the doorway.

"What are you guys playing?" Colin asked, now that he'd been discovered.

Parker's head popped up from behind the five cards in his hand. "Hey, Colin. I didn't see you there." He paused as if trying to remember the question. "We're playing five-card draw."

"You're playing poker?" Colin laughed. "How old are you again?"

"Eight, but I'll be nine in three months. So I'm practically nine."

Lily diverted her eyes from the deck she'd started shuffling to give Parker a skeptical look. "No you're not. Three months doesn't make you practically nine. That's an entire quarter of a year."

"What?"

"It's basic math. There are twelve months in a year. A quarter of that—"

"Okay, Lily. I don't think Parker wanted a math lesson."

Parker blushed. "I was just saying that I'm old enough to play poker," he said defensively.

Colin gave Lily a stern look. "Hey, Parker, can you let me talk to Lily alone? I'll only be here for a few minutes. You guys can go back to playing your game in a little bit."

"That's okay. I'm actually pretty fatigued." Colin chuckled at Parker's medical terminology as Parker got up. "I'll see you later, Lily."

Once Parker had left, Colin moved toward Lily and sat in the chair Parker had left warm. She stuffed the deck, which looked more worn than ever, back into the cardboard box. Colin waited till she'd finished.

"You were kind of mean to Parker just now," he said. "You know why his math isn't good—he's been stuck here since he was six. Do you think you could cut him a little slack?"

"He can learn math here; he just doesn't want to."

"Look, I know you're upset. You have every right to be. I'm upset with Dad too. I haven't talked to him in five months. But that's not Parker's fault. He's your only friend here. You should go a little easier on him if you want to keep him as a friend."

Lily looked out of the window like she always did when she was trying not to cry. "It's not just Dad."

"What is it then?"

"I—" She looked at him with tears in her eyes. "I'm never going to get out of here, am I?"

Dr. Long walked in the room before he could try to come up with a good enough answer. She asked Colin if she could speak with him alone in the hallway. Lily wiped her eyes and looked out the window again.

Colin followed Dr. Long down the hallway. Her voice hadn't sounded as happy as it usually did when she was in Lily's room. She walked past the nursing station, and the recreation room, then Parker's room, and kept going. They were way too far for Lily to hear, unless Dr. Long didn't want Parker to hear either. "Is something wrong?" Colin asked.

Dr. Long stopped walking. She turned toward Colin and slid her glasses into her curly red hair. "Colin, I'm afraid I have some bad news. As you know, Lily's on bed rest because she had a seizure last week, which is fairly normal for this type of tumor, but we ran some tests just in case. I just finished looking at the images I got back from the MRI. The glioma has metastasized, meaning it's spread to other parts of her brain." She sighed.

159

"We can increase chemo and radiation therapy. Unfortunately, that will only prolong her life by a few months at best, and get rid of any quality of life she might've had. We'll continue giving her palliative care to relieve the symptoms, but I'm recommending she be put on hospice care in addition."

His legs felt weak. He leaned against the peeling teddy bear wallpaper. "I need a moment to think."

Dr. Long spoke softly. "I'm going to make sure she is very comfortable, Colin. I'm sorry I don't have better news."

Colin rubbed his temples. "I'm just trying to understand this. She's dying?"

"She has three months, at most."

Colin scoffed. "Three months." He started to pace. "And you're positive?"

Dr. Long nodded.

"Can you remove the tumor? I know it was too dangerous before, but if she's going to die anyway—"

She reached out for Colin's hand. "The glioma is inoperable, Colin. If there was any other way, I would tell you, even if it was high-risk."

"Why is this happening?" He raised his trembling voice. Suddenly he remembered something. "About a year ago, my mom told me there was a cure out there. She'd read about it online or something. I know it would be expensive, but I don't care. I'll make payments for the rest of my life if I need to."

"Colin, I know you want to save your sister ... but this disease is incurable, for now. I'm truly sorry."

Chapter 33: The Plan

His mom's old laptop was slow, but it was his only option if he was going to find the cure. Colin waited for it to turn on. It asked for a password. He typed "Lily2014." It processed his request. After a few minutes, the home screen appeared. He waited for the icons to pop up. He exhaled. This was torture. The icons appeared on the screen one by one like kernels of corn popping—pop, pop, pop—until eventually the entire screen had been filled. He clicked on an icon that represented the search engine, whose home page appeared white on the screen as it loaded. He grunted. How had his mom used this all the time without slamming it into a wall? The search bar appeared just as he was thinking about giving up, or hitting it with a hammer. He went to her browsing history. It felt like a violation of her privacy, but he needed to find the cure she'd mentioned when she was still alive. As soon as he found what he was looking for, he would close her laptop and never open it again.

While he waited for the search engine to load her history, he walked to the kitchen and poured himself a glass of sweet tea. By the time he got back to the desk, the results had loaded. He could see the love his mom had had for Lily as he scrolled down the dozens of articles she'd read. It was clear to him that his mother had been just as desperate, if not more so, to find a cure. He skimmed through the articles until one stood out. He clicked on the link. It was a transcribed interview with a doctor named Harold Lloyd. The name sounded familiar. It had to have been the same guy she'd told him about. Colin closed her laptop and turned on his phone. The search engine popped up instantaneously. It was nice to use technology from 2026 again. He typed on his phone's keyboard: Dr. Lloyd. The results loaded immediately, and he found more recent interviews with the doctor. One, in particular, caught Colin's attention. The title was "The Cure Worked!" The interview was only a few weeks old. Colin threw his feet on the desk and leaned back in the swivel chair as he clicked on the video. He jumped as the chair almost fell backward and then moved to the couch instead.

He listened impatiently, as the interview went on and on, for the doctor to say where the cure could be found. Finally, the old doctor explained that they hadn't begun clinical trials yet, due to the government suspending their funding. He said the government didn't want to get their hands dirty with all the lawsuits. Colin's heart sank at the doctor's blunt but honest words. The video concluded with the doctor saying the cure worked, and he hoped that when the lawsuits ended, the funding would start again so they could begin clinical trials. After that, the video ended.

Colin's mind worked rapidly to figure how out he was going to get the cure. It existed. The cure wasn't available yet, but the doctor said it worked. Somehow, he had to get his hands on it. But how? The doctor was obviously American, by his accent, and so was the interviewer. That narrowed it down some, but not enough. There had to be more information on the cure out there. In the interview, the doctor had never mentioned where his lab was, only that they'd been sued for testing on animals. He knew that animal testing had already been outlawed in every state except for two: Texas and Georgia. The doctor wouldn't have been so open about doing something illegal, so he had to be in one of those two states.

Colin clicked on a profile of the old doctor that said that Dr. Harold Lloyd was born in 1958, in Jackson, Florida. He attended medical school at the University of Central Florida College of Medicine, then later attended the University of South Florida to specialize as an oncologist. In his late twenties he met his wife, Jenny, and moved to Atlanta. Colin's eyes got bigger when he saw the word Atlanta. The doctor was closer than he'd thought. Dr. Lloyd and his wife had a son named Jackson Lloyd. At the age of five, Jackson was diagnosed with leukemia. That's when Dr. Lloyd began working at the Emory Cancer Institute of Research, a nonprofit cancer-research lab based outside Atlanta. His son lost his battle to leukemia at the age of ten. Dr. Lloyd left the ECIR lab and quit practicing medicine for almost five years. Later he opened his own lab based out of Atlanta called the Jackson Hope Institution of Cancer Research, where he continued his research for a cure.

Colin sighed. It was a sad story, but it didn't change the fact that Lily needed the cure—one way or another. He searched for the address of the doctor's research lab. The latest online images showed pictures of protesters holding up signs outside the large square building. One image showed two guards pushing the angry crowd away from the entrance of the building as they tried to force their way in.

He knew it was too dangerous to try going to his lab, which would have security guards and cameras everywhere, not to mention the crowds of people protesting. Considering how many people the doctor had ticked off, he was probably a well-protected man to still be alive. Besides, it wasn't like the doctor was going to willingly hand over his life's work to a complete stranger. Even if Colin could get into the building, he would never get out with the cure. He'd probably be arrested before he could reach the door. If only there was another place he could get it that wouldn't be so public. Even if Colin was crazy enough to follow him, the doctor obviously wouldn't carry cases of the cure in the back seat of his car when he drove around. Colin rubbed his head. He needed to take a break. He was exhausted—emotionally and physically.

He looked at his phone. His dad had no idea what he was going through—what he'd left him to deal with. He could call and tell him about Lily, but why would a man who'd deserted his own family deserve to know anything? Colin paced. It felt good to stretch out his legs. His eyes were tired from straining to look at the screen. His body ached from sitting for two hours. Maybe his dad didn't deserve to know, but still, Colin would never be able to forgive himself if he didn't call. He picked up his phone.

A few minutes later, the receptionist at the rehab told Colin there weren't any patients by the name of Thomas Durnin staying there. Colin checked to make sure he'd called the right number. It was. When he asked if she could tell him how to contact his dad, she told him she could not. He told her it was an emergency, but that only led to her repeating her previous statement with more irritation in her voice the second time. He hung up. At least he'd tried. It wasn't his fault if his dad didn't know what was going on with his own daughter.

Colin's stomach growled. He hardly felt like eating, but he needed to. He looked at the time on his phone and tried to remember the last time he'd eaten. It had to have been sometime that morning before he'd visited Lily. It'd been almost eight hours since he'd eaten anything. He walked to the kitchen and rummaged through the fridge. Leftovers from Al's. He couldn't remember how old the cold spaghetti was, but it smelled safe enough to eat. He stuck the container in the microwave and watched it spin in circles. The microwave beeped. His phone rang. Colin pressed the button on the microwave to answer the phone. "Hello?"

He realized he was speaking out loud to the microwave. "Don't hang up. Don't hang up. Don't hang up."

Colin grabbed his phone and answered before they hung up.

He answered it. "Hello?"

"Hey, umm, it's me, your dad. The receptionist at the rehab called and told me you had called about an emergency."

"Why'd she say you weren't there?"

"Because, it's complicated. I—"

"Don't worry about it, Dad. You're not at the rehab, you're not at home, and you're not at the hospital with Lily, so I don't want to know where you are. I can imagine." Colin took a deep breath. "I only called because, regardless of my personal feelings, I think you should know that Lily's not doing too well. She's doing pretty bad, actually."

"I'm sorry to hear that." He said it as if Colin had just told him their pet gerbil was sick. The line was silent long enough for Colin to hear the sound of voices and music in the distance. It sounded like his dad was calling from outside a bar. Colin was about to hang up when his dad's voice stopped him. "What's going on with her?"

"Her cancer is spreading. She's on total bed rest now. I told her you were on a business trip, but I think she's starting to realize I lied. You've been gone for five months, Dad. When are you coming back?"

Thomas hesitated. "I don't know—"

"Well, figure it out, Dad! While you've been gone, Lily's been stuck in her hospital bed, missing Mom, and now missing you too. And this morning Dr. Long said she's going to die—"

"What do you mean, she's gonna die?"

"Well, we knew this was going to happen eventually, Dad. She has cancer, or did you forget? You wouldn't be so surprised if you weren't off at some bar pretending you don't have a daughter."

"Colin, that's enough! You've been an amazing son for taking care of my burdens, but you still don't get to talk to me like that. I'm sorry for the way I left, but I can't do anything about that now. I needed help, and besides ... you two were better off without me."

"Yeah, I'm sure your dying thirteen-year-old daughter will understand that she was better off without you."

"You know why I left. I already feel guilty enough about that." He paused. "Just tell me what her room number is."

"Room 12. And she's not a burden," Colin retorted.

"What?"

"You said I've been taking care of your burdens. Lily isn't a burden."

"I wasn't saying she's a burden. I meant—I was talking about the house and... You know what, I don't have to explain myself to you. I did what I thought was best." His dad paused. Colin could hear people laughing in the distance. "Are you doing okay with money? Do you need help?"

"No, I didn't call for money. I just called to tell you about Lily, and now I have, so ..." Colin thought about the cure, which he had almost given up hope on. Maybe it was the tiredness taking over, but an idea popped into his head. "Actually ... I could use your help finding a lead."

"A lead?" His dad laughed for the first time since he'd called. "On what?"

A moment later, Colin was scribbling furiously onto the back of an old envelope as his dad gave him instructions: GIS—property profile—search by owner name. Got it. He told his dad he just needed to ask the guy if he knew anything about the so-called cure. When his dad asked who "the guy" was, Colin told him he was someone who knew a lot about the cure and had talked about it in interviews online. Colin was telling the truth, but he left out a few details. His dad was an old cop. There was no way he would help Colin if he knew the whole story. His plan was dangerous and stupid, but it was necessary if he was going to save his sister.

He followed his dad's instructions on his phone and typed in the old doctor's name. The results loaded immediately, and then he was staring at the doctor's address: 1142 Pine Lane, South Fulton, Georgia. It seemed too good to be true. How had it been that easy? There had to be a catch—a guard dog, a security system, cameras.

If he was going to do this, he needed a plan. The doctor wasn't going to welcome him into his home with open arms. If the cure was at the doctor's house, as Colin hoped, then he needed to be prepared for every scenario. Colin would need to know his way around the neighborhood, by foot and by car. If the cure wasn't at the doctor's house, then he would have to "persuade" the doctor to take him to his lab and get it—assuming it hadn't been shut down since the publication of the interview three months ago. Colin was going to need something to persuade the doctor with. He couldn't just waltz into his home demanding things and expect to be given them.

Colin walked to the hallway and looked up at the little bit of rope sticking out of the attic door on the ceiling. The ladder unfolded as Colin pulled on the little dinky rope. Dust fell down as the ladder noisily became unhinged. The thing looked like it hadn't been touched in years. He wondered if the wooden steps would hold him as he walked up the rickety old thing. He waited a moment before climbing to the next step.

His eyes looked around the dark space, scanning for the box. He could see that the boxes and containers had been thrown around in every direction. He climbed into the cramped, dusty space and moved a few boxes around. Too big, too small. He would know it when he saw it. When he was a child, he'd played with that box all the time.

Aha! He found it. For a moment, he could have kissed the flimsy cardboard. But it was dusty, and he knew that kissing a box was crazy, especially one that had been sitting in the attic for years. He opened it and found an old uniform with a few holes in it where moths or mice had eaten through. There it was—the dusty holster was still in the corner of the box. He reached in and picked it up. Just in case.

Was he seriously thinking what he was thinking? The cure might not even work. He could be caught and thrown in jail. If Lily recovered, then who would take care of her? With Mom gone and Dad playing hooky, he was all she had. He couldn't think about any of that now. Lily was going to die if he didn't do this. He grabbed the box and descended carefully back down the old ladder.

Chapter 34: The House

It didn't take a genius to figure out why they'd named it Pine Lane: tall pines lined both sides of the narrow road. Colin looked for the number 1142 on mailboxes as he drove past. Each house seemed larger than the last. He took his foot off the gas as he drove past a mailbox marked 1142, then stopped. This was the doctor's home.

Through the row of hollies that made sort of a natural fence around the yard, he could see the colonial-style house sitting behind an acre or two of rolling green grass. It smelled like it'd been freshly cut. The only vehicle in the driveway was an old pickup truck with a trailer attached. It was probably the landscaper's, even though there didn't appear to be anyone around. The house looked quiet: no lights on, no grandchildren playing in the freshly manicured grass, no women gossiping on the porch swing over a glass of sweet tea. It had to be the doctor's. To Colin's surprise, there was no gate, no cameras, no guard dogs. Why did it look so unguarded?

A man came around the house on a riding lawn mower. He wore a hat and scarf to cover his head and face, but Colin was confident it wasn't the doctor. The man's stature seemed young and lively, if there was a way for someone to ride a lawn in a lively way. Besides, why would Dr. Lloyd be mowing his lawn in the middle of the morning? Judging by the fact that he was in the South and the man didn't wave to him, Colin figured he must not have noticed him watching from the road. He made a loop around the large magnolia tree, then followed the walkway to the front door. The man again didn't wave as he made another loop around the house, so he must have been oblivious to Colin's presence.

An old woman drove up beside him in her car and stopped. She rolled her window down and waved at Colin. He sighed. She was probably just a nosy neighbor. He smiled and rolled down his window.

"Are you looking for someone?" she asked.

"No, ma'am. I was just admiring the house here. I was about to be on my way."

She squinted at him, probably to get a better look. "I've never seen you before. Do you live around here?"

Colin gulped. "No, I was—just driving through. The GPS is having me take back roads, I guess."

"Where are you trying to get to?"

"Oh, umm, Cedar Crest Drive."

"Hmm, I'm not familiar with where that is"—(because it's made up, Colin thought)—"but this road dead ends, so you're not going to get there from here unless you turn around."

"Oh—okay. Thanks."

She nodded. "Have a nice day."

She rolled up her window. Already, his trip had been useful. He'd learned that the drive was a dead end, that the long gravel driveway would probably be too loud for him to drive on if he didn't want to alert the neighbors' dogs (assuming they had dogs to alert), and that the doctor hired workers to take care of his lawn in the daytime. Colin's mouth dropped open as the woman he'd been speaking to drove into the entrance of the driveway to 1142 Pine Lane. He'd read that the doctor was married and had a son who'd died several years back, but he hadn't thought about the doctor still having a wife—assuming she was the wife, since she looked to be about the right age.

The man on the lawn mower waved as she got out of her car with a bag of groceries. Suddenly, Colin realized he was still sitting in front of their house watching her as she looked back curiously at him. He reached for the steering wheel and drove farther down the lane before finding a driveway to turn around in. He hadn't thought about the wife being there. That changed everything. Maybe he could convince her that he worked with her husband and that the doctor had sent him ... no, that didn't make any sense. Someone honked as Colin pulled out in front of them onto the main road. He waved in apology and went back to his scheming. He remembered the box in the attic with his dad's old uniform. It had a few holes, but nothing he couldn't patch up or hide. Maybe he wouldn't have to take the cure by force after all.

When he got home, he pulled his dad's old uniform out of the flimsy box he'd left in the living room and tried it on. Colin was six foot two, but still his dad was almost three inches taller than him, so the pants dragged down onto the carpet and the shirt sat sloppily around his waist. There was no way he could impersonate an officer looking that way. He changed back into his regular clothes and looked over at the jacket sitting in the box. He tried it on over his tank top. The cuffs hung down past his wrists, but it looked good enough. The doctor and his wife were old. They probably wouldn't be able to tell if he was wearing the full uniform or not. The jacket would look convincing on its own, if only he had a badge to show. His father had turned his in when he'd resigned. It couldn't be difficult to find a fake badge. He stared at the mirror, the reflection of a man with blond hair and blue eyes wearing a police jacket looking too much like his father. He pulled the jacket back off.

Chapter 35: The Heist

Colin stood in the driveway, watching the shadow move across the curtain upstairs. Downstairs, the doctor had just walked through the kitchen into a room toward the back of the big house. Colin could no longer see him, but that didn't matter, because he knew the doctor's wife would be out of the way now. This was his chance. Colin had planned this moment for the past three nights. He would've preferred to plan his first and only robbery for a little longer, but he had no time to lose. Lily was fading a little more each day.

The moonlight illuminated the winding driveway more than he liked. He hadn't left the shadow of the mature oak tree for the past hour. It was the perfect place to see without being seen. It'd been thirty minutes since the doctor had walked from the dining table to the living room sofa. He'd been reading the newspaper ever since. The curtains were still open in most of the rooms.

A movement upstairs caught his eye. The doctor's wife was drawing the bedroom curtains shut. He would have to make his move now or never.

What was that? Nearby, a puddle rippled. He took a deep breath to steady his nerves. He wasn't usually this jumpy. Something about the feeling of cold metal against his hand was making him more nervous than usual. His finger searched for the trigger, which made his heart race faster. He'd never pointed a gun at anyone before. Of course, he didn't intend on using it tonight. Nobody was going to get hurt. Get in. Get the cure. Get out.

The rain had stopped over an hour ago, but the air remained damp. Could it be any muggier? The frogs seemed to be delighted by the July weather. They sang so loud it hurt Colin's ears. Any other night, he would've appreciated the symphony coming from the different nocturnal creatures all around him. Tonight, of course, was different. He needed to concentrate.

With every step, Colin's legs felt heavier. Sweat, along with the humid air, clung to his skin. Was it the heavy air or the pure adrenaline coursing through his body that was making it harder to breathe?

Croak. Colin jumped. It was just a toad. As if it were copying him, the unusually large toad jumped out of the way. He crept forward, feeling even more nervous than before. Stupid toad had almost made him soil his pants. How was he going to pull this off if he was jumping at everything on God's green earth?

A large cloud drifted across the sky, obstructing the moon's creamy light. The uneven gravel driveway went black. He stumbled over something hard—a rock, most likely. The Glock jiggled in his dad's old jacket, reminding him of its presence. Whose idea had it been to not put lights along the driveway? It probably wasn't right to complain. After all, he was the one who was breaking the law.

The gravel crunched underneath his feet rhythmically. More than once he tripped and stepped in a puddle. It was impossible to see anything. The full moon reappeared from the clouds. He was grateful to be able to see the gravel driveway again, even though it meant he would be more visible. He tried to walk faster in case the moon decided to disappear again.

Water splashed onto his pants from a small puddle he'd stepped into. He wasn't bothered by water sloshing around his new shoes. The singular thought went through his mind as he walked toward the colonial house: Will the cure work? Tonight was his only chance. If this didn't work, nothing would.

Hoot hoot! A barn owl announced its presence from a nearby magnolia. He jumped again. What was up with these animals? Did he look like Snow White or something?

After what felt like forever, he stood facing the oversize french door at the back of the house. His heart stopped. A woman's voice yelled out something. It must've been the doctor's wife. She must have come back downstairs for something. The house got quiet again.

He stood, frozen in place. Come on, knock. His hand weighed a ton as he tried to lift it. On the other side of the door, Colin could hear what sounded like footsteps against a floor, or maybe someone was using a cutting board. His hand banged against the door. The sound of footsteps drew closer.

Next to the door, he could see a shadow move behind the curtain. He called out, "Police! Open up."

The sound of the metal bolt turning came from the door. They'd taken the bait. The bolt made a sharp grinding sound as it was turned from behind the door. A woman stood in the doorway with a puzzled look on her face.

"We need to search your house," he said.

She stepped to the side to let him in. He could feel her studying him, looking at the old police jacket. "You look a little young to be a police officer. I'm guessing you can't be older than twenty-two." Her eyes traveled down to his shoes and stopped. "Oh, my word. Your shoes are soaking wet. Were you standing out there for long? I didn't realize it was raining outside." She peered around his shoulder at the driveway. "Did you say you were a police officer? You look familiar. Did I see you the other day in front of my house?"

"Ma'am, is your husband here? I need to speak with him."

Before she could answer, a door on the other side of the room swung open. A man walked in. Judging by the look on his face, he was surprised to see Colin standing in his house.

"Who are you?" the man asked.

"Police. I have a few questions to ask you, Dr. Lloyd."

"What's this about?"

It was clear that Colin was not welcome. He couldn't blame him for their hostility. He knew how this must look: showing up at a stranger's home in the dead of night could only look one way. Unfortunately, any of their suspicions were right this time.

Before he could stop her, the woman was rushing toward the same door her husband had just come through. She was faster than she looked. And if she had any brains at all, she'd be calling the cops now.

Colin looked at the doctor. "Sir, I'm going to need to search your house."

"Is that right, Officer."

Colin skimmed the room quickly. He wanted to dash toward the cabinets and look for the cure himself, but he didn't know what it might look like. Was it a pill? Something in a beaker? He needed the doctor's cooperation.

Colin tried to look offended. "I'm a police officer. Did you know that it's a crime to withhold information from the police?"

"You're not the police. What do you think, I was born yesterday? Gimme a break." The doctor squinted at him. "Who sent you? Pet Safe? Do No Harm? No, let me guess. You were sent by one of the guys at the chemo corporation."

Colin held his breath as he pointed the handgun at the doctor's plaid shirt. "I don't have time for this. Show me where the cure is or I'll shoot."

Dr. Lloyd squinted as if he couldn't make out what was in Colin's hand. "Put that away, kid, before you hurt someone. You'll have to shoot me before I give you what you're asking for. What even makes you think I'd keep something like that at my house?"

"Come on, Doc. This isn't exactly a kitchen. Unless your wife uses a microscope to bake bread." Colin lowered the gun. "Look, my sister is going to die without that medicine. I didn't want to do it this way. If you just give it to me, I'll go."

"The cure hasn't been tested on humans yet."

"I know you want to know if it works on humans or not. I have to take that chance. She can be your clinical trial." Dr. Lloyd didn't budge. "Without it, she will die. So either give it to me or I'll shoot you and look for it myself." Colin waved the gun at him and hoped he wouldn't call his bluff. "I don't have all day."

The old doctor walked to a fridge with a glass door and pulled out a vial. "Take it and leave."

"How do I know if that's really the cure?"

The doctor smiled faintly. "You don't."

Colin reached for the vial slowly. The doctor glanced down at his hands, which were shaking.

"Son, you must love your sister a lot to be this crazy. What if she dies sooner because of this? What if she suffers because of the medicine you gave her? Would you be able to live with yourself?" Colin didn't answer. It was a question he'd asked himself many times over the past couple of days. Instead, he stuck the vial into his breast pocket and backed toward the door

177

slowly. The doctor continued. "I gave the cure to my own child before it was ready. I told myself he was going to die without it anyway, just like you're telling yourself right now. I've had to carry the burden of killing my own son ever since. It's a burden I wouldn't wish on my greatest enemy."

Colin took another step back and stumbled over the doorframe. After a quick recovery, he ran away from the house. With a glance over his shoulder, he could see that the old man was still standing in the doorway. Colin stopped running and called out to him: "I'm sorry!"

The doctor closed the door without responding. Colin turned and ran into the darkness, toward the hollies. The vial sat safely in the inside pocket of his jacket. Maybe it was from running, or from robbing an old couple, or from not eating all day, but he suddenly started to feel like he was going to puke. He couldn't slow down yet. The car was only a few yards away. He needed to get far away before the police showed up. Why had he thought it was a good idea to park so far away from the doctor's house in the first place?

The narrow drive was still empty and dark. His feet pounded against the gravel as he sprinted. He couldn't trip, or all of this would have been for nothing.

* * *

The speedometer climbed. Sixty. Seventy. Eighty-five.

He reached into his coat pocket and pulled out the vial of medicine. The tube was smooth and small. He gently rubbed his thumb over the vial and glanced down, just to make sure it was real. He was mesmerized by the copper liquid that had taken on the color of the lights on the dashboard. The doctor's words

178

haunted him. What if she suffered because of the medicine he gave her? What choice did he have? She would die if he didn't give her the cure.

The sound of a car horn brought him back to the present. Instinctively, he reached for the steering wheel and yanked it to the right, managing to swerve back into his own lane before hitting the car in the lane beside him.

Crap. Where was the vial?

He leaned toward the passenger seat and gently slid his hand across every crevice and stitch. It wasn't there. The cup holders and center console gave the same results: nothing. Before he could search further, he heard the faint sound of a police siren growing louder.

Colin glanced at the dash. The speedometer showed ninety mph. His foot hit the brake, but he was too late. In the rearview mirror, he could see the blue and red lights flying up behind him. There was no way he could outrun them in a Prius. He pulled off the exit and waited.

A moment later, the cop was tapping his knuckle against his window. He rolled it down. "Colin Durnin?"

Colin looked up to where the familiar voice had come from. "Officer Digger?"

"Colin, what are you doing way out here?"

"Oh ... I was just ... meeting someone."

"Well, I don't want to hold you up, but kid, do you know how fast you were going?"

"I was thinking about a lot of things. Sorry. I know that's not a good enough reason."

"You were going ninety miles an hour." He paused. "I hate to even ask you this, but ... have you been drinking tonight?"

"What? No. No, sir ... definitely not."

"If I was off duty, I would just tell you to drive more careful, because I know you're good people. But unfortunately, I can't just act like I didn't see you racing down 85 South, swerving like you're a NASCAR driver." He sighed. "I have to ask you to step out."

"Sir, I swear—"

"This isn't personal. If you've been drinking and I let you get back on that road, and you hurt someone—or, worse yet, you kill someone—that would be on me. And I couldn't live with that on my conscience. So again, I'm gonna have to ask you to step out."

A female voice buzzed over the handheld transceiver. "Code 211. White male. Twenties. Seen last at—"

Digger turned the dial down and stared at Colin.

Colin's heart raced. He felt around his seat subtly before opening the door. Where could that vial have gone? Digger stepped back as the door opened. Colin swung his leg out slowly and glanced down at his lap. The blue strobe lights from Digger's car were so bright that he couldn't make out anything. He stood slowly and tried not to look as he heard the clinking noise of a small object hitting the ground. Digger glanced at the ground.

No.

Digger looked back at Colin and held out an object. "This is a Breathalyzer. I need you to blow into it for me."

Colin placed his trembling lips around the tube and blew into it. His heart pounded in his chest as he heard a noise that sounded like the object rolling under his car. He coughed to cover the sound. He realized how it all must have looked—all the signs added up: the vial of copper liquid on the ground, the sweat beads forming a blanket over Colin's face, the excessive trembling, the speeding and swerving. Digger had every reason to suspect Colin of being a meth addict. Digger looked at him and went back to reading the numbers on the Breathalyzer. Colin took a deep breath.

"You're all good," Digger said, looking up finally. "Hey, I'm not gonna write you a ticket this time, but listen to me—you're going to kill yourself, or somebody else, driving like that. If I was some other cop, they could've taken your license. If you'd been going much faster, the cops could've hauled you in to jail."

"I'll slow down. I promise. Please don't tell my dad about this. He's going through a lot right now."

Digger didn't look surprised. And for the first time, Colin realized he knew about the rehab.

"You know, don't you?"

Digger nodded. "He told me before he checked in."

Colin's anger toward his dad suddenly turned to Digger.

"If you knew, why didn't you stop him?"

"Colin, your dad's a grown man, and I'm not about to stand here and talk bad about him to his son. I can't say I agree with what he did, but I can say he was trying to do what he thought was right. Even good people make bad decisions sometimes." His words struck Colin hard. "And listen, I won't tell him this time, but you better believe if I catch you driving like a maniac again, oh, he's getting a call. Understand?"

Colin nodded. It was more than fair. Digger had worked himself up so much he'd lost his breath, and now he breathed like he was trying to catch it again. "This is exactly why I didn't have kids. My blood pressure is already shootin' up." He shook his head. "Well, I need to go check out this call we got about a suspicious guy in one of these rich neighborhoods. Probably just another one of these stupid high school kids. They're always getting into one thing or another. You be safe and slow down."

Digger smacked Colin's shoulder, making the metal in his dad's jacket jiggle. Colin had forgotten about the gun. Maybe Digger didn't hear it. Digger glanced at his jacket. Crap.

"Uh, yeah, you too," Colin said to distract him.

Digger nodded and turned to walk to his car. Colin looked at the ground. He couldn't see anything, but it had to be the vial that had fallen out. He jumped at the sound of Digger's voice. "Colin, what did you say you were doing out this way again?"

"Oh ... meeting someone."

Digger squinted. "Try to get there in one piece." He walked back to his car and drove away.

Colin got in his car and waited till he was far enough away not to see him in his rearview mirror before hopping back out to look for the vial that held his only hope of saving Lily. He got on his hands and knees to get a better look. If it was the vial that had rolled, it was probably under his car, hopefully still in one piece. He could kick himself. He should've been more careful. How could he have let that happen? Stupid, stupid, stupid.

The asphalt felt sharp against his hands and knees as he lowered his head. Something small shimmered on the other side of his car. Colin jumped up and ran to the other side. Once again, he found himself on the ground, reaching blindly around the front tire. His finger felt something smooth. He grabbed it. Please be it ...

Chapter 36: Lily

The morning after the heist, Colin arrived at the hospital at nine a.m. He sat on a bench near the entrance of the building, eating one of the muffins he'd gotten on the way. Visiting wasn't allowed until ten, which was normally when he arrived. But he had to do something other than pace around that house, debating whether or not he should give the cure to Lily, then hating himself for debating. He was driving himself crazy. Of course he should give it to her, after everything he'd gone through to get it. He shook his head. Just because he'd stuck his neck out to get the cure didn't mean he should give it to Lily. Still, he had gone through so much to get it, because she needed it. He was just worrying too much, or was he? Maybe feeling worried was a sign that he shouldn't give her the cure. Maybe something inside him knew it was too risky. What did risk matter when she was guaranteed to die?

He put the baggie with the other muffin back into his backpack. The bottle of apple juice laced with medicine sat at the bottom. He'd forgotten to ask the doctor how the cure needed to be delivered—not that he would've answered. Besides, it wasn't like he could ask the nurse to give Lily a mystery medicine intravenously. Having Lily drink it was his only option. He hoped it would work.

Someone in scrubs covered with rainbow-colored balloons walked out of the sliding glass doors. Colin checked the time on his phone: 10:02 a.m. He put the baggie back into the backpack he'd brought. He got up and walked toward the automatic doors.

Lily smiled as her brother walked into her hospital room. She didn't look much like herself anymore, but her smile was untouched. He sat in his usual spot—the recliner—and looked around the room and thought about all the days Lily had spent there, instead of in her own home. The walls were decorated with flowers and bears. The lamps were round and yellow to look like the sun, or a yellow balloon. They did their best to make the rooms look happy, although the decorations almost seemed to have the opposite effect on Colin. The place reminded him of the childhood Lily was missing out on. Colin managed a weak smile. He realized Lily had been staring at him while he looked around her room as if he'd never seen it before.

"You look rough."

He laughed. "Gee, thanks. Good morning to you too."

He ruffled the water out of his wet hair.

"Is it raining outside? I didn't think it was."

"No. I just took a shower before I headed this way."

Her head tilted to one side. "You look upset. Is something wrong?"

He shrugged. "Nope."

"You look like you're thinking about something."

"I just didn't sleep well."

"Why not?" She was persistent.

He smiled. "Stop worrying about me. I'm older than you are, so it's my job to worry about you. Got it?"

"Fine." Lily rolled her eyes. "Why'd you bring a backpack? Did you bring me something?"

He had her favorite breakfast: a chocolate chip muffin.

Colin laughed. "Why are you so observant today?"

"It's so boring here. Parker had to have surgery. He's fine, but now he can't come by to play cards with me for a few days."

"Do you want to play cards with me?"

"No, thanks."

Colin smirked. "Why not?"

"It's not the same."

Lily hadn't taken her eyes off the backpack. "So you never answered my question. What's in the backpack?"

"I got you something. Close your eyes."

Lily's eyes squeezed shut obediently. Colin grabbed the bag with the muffin. His hand hovered over the bottle of apple juice. He glanced at Lily to make sure her eyes were still shut and noticed the blue veins showing through her translucent skin. She looked so frail. He left the bottle in the bottom of the bag. It was just too risky.

"Open your eyes."

Her eyes opened. She smiled wide, showing off her dimples on both sides of her face. She reached out and grabbed the bag from him. She wasted no time in tearing the top off the muffin. Colin chuckled as she stuffed a piece of muffin into the side of her cheek, like a squirrel. "Thanks. Did you get anything to drink?"

"You're going to choke if you keep trying to talk with food in your mouth."

He reached into the bag slowly. He could do this. It was her only chance. If he didn't give it to her, she would die. His hand touched the bottle of apple juice laced with untested medicine. He couldn't think about what that old doctor had said now.

Lily took the juice from him excitedly. Colin watched closely as she opened the lid. His stomach turned. In less than twenty-four hours he might be a thief *and* a murderer.

"Did you drink from this already?" she asked.

"No. Why?"

"The thing you pull off the lid was missing. You drank out of it already, didn't you?"

"Why would I do that?"

"Eew! You did drink it already. You're such a bad liar."

"Lily, just drink the juice."

"It has backwash in it. You can have it back."

"I promise I didn't drink out of it. So drink it or I won't bring you stuff anymore."

Lily looked surprised by her brother's tone.

"I shouldn't have snapped. I'm sorry."

"You get it from Dad."

Colin shuddered at her comment. Lily seemed oblivious to the effect her comment had had on her brother. She seemed too preoccupied with the apple drink she was examining for backwash.

"This tastes funny. Maybe it's expired."

"What does the expiration date on it say?"

"September twentieth, 2026."

"Okay. It's only June. So drink it."

"But it tastes funny."

"It's not expired. If it tastes funny, it's probably because your taste buds are off from the chemo. It's not the juice, it's you."

Lily stopped peeling the wrapper off the bottle and stared at him.

"Lily. I shouldn't have said that. Geesh. I'm on a roll today, huh? It's just that I think the vitamins will do you good. Plus, you're always begging me to get you stuff; then, when I do, you act like you don't want it. And like I said, I'm tired."

Colin watched Lily drink her apple juice to make sure she finished it down to the last drop. It took her almost an hour to finish the entire bottle. Colin didn't have much to say as he sat and watched her, since his mind had been on one track recently. He couldn't seem to find anything else to think about other than the cure, the doctor, and the heist. Colin wanted to tell someone about the secrets that had been burning through his conscience, about the felony he'd committed, about the old man he'd robbed. He wanted to confess his sins to someone and relieve his guilty conscience. He wished he could tell Lily about the medicine she was currently trying to keep down. It would make things easier. It was just too risky. Lily didn't have the best track record for keeping secrets.

She drank slowly to make sure it wouldn't come back up. He knew her stomach had been sensitive lately, and it probably didn't help that she found the taste of the medicine repulsive. He'd worried about a lot of things over the past four days, but none of them included Lily throwing up. If she did, would the cure still work? It seemed unlikely. He should've asked the doctor how to administer the medicine—again, not that the doctor would've told him. At last, she finished. It was 11:14 a.m. Colin swung the backpack over his shoulder and stood up.

"I need to go to work."

"Already?"

He nodded. "Yeah, sorry. I was late three times in a row. I can't be late today."

He leaned over her bed and hugged her goodbye. Please don't throw up, he thought.

Chapter 37: Eavesdropping

Colin watched the blood and water mix in the sink and run down the drain. He turned the knob and reached for the gauze that was still there from the last time he'd cut himself. The bleeding didn't stop completely, but the gauze slowed it down enough for him to go back to chopping zucchini. He stuck another glove on his hand and grabbed the knife. He'd been distracted all day, worrying about Lily. It had only been a few hours since he'd given her the cure, but it felt like forever. He kept his ringer turned all the way up, which was against kitchen rules. Any minute now, he could get a call from Dr. Long. Being on edge hadn't helped while he was holding a knife. He scraped the zucchini into the skillet and looked over at Bob's station. Al had hired him a few weeks ago, and he still hadn't learned how to do much more than make a salad. Sometimes Colin wondered if this was Al's way of getting back at him for taking all that time off.

Bob had been preparing a salad for almost fifteen minutes. Colin was starting to lose patience for these trainees. Bob looked over at Colin's hand, which was wrapped by a bandage that was slowly changing from white to red. The corners of Bob's mouth started to creep up into a smile. He laughed and joked that maybe he should be training Colin how to use the knife safely.

Yeah, like that's ever going to happen, Colin thought. Colin took a deep breath and tried to tune out his obnoxious trainee. If he had the power to fire him, he would've already, but he didn't. Things had been awkward enough in the kitchen between him, Olivia, and Rob. The last thing Colin needed was tension between him and Bob. Although Bob probably couldn't tell if someone disliked him if they slapped him in the face.

He slid the plate of chicken parmesan through the kitchen pass toward Rob and Olivia. They stopped talking about whatever it was that was making Olivia giggle so much and looked at Colin with the same unwelcoming expression. Rob took the plate and disappeared through the doors. Colin smiled at Olivia. She gave him a half smile back. "Hey."

"Hey," she said.

"This new cook is driving me crazy," he whispered. "The guy really isn't the sharpest knife in the kitchen, pun intended. Where does Al find these guys?"

"Probably the same place he found you."

Before Colin could say anything else, she'd grabbed a pitcher of tea and left. She'd given him the cold shoulder for months, ever since he'd stopped returning her calls without explanation. He couldn't blame her. Still, it had been harder than he'd expected to try to fix things between them. One night, back in December, he'd texted her that he missed her, but she'd never replied. Who could blame her?

Colin turned and began chopping the tomatoes carefully. Bob still had that stupid smile plastered across his face.

"I don't think she's into you, Colin. There's other waitresses here. Why don't you ask one of them out?"

"And hurt your chances of getting a date? No way," Colin said sarcastically.

189

"Wow, thanks, man." Bob sounded completely genuine.

Colin glanced down at the salad Bob was working on.

"Bob, tell me that is not the same salad you've been working on for the last twenty minutes."

"It has to be perfect."

Colin reached over and grabbed the salad. "Chicken salad." He slid the bowl across the pass. Rob and Olivia were standing on the other side again. Colin told Bob to make the salads faster and started chopping the onions. The fumes burned his eyes as they rose from the onion. He turned his ear toward the pass to try to hear what Olivia was saying to Rob.

"If you trade tables with me, I'll give you all of my tips tonight ," Olivia said, laughing flirtatiously. Colin rolled his eyes.

"Have you told him?" It was Rob's voice.

"No. Shh. He's standing right there."

Colin glanced over his shoulder. They didn't see him as they stood close to each other, whispering. Olivia reached out and touched Rob's arm. Colin's stomach turned. It was obvious something was going on between the two of them.

"I think one of us should tell him. He's probably already figured it out. Wouldn't you like to stop ..." His voice got too quiet to hear.

"I guess, but he should hear it from you."

"Why? It's awkward enough ever since he moved out, but this'll make it so much worse."

"Because you've been friends for years, and if you ever want to be friends again, this needs to come from you."

"I can't understand the handwriting on Olivia's order, Colin. What's it say?"

Bob's voice startled Colin, almost making him cut himself again. He glanced at the ticket.

"It says one lasagna and one house salad—no croutons, no cheese."

Colin looked back toward the pass. Olivia was gone. Rob looked up and nodded. Colin nodded back and turned around. He pulled his gloves off and checked his phone again. It was only 7:09 p.m. He couldn't wait around to get a call. He opened his old messages.

Colin: What's up?

Lily: Watching TV

Colin: You feel okay?

Lily: Yes lol

Colin put his phone away and grabbed a fresh pair of gloves. He glanced back over at Bob, who was neatly placing croutons on the house salad. Seriously, what was up with this guy?

"Bob, no croutons. They might be allergic. Make a new salad. *No* croutons this time."

Chapter 38: BO

The next morning, the empty pudding cup sat on the side table next to the deck of cards. Lily's hospital room was bright, like it always was in the morning, since her window faced the sunrise. She'd learned once that that meant it was facing east, but it was hard to remember for certain. Many things she'd learned in school felt far away, as if she'd learned them years ago instead of six months ago. Really, it'd been nine months since she had truly learned anything from school, since she'd only attended seventh grade for a few days. At first, it was fun not having to go to school, but she was starting to miss the eight-hour days, the uncomfortable wooden chairs, the bumpy bus rides, her heavy backpack weighed down by twenty pounds of books. Her heart ached. Thinking about school always made her miss her mother, since school had always been so important to her. Lily never would've gone this long without learning something if her mother were still alive.

Lily looked at the clock. She'd tried all morning not to worry about Colin, but he was late for his visit and hadn't called, which was unusual. Before she could imagine the worst, the door opened. Her eyes darted toward it so fast she got dizzy.

Colin walked into the room. "Sorry I'm late." He yawned. "I slept through my alarm."

She took a deep breath and smiled. She'd gotten herself worked up over nothing. "It's okay. You look tired." She watched him as he moved across the room and sat on the recliner next to her bed. She could smell the Italian food coming off his wrinkled clothes. He must not have taken a shower, or even changed clothes, since yesterday. "You could've slept in, or showered, instead of coming today. If you needed to."

Colin frowned. "Do I smell that bad?"

Lily laughed and pinched her nose. "Oh, yeah."

"All right, drama queen. How are you feeling? And don't say you're feeling like throwing up because of my BO."

Lily smiled. "Actually, I feel pretty good today ... despite your BO."

A young nurse walked into the room. Colin didn't seem to notice, much to Lily's surprise. He stretched out his arms and yawned. The nurse appeared to be taking her sweet time checking Lily's numbers on the monitor. Could she move any slower?

After a few minutes, she smiled at Colin and asked him how he was doing. Apparently, she thought *he* was her patient.

He does look worse than me, though, so who could blame her for the confusion? she thought.

Colin answered in monosyllables. Fine. Good. Thanks.

He didn't seem to care that a pretty nurse was flirting with him. She must've run out of excuses to be in Lily's room, because she left, looking defeated.

"That nurse was flirting with you."

"She was just being nice. Why do you always assume every nurse is flirting with me?"

"Because when you leave the nurses ask me questions. 'How old is your brother? Is he single?' Blah, blah, blah. Sometimes I

193

tell them you're married, just to mess with them."

"Wow. You're a terrible wingman."

Lily scrunched her face. "What's a wingman?"

"It's a—never mind." He looked serious suddenly. "How are you feeling today?"

"Why do you look so worried? I feel fine."

"So, you've been feeling better since yesterday?"

"Yeah, I guess so."

"Have you had any weird ... symptoms?"

"Umm, no? Like what?"

"Fever, nausea ... stuff like that."

Lily tilted her head. "Not really. Why?"

"Just making sure."

"Making sure of what?"

"Nothing, Lily. I was just wondering."

"Why are you acting so strange?"

"I'm not. I just wanted to make sure you're doing okay."

Lily watched him close his eyes and wrap his arms around his chest, then pull them up and support his head, then drop them again and open his eyes. He seemed restless, and not just today, but for the past four days—ever since Dr. Long had asked him to step out into the hallway. She wondered what Dr. Long had told him, but there was no way Colin would ever tell her.

Something was wrong. It was either her health or money problems. Dad had always gotten stressed about money. Lily chewed on her flimsy fingernail as Colin pushed the recliner back, making his feet pop up. He closed his eyes again like he was about to fall asleep right there. Colin's chest rose and fell slowly. He seemed to be drifting off.

"Colin?"

"Hmm."

"Are you stressed about money?" His eyes opened. "Because Dad was always worried, and now he's been gone for five months on that business trip."

"Lily, calm down." He stood and walked to the bed. "I'm not stressed about money. Well, I mean, I am, but that's not why I'm stressed. I'm just dealing with adult things right now."

"Why can't you tell me?"

Colin sat on the edge of the bed and held her hand in his. "Look at me." She looked into his blue eyes that looked like their parents' eyes, and her own of course. "I promise I'm not going anywhere—well, except for work in a minute. Sorry I worried you."

Colin kissed her on the forehead and left for work. The room was quiet once again. He hadn't closed the door all the way, so she could hear laughter outside her room. It sounded like the other kids were having fun in the recreation room down the hall. She stopped worrying about Colin and let her thoughts wander. It had been almost a week since her friend Parker had visited her room. She missed hanging out with him. He wasn't all that annoying for being an eight-year-old. She picked up her phone and typed the message.

Lily: You wanna hang out?

Parker: How ?? We're both on bed rest

Lily: I feel better

Parker: Okay, sure!

She scooted toward the edge of her bed. Dr. Long had put her on bed rest, but she was feeling better now. Walking would probably help. Her arms ached as she pushed herself off the bed. She slid down gracefully until her feet touched the floor. Her legs trembled, like a baby deer trying to stand for the first time. It had been too long since she'd used them. She let go of the bed to see if she could stand. Her knees buckled. She grabbed the side of the bed before falling. Suddenly, two hands were helping hold her up.

"What are you doing?"

"Oh. Hey, Dr. Long. I didn't see you there."

"I see that. Were you trying to walk?"

"Yes. I'm feeling better. I'm going to go see Parker."

Dr. Long helped Lily back into the bed. After a quick doctorly lecture, she smiled at her. "You look like you're feeling better."

"I am. I think it was the chocolate muffin that did it—maybe that should be on my chart."

"You are so silly." She pulled the covers over Lily in a way that reminded Lily of her mother. "You'll see Parker when he's fully recovered."

Chapter 39: It's Over

Colin's hand trembled as he signed and dated the last page of the pile of paperwork in front of him. He handed the clipboard back to Dr. Long. Was this really happening? After seven months of worrying every day that Lily wouldn't wake up the next morning, was it really over?

Lily wasn't suffering anymore. It was over. And all Colin could think about now was his mom. He couldn't deal with all of this on his own. More than ever, he needed her help. In a sense, he was responsible for everything. When he'd given Lily the cure, he knew it could have gone one of two ways. Was he strong enough to do what needed to be done now?

Dr. Long reached for his hand. She held it and waited until he looked her in the eyes to speak. "I'm sorry that your mother couldn't be here today. I know this day is bittersweet for you."

He nodded.

"Dr. Long, am I going home today?" Lily asked.

"Yes, Lily, you are."

Colin stared at the floor. Why wasn't he jumping up and down with excitement? He signed the discharge papers as if he were signing a DNR form.

"Colin, do you have a moment? Outside?" Dr. Long asked.

"Sure." He followed her to the hallway, to their usual spot

where they went when Dr. Long wanted to talk without being overheard. She stopped walking when they passed the nursing station and turned. "Colin, I wanted to apologize."

Colin tried to think. "What for?"

"For telling you that Lily only had three months to live, and then ..." She was crying at this point. "I was wrong. I've been looking over her test results, trying to figure out how I could've been so off." She shook her head. "It makes no sense. I want you to know that I never would've told you that if I hadn't been sure. The only way I can explain Lily's recovery is to say it was miraculous." Colin wanted to tell her about the cure, but instead he listened and nodded. "There's no other way to explain it."

"It's okay, Dr. Long. I know you're a good doctor."

"It's not okay. I just can't understand." She shook her head. "The results were ... unless the MRI machine is faulty. I'll have it checked."

Colin was screaming on the inside.

"It was probably just ... a fluke or something. I'm sure this kind of stuff happens sometimes."

Dr. Long looked dumbfounded. "Colin, you're handling all of this remarkably well, not just for someone your age either." She looked down. "I feel like you and Lily are my family, so forgive me if I'm out of line, but are you going to be able to take care of Lily? I—I know your dad is still gone. Lily told me."

Colin sighed. Of course she had. She couldn't keep a secret to save her life. "Oh—I would've told you. It's just that, I wasn't sure how long he'd be gone and—"

"You don't need to explain." She smiled warmly. "I didn't mean to put you on the spot. I just want to make sure you're going to be okay taking care of her. You're taking on a lot—raising a preteen. If you need help, I'm a call away."

"Thanks."

"Colin, as you know, I don't have any children of my own. But if I had ... I would've wanted them to be just like you and Lily. Your mother would've been very proud of you."

"That means a lot."

"I'm really going to miss her around here, but that's the selfish side of me talking. You two go have fun and celebrate her miraculous recovery."

Gulp. There was that word again. "Will do."

* * *

Lily stared out of the car window, watching the trees flash by. She was enraptured by the view she'd seen a million times before. It'd been so long since she'd been outside that it almost felt new all over again. All the small things she'd never noticed—like the pigeons sitting on the billboards and the planes flying away from and toward the Atlanta airport, like shooting stars. The sky was perfectly blue, with not a cloud in sight. Colin turned onto the exit for their home. Lily felt a burning sensation in the pit of her stomach. "Can we get some ice cream before we go home? My stomach hurts a little. I think ice cream would help." Colin stared straight ahead without answering. His expression didn't change.

"Are you listening to me, Colin?"

"Huh?"

"Did you hear what I said?"

"I'm sorry. What'd you say?"

"Can we stop and get ice cream? I'm hungry."

"Ice cream isn't real food."

"Please, Colin. I don't want real food. I haven't had ice cream in forever."

"Didn't you have it last week?"

"That wasn't real ice cream. That was frozen water."

"Hmm. Fine."

He had been quiet for most of the drive home, but Lily hadn't minded, since she'd been busy observing and sightseeing. She began to wonder if he wasn't just being quiet, if maybe he was upset. "Are you all right?"

"Yeah. Why?"

"You just ... seem upset again."

"I'm not upset. Just tired."

"You keep saying that, but I know you're lying to me. Why won't you tell me what's wrong?"

"Nothing's wrong."

Lily crossed her arms over her chest and stared out the window again. This wasn't the way she'd imagined her first day out of the hospital going—arguing with her brother. Colin started to talk.

"I'm just thinking about Mom."

Lily turned back to Colin. "You are?"

"She would've been so happy today."

Lily smiled, even though thinking about her mom was painful.

"This was what she fought so hard for—to see you healthy again. I'm just sad she isn't here to see it."

Lily was crying now. They pulled into the parking lot for ice cream. Lily laughed. "I can't go inside crying."

Colin unbuckled his seat belt. "I'll go in and get whatever you want. I'm partially responsible, after all."

"Cookies and cream, please."

After finishing her ice cream, Lily was too excited to sleep when they got home ten minutes later, despite being exhausted.

After Colin carried her suitcase to her room, he hugged her and told her he needed to take a nap from all the sugar he'd eaten. A moment later, the light coming from under Colin's door turned off and the house was completely quiet. She looked around as if she were a guest staying for the first time. Nothing had changed since she'd left, but somehow it felt like she'd never been there before. The home she'd grown up in now felt colder and stranger than the hospital ever did. She yawned and realized she could actually go for a nap after all.

She quietly walked down the hallway to her room to not wake Colin. The door to her parents' bedroom was open. She stopped walking and looked in. Their room, like the rest of the house, appeared to be unaltered. Without realizing it, she'd walked to the doorway and was leaning in. It felt as if there were two magnetic forces at play on her. One was drawing her into the room. The other was keeping her out of it, holding her at the doorway as an unwelcome guest.

The floor creaked softly as she stepped into the room and turned the light on. It was still light outside, but the blackout curtains kept their room dark. She looked around the room—at their soft gray walls, their pure white comforter, the antique furniture her mom had inherited from her deceased parents. The smell of her mother's perfume subdued her other senses. It was as if time had turned back suddenly. For a moment, she could imagine her mother was still there—inviting her in, stroking her hair, and singing a lullaby softly, comforting Lily after she'd had a nightmare. Then, without warning, the room was silent again. The memories were only memories once more. Lily moved across the room cautiously, as if at any moment she might step on another memory landmine and be hit with a less pleasant flashback. The last ones had seemed so real; she was afraid of what other memories she might relive suddenly.

The vanity was untouched. Her mother's makeup was still sitting in front of the antique mirror. She'd played with dolls at her mother's feet hundreds of times there while her mother applied lipstick in front of that rusty mirror. Sometimes her mom would let Lily wear lip gloss if it was clear or pink, but never red. Suddenly, she remembered the day her mother had shaved her hair off—her mother's voice saying, "You are so brave."

The memories stung like little bees around Lily's heart. Salty tears came to her eyes. She stumbled toward the bed and collapsed onto it. Her body shook as she sobbed into her mother's old pillow. It smelled like her. Lily inhaled deeply between sobs. For a moment, she wanted to be back at the hospital with her friend Parker and Dr. Long. And most of all she wanted to be far away from the painful memories in this room ...

Lily stretched her arms over the soft silk pillow. Glancing around, she realized she'd fallen asleep in their parents' bed by accident. She sat up and listened carefully for any sounds. Nothing. Colin must've been asleep still.

The floor creaked softly as she walked to the doorway and peaked out into the hallway. She looked around. Everything was quiet and still. She tiptoed past Colin's room, which was dark. She glanced out the window in the living room. His car was still in the driveway, so he must've been asleep. A squeak came from Colin's door. A moment later, he was in the living room stretching his arms overhead.

He yawned. "How long was I asleep for?"

"Uh, I'm not really sure."

"Hey, you okay?" he asked and then rubbed his eyes.

She walked up and wrapped her arms around his waist so he wouldn't see the tears in her eyes. "I thought I'd be happy to be home, but without Mom or Dad here, it doesn't feel like home anymore."

He held her tight. "It's just a house now, isn't it?"

She nodded. "Yeah."

He pulled her away so she could see him. "Hungry?"

She nodded and smiled.

She followed him into the kitchen, where he cracked two eggs against the side of a frying pan. They spilled open simultaneously. Lily watched his every move. Bacon popped violently, sending drops of grease flying into the air and occasionally landing on Colin's skin. Amazingly, he didn't flinch.

She swiveled back and forth on the barstool. "You're making breakfast for dinner?"

"Yep." One of the larger grease bubbles exploded.

"That's weird."

He handed her a piece of bacon. "Bacon's never weird."

She rolled her eyes playfully and stuffed a piece of bacon into her mouth. He was right: bacon was never weird.

"So, what do you want to do tomorrow?" he asked.

"Tomorrow's Tuesday. Don't you have to work?"

"I took the day off."

Lily chewed on her greasy food. It was heavenly.

"I need clothes for school. I outgrew my old ones."

"So, the mall?"

"Okay." Her answer came out flat. She couldn't figure out why, but she wasn't excited to go to the mall. She used to love going to the mall, but she'd outgrown a lot of her favorite things. Maybe it was part of getting older and more mature.

She devoured another piece of bacon and spun the stool in

a full circle. This was how she'd pictured her first day home. She pulled out her phone and opened her messages. She texted Parker.

Lily: Hey, I made it home safe.

Parker: Awesome. It's boring here without you, though.

Lily: Yeah. Sorry.

Parker: Did you get the ice cream?

She looked up when Colin laid a plateful of food in front of her. It smelled amazing.

"Who are you texting?" Colin asked.

"Parker. He said it's boring there."

"Well, maybe we can visit him after we finish shopping tomorrow. If you have the energy."

Lily smiled. "Ohmigosh, really? You're the best brother ever."

Chapter 40: The Mall

The dressing room door swung open. Lily stepped out with a pile of clothes across her forearm. She told Colin she didn't want any of them. He took the clothes from her, wondered how she had carried them, and hung the clothes on a rack and walked away. Colin followed her as she turned left out of the store and back into the main mall. She walked straight for a while. Turned left. Straight. Right. After five minutes, they had made a full circle.

"Where are you going?"

She continued walking.

"Lily, stop."

"No."

"It's almost twelve. Let's take a break."

"I can't. I need to get clothes."

"You need to eat. You'll feel better after."

"I can't eat!"

"Why not?"

Lily stopped walking.

"I'm fat! That's why nothing fits me."

He rubbed his temples.

"What are you talking about? You're not fat."

Lily became hysterical. She continued to list every reason

why she was fat, ugly, and stupid. He was a boy, so he couldn't understand. The last thing she needed was to eat! People walking by gave Colin a concerned look. They stared at Lily like they would stare at a baby screaming, wondering, *Why doesn't he get that girl to stop making a scene?* He wished he could. Colin tried to tell her to lower her voice, but it only made her more hysterical. It was the first tantrum she'd thrown since she was a little girl, and he had no idea what to do. After she'd run out of steam, Colin convinced her to at least eat a salad. Finally, she agreed, since a salad wouldn't make her fatter than she already was.

By the time they'd gotten to the food court, she'd changed her mind about the salad and had decided on a sandwich with a side of fries instead. Colin shook his head and muttered, "Women."

Lily licked her lips at the greasy plate in front of her. She chewed on a french fry happily. The tantrum was over, just that like. Colin stood up. "I need to go make a call. Be right back." She didn't seem to notice.

* * *

Colin walked until he was sure Lily wouldn't overhear him. He kept his eyes on her while the phone was ringing. His palms started to feel sweaty. He should just hang up. It was a stupid idea. Why hadn't he hung up yet? He could figure out another way to help Lily. This wasn't a good idea. He would hang up now. It was decided. Later, he could say he pocket dialed.

Her soft voice spoke. "Hello?"

"Hey, Olivia?"

"Yeah. Are you okay? You sound strange."

"Yeah ... I'm good. How are you?"

"Good." The line went silent. "What's up?"

"I was going to ask you something, but I just remembered you're working today. So never mind."

"I'm not working. What'd you want to ask?"

He explained the situation, adding "I'll understand if you say no" to the end of every sentence. She listened and said she wanted to help, much to his surprise.

He hung up and walked back to the table, where Lily was already finished with her fries and had started on her sandwich.

"I can't finish this. You want it?"

"I'm not hungry, but let's take it to go." They got the takeout box and walked around the mall some more. Suddenly, tears came to Lily's eyes. Oh, boy. Why was she upset now?

"Lily, you aren't fat."

"I know. It's not that."

"Oh. What is it then? I thought you wanted to come to the mall."

"I thought so too. It's just ... I thought I was upset because nothing was fitting, but it's not that." Tears were rolling down her face now. "Mom isn't here. She's supposed to be here. She always picked out my clothes, and I don't know how to do it without her."

Colin thought for a moment. "Oh. I hadn't thought about that. I'm sorry I can't be Mom." He paused, remembering his call to Olivia. "Lily, don't be mad at me. I thought you were just upset about not finding clothes, so I called someone I thought could help you."

Lily sniffled and squinted at him. "Who?"

* * *

207

Colin had thought about calling her back and telling her not to come after all, but this was the first time they'd had a chance to talk in almost a year. If he'd canceled, he'd probably never get another opportunity. Lily had said she didn't care if Olivia helped, but Colin was starting to think she did. She stayed ahead of them by a few feet as they walked through the mall aimlessly. Colin noticed that she hadn't said a word since Olivia arrived.

"What places have you already tried?" Olivia asked.

"All of them," Lily finally replied.

Olivia cupped the side of her mouth with her hand and looked at Colin. "Did I ruin brother-sister day?"

"How could you have ruined it? I asked you to come."

"Lily seems upset."

"She misses Mom."

"Oh. Of course she does." Olivia sighed. "Should I leave?"

"No, please don't. Neither of us know how to shop. You're our only hope."

"Wow. Very dramatic, but it worked. Okay, I'll stay."

Colin laughed. "You have no idea how much it means to me. Lily will come around—just give her time."

"What places have you already tried?"

"All of them. And to be honest, I don't know how I'm going to afford fifty-dollar jeans with holes in them."

Olivia leaned closer to him like she was telling him a secret. "There are a lot of places that give cancer patients free or cheap clothes. Have you tried any of those yet?"

"No. I completely forgot about that. I think my mom took Lily to one of those places once. It was called the American Cancer Shops, or something." He noticed Lily turn her head so her ear was toward him. "Aren't the clothes used, though?"

"The clothes she's trying on here have all been worn. What's the difference?"

"I guess you're right."

She smiled. "I know I'm right."

He reached out to touch her arm. "Thanks for coming. It means a lot to me."

She pulled her arm away gently. "It's no problem."

He blushed. "I didn't know who else to call—"

"It's really no problem."

"And I've missed you."

It was her turn to blush. She looked down and didn't say anything. Lily had slowed down, either from getting tired or trying to eavesdrop—not that there was much to hear. Colin could see relief up ahead in the form of a neon exit sign. They were almost to the parking lot. Olivia looked away from her shoes to look at him.

Colin asked, "So, am I going to drive with you or—"

"Actually, I think separate would be best."

Colin noticed she wasn't smiling any longer.

"Can I ask you something?" she asked.

"Of course."

"Why did you just cut us off? Rob and me, I mean. We were trying to be there for you, and you just pushed us away."

Colin rubbed his forearm. "Wow. I didn't see that coming." He paused. "I just had a lot going on in my life. It was hard for me to talk to anyone after—you know. I meant to apologize to you a long time ago for the way I treated you. I didn't know how to deal with it all, you know?" He paused again. "I shouldn't have pushed you and Rob away. I'm sorry."

The automatic doors slid open. The heavy heat washed over Colin. They all walked toward the parking lot silently for a minute. Colin felt exhausted. Hopefully, no more emotion bombs would be dropped for the remainder of the day.

"Was I the reason you and Rob stopped being friends?" Olivia asked out of the blue.

"No." Colin thought about it. "I mean, I was upset that you talked to him about our issues, but ... I understand why you did." He paused. "So Rob told you we're not talking?"

She nodded. "Colin, I should've told you before." Olivia frowned. "Rob and I are engaged."

Before Colin could respond, Lily spun around with her mouth hanging open. "You and Rob are engaged?" Lily gasped. She no longer seemed to be upset that Olivia was there as she walked next to her and asked questions: When's the wedding? What are you wearing? Where are you getting married? What are the bridesmaids wearing? Do you have a ring? Can I see it?

Olivia glanced at Colin apologetically as she answered Lily's questions. She held up her hand for Lily to study the ring, which he'd somehow not noticed until now. His eyes were drawn to the small sparkling diamond on her finger. Rob probably couldn't afford a larger diamond, but it was still a decent-size rock. Suddenly, Lily squealed. "Your ring is so pretty!"

Lily seemed to forget that Colin was there at all as she began walking between him and Olivia, going on and on. It was so romantic that Rob was getting married. He was so handsome. Olivia would be such a pretty bride.

When they got to Olivia's car, Lily asked if she could ride with Olivia, who didn't seem to mind, and neither did Colin. The day had taken too many unexpected turns for him. Colin needed a moment to gather his thoughts, so he happily agreed. After they got in Olivia's car, he headed toward his Prius, on the other side of the parking lot. Olivia rolled down her window and said, "Hey, want me to drive you to your car?"

He turned around. "No, thanks. I'd rather walk."

"Suit yourself. It's a hundred and two out today."

"I don't mind. I need time to think."

"Sorry, I wanted to tell you."

"It was my fault. I waited too long."

He turned and walked away. In the distance, he could hear Lily still yammering on about the wedding. Needless to say, the day hadn't turned out the way he'd hoped, but at least Lily was happy. Today was her day, and he still had one more surprise left for her that she didn't know about.

Chapter 41: Dress-Up Day

After shopping the day away, Olivia went home. Colin asked Lily if she was up for one more surprise. Her eyes lit up at the word "surprise." Now Lily was looking at him skeptically as he pulled into the hospital parking lot. He smiled.

"Why are we here?"

"It's a surprise, remember?"

"What kind of surprise?"

"The good kind. Bring your bags with you."

A few minutes later, they were in Parker's room. Parker's eyes hadn't left the bathroom door since Lily went in to change. She'd decided to put on an impromptu fashion show for Colin and Parker. Lily hadn't given Parker much of a choice, and being that he was on strict bed rest still, it wasn't like he could escape. To Colin's surprise, Parker didn't seem to mind. Lily's voice yelled through the door, "One more second!" They waited for her to come out. "Ready?" Lily yelled.

Colin noticed that Parker was blushing. It made sense suddenly.

"Yes, Lily. Visitation ends in five minutes—hurry up!" Colin yelled back.

The bathroom door opened and Lily stepped out. She had

put on a frilly white blouse with bell-shaped sleeves with a pair of faded jeans that clung tighter to her legs than Colin liked. Olivia told him it was the style, and he would have a difficult time trying to find pants that weren't skin tight. Parker was speechless. Colin spoke up when he noticed Lily getting nervous from the silence.

"You look nice."

"Yeah? Do you like my new outfit, Parker?"

Parker stuttered. "I—y-you look really nice, like Colin said."

She smiled ear to ear. "Thanks! Look at my shoes." She propped her foot on the edge of his bed. "Converse, almost brand new."

"Those look wicked cool."

Lily laughed. "'Wicked cool'? Who says that?"

Parker's face turned a bright shade of pink. "Oh, it's a northern thing. My mom is from New Hampshire and says it all the time."

Lily shrugged. "Why's your face red? Do you have a fever?"

Colin stepped in. "Hey, Lily, how about you say goodbye, since visiting hours are up."

She stuck her bottom lip out and pretended to pout. "Fine. Bye, Parker. I miss hanging with you. It sucks that you're on bed rest still."

"Yeah. It's not all bad, though. I get to watch SpongeBob all day, which is wicked cool."

She leaned over and hugged him. His face went from pink to red. Fortunately, Lily didn't seem to notice.

"Bye, Parker."

"Bye."

As she closed the door to Parker's room, Colin smiled at her. He knew she was in a good mood, because she was humming quietly as they walked to the elevator like their mom used to do. When they stepped inside and the doors started to close, he chuckled. She glanced at him curiously. "What?"

"Parker likes you."

"What!"

"He has a crush on you."

"That's disgusting." She punched his arm playfully. "He's four years younger than me."

"Boys like girls that are older than them all the time. I used to have a huge crush on my babysitter." He noticed her eyes had opened wider. "It was before you were born. She was fifteen and I was seven. I thought she was the prettiest girl on earth."

"What happened?"

"She eventually got a real job. My heart broke. Then I was over it a month later when I decided the prettiest girl in the world was actually Rachel McAdams."

"Who?"

"An actress. Anyway, my point is ..." The elevator dinged. The doors opened, and they stepped into the main entrance of the hospital. "It's normal for boys to like girls that are older than them, and Parker definitely likes you. Be nice to him, but not too nice. That's all I'm saying."

"What do you mean, don't be too nice?"

Colin sighed. "You don't like him, right?"

"No way!"

"So don't be mean, but don't be too nice either. Make sense?"

"I guess so." She sounded confused.

Colin thought about their conversation as they left the building. Lily hadn't said anything for a few minutes. She seemed to be deep in thought too. It concerned him that she seemed so naive about boys. He wanted to say something more helpful about how she was turning into a young woman and boys were going to start noticing her, but he felt too awkward. How had his mom done it when he was thirteen? Lily was about to be an eighth grader, and she still had no idea that most teenage boys thought about nothing but girls all day. He was sending a gazelle into the lion's pit without a fair fight. He looked at Lily, who had started humming again quietly.

It was still hot outside, even though the sun had already started to set. It looked like a pat of butter melting over the edge of the world. As they walked to the car, gnats encircled them like a force field. One darted up Colin's nose and made him sneeze. He unlocked the car and threw Lily's bag of clothes in the back seat.

"Lily, did Mom ever have the talk with you?"

Her eyes got big. "What talk?"

"You know ... the talk."

"Yes. Why?" She looked disgusted.

"Okay. That's all I needed to know." Her face had contorted until her eyes, mouth, and nose all met in the center. He remembered making the same face at his mom. "Sorry, I won't ever bring it up again ," he added. He slid into the driver's seat. She slid into the passenger seat a moment later. "It's just that you're going to school in less than a month with teenage boys, and I was a teenage boy once. So I know what they think about all day. It's just ... I'm not comfortable with you dating. I know I'm not Mom or Dad, but I'm the one taking care of you now, and I just think you're too young to date."

"What are you talking about? I'm not going to date Parker!"

"Not Parker. I'm talking about boys at your school. Mom didn't let me date until I was eighteen, and I don't think she would've let you either—if ever."

"Boys are gross. I'm never going to date."

Colin laughed and started the car. "If only that were true."

Chapter 42: First Day

Lily's eyes looked at him accusingly. "You sure this outfit is right for my first day as an eighth grader? It doesn't look too … immature?" Lily stood by the front door in her long pink shirt, black leggings, and flats. She looked younger than most thirteen-year-olds, but Colin was grateful for that.

"Parker thought you looked good." It was almost too easy to upset her.

Lily rolled her eyes. "Whatever."

"Seriously, you look very nice."

"Just nice?"

"You'll be the most beautiful girl in the entire school. Happy now?"

"Yes." She curtsied and stuck her tongue out.

"Very classy." He looked out the door. "What time is your bus supposed to be here?"

"I don't know. Hey, do you think anyone will notice I'm wearing a wig?"

"No, I think it looks natural." Colin looked toward the end of the street. "The bus must be running late."

"You're not even looking at me. How do you know my wig looks natural?"

"Because…. The bus just turned onto our street … thank

goodness," Colin mumbled.

"What?"

"Nothing, go outside so the bus doesn't leave you."

"Colin, I'm nervous."

"Everyone gets nervous on their first day. You'll be fine. Now go catch the bus."

Lily rushed out the door and waved at Colin. "Bye, Dad—Colin. I meant Colin. Not Dad." Her face turned red. Colin tried not to look surprised by her slipup.

He waved. "Bye, munchkin."

She smiled and ran toward the bus. He waited until the bus drove away to go back inside. The house was empty for the first time in a month. He went back to his room and crawled under the covers of his bed. He closed his eyes.

* * *

Lily thought she would be more familiar with the layout of Coweta Middle School as an eighth grader, but she was just as lost as she had been in seventh grade. Finally, she found a door labeled SPANISH 101 and opened the door slowly to peek in. An old pale teacher was announcing to the class that her name was Mrs. Toliver. Lily glanced back at the label on the door to make sure she'd read it right.

"May I help you? Are you lost?" the old teacher asked.

"Oh. I was looking for Spanish 101."

"Take a seat."

Lily could feel the eyes on her as she looked for an open desk. It was like déjà vu of her first day of seventh grade. Lily slid into it and listened to Mrs. Toliver greet the class in Spanish.

"Hola."

The class mimicked.

"Hola."

"¿Como están?"

After an hour of the class repeating the teacher like parrots, the bell rang. Seats were slid under desks. Backpacks were slung over shoulders. Feet shuffled through the door. Lily rushed to her next class. The bell rang again.

"Welcome to art class. My name is Mrs. Bell. You'll see a variety of supplies placed at your stations." Lily watched the teacher closely as she explained what each brush could be used for. The teacher smiled. "Okay, class, you may spend the remaining twenty minutes becoming familiar with the tools we just discussed. Feel free to paint or draw, but be sure to clean up after yourselves before the bell rings. Today, you'll be getting familiar with these supplies. Tomorrow, you'll start painting your first masterpiece."

Lily stroked the bristles with her fingers. She jumped as the boy next to her leaned closer and whispered, "You must be an artist."

She blushed. "Uh, not really. Why?"

"You just seem really into those paintbrushes you got there."

Lily glanced at the brush in her hand. "Oh. No, it's just—"

"I was teasing." He squinted suddenly. "Hey, I don't think I saw you last year. Are you new?"

Lily jumped as the bell rang.

The boy smiled. "Guess you can tell me tomorrow."

Lily blushed. "Okay."

She thought about what Colin had told her that day they'd visited Parker at the hospital. Boys were different in eighth grade. They were weirder.

* * *

The class started to move as one around the gym like a herd of cattle at the sound of Coach Farsi's whistle. Lily's heart protested as she tried to keep up with the group.

"Lily?" a girl asked as she jogged up to her.

Lily looked. "Hey, Makayla!"

"Oh my gosh! I can't believe it's really you." She jogged next to Lily. "So where have you been?"

Lily thought back to her last visit with Dr. Reece. You don't have to talk about anything you don't want to, she thought. Lily answered. "Mostly the hospital." She decided to leave out the parts about her mom dying and her dad never coming back from his business trip.

Makayla gasped. "Why? Are you okay?"

"I'm okay now." Lily tried to catch her breath as they jogged faster. "I had cancer."

"No way. Are you serious?"

Lily panted. "Yep. I'm okay now, though."

"Hey, are you sure you're okay? You're breathing kind of heavy."

Lily nodded.

She then looked as the boy from her art class passed her on her right. She blushed as he smiled at her. Makayla was suddenly whispering something to Lily.

"See that boy that just jogged by us?"

"Yeah."

"His name is Bryce. I've had the biggest crush on him since like fourth grade."

"Fourth grade. Wow." Lily panted. "Hey, is the room moving?"

"Umm, no. Hey, you look pale. Are you sure you're—"

She opened her eyes slowly. Coach Farsi was kneeling over her, holding up his fingers.

"Lily, can you hear me?"

Lily grunted.

"How many fingers am I holding up?"

"Two."

"Good. We need to take you to the nurse. Can you stand?"

Lily sat up slowly. She could hear the wave of whispers and giggles around the gym. Suddenly, a voice announced to the entire gymnasium, "What's that on the floor?"

Everything went silent. All eyes were on her. She turned and looked at the floor behind her. There it was—a pile of blonde hair. Her worst nightmare had happened. She reached up and touched her head. She could feel the short pieces of hair that had grown back over the past couple of months against her fingers. A wave of heat came over her entire body. For a moment, she felt like she might pass out again. She snatched the wig off the ground and brushed it off. She could hear them whispering and giggling around the gymnasium.

Coach Farsi blew his whistle. "All right, get back to your push-ups!"

Chapter 43: Careful

L ily walked straight to the fridge when she got home. There was a note on the fridge: "Dinner's inside the container."

She opened the fridge door, spotted the takeout container of spaghetti that Colin had left for her, watched the red sauce pop as the bowl rotated in the microwave, and then plopped on the couch while balancing the hot bowl in her hands.

The screen lit up on her phone with a message from Colin. She swiped the screen to open it.

Colin: See the note on the fridge?

Lily: Yep. Thanks. Hey, Colin?

Colin: Don't worry about this morning. I know you didn't mean to call me Dad. You told me twice already.

Lily: ... [typing]

Colin: BTW, you're not eating on the couch right?

Lily walked to the kitchen.

Lily: Nope.

Colin: How was the first day of school?

Lily: Passed out. Wig fell off. Everyone laughed. Never going back.

Colin: Are you serious??! Are you okay??

Lily: My pride's hurt.

Colin: Why didn't the school call me?
Lily: Don't know.
Colin: I'm going to come home early.
Lily: :-)
Colin: We need to go to the hospital to make sure you're okay.
Lily: :-(

* * *

Lily went to her room and lay on her bed when they got back from the hospital. Colin was relieved that Dr. Long said she hadn't suffered a concussion and could keep going to school, but the fact was, Lily had passed out. Dr. Long said it was probably just that Lily was not used to that level of exertion, and she advised her to take it slow and rest for a few days. She was probably right, but something nagged at the back of Colin's mind. What if it was more than that ...?

Colin stood in the doorway of her bedroom. She had the pillow over her face, like she often did when she didn't feel good. He knocked softly.

"Lily, I know you're tired, but I need to talk to you for a minute."

"Hmm?" Her voice sounded muffled through the pillow in her hands.

"Have you been feeling dizzy before today?"

She pulled the pillow off her face and propped herself onto her elbows. "Sometimes ... if I stand too fast, or bend over, or don't eat enough."

He thought. "I need to tell you something. Do you remember the apple juice I gave you that you thought I'd backwashed in?"

"Aha!" She pointed at him. "Are you finally ready to admit

223

that you backwashed?"

"No. I need to tell you something about it." She listened. "There was some medicine inside it."

Lily stared blankly.

"It was a cure … for cancer."

"Sure it was." Lily rolled her eyes.

Colin sighed. "You don't have to believe me, but I need you to be more careful."

She sat up straight. "You're being serious?"

"Yes."

"Okay, where would you have gotten a cure for cancer from?"

"I can't tell you where I got it, and you can't tell anyone about this conversation. It wasn't exactly … legal."

Her eyes got bigger. "Colin, you broke the law? You're making this up!"

Colin shook his head. "Lily, I was going to lose you. We'd just lost Mom, and then your health was declining." His voice cracked. "And I was desperate."

She didn't say anything for a moment. It felt good for Colin to finally have the burden lifted from his shoulders, but by the look of it, his burdens had just been transferred to Lily. He waited for her to process everything.

"So you're seriously telling me that inside of that bottle of apple juice was a cure for cancer that you got somehow, but it wasn't legal, and you can't tell me how?"

Lily's expression said, *You're losing it.*

He sat on the edge of her bed. "Lily, I've worried every day since I gave you the cure that something was going to happen to you, and it would be my fault. Then today, you passed out."

"Dr. Long said it was because I pushed myself too hard."

"And I hope she's right, but I need you to be careful. The cure hasn't been tested yet."

"What do you mean?"

"You're the second human to ever receive it." He decided to leave out what had happened to the first kid.

"So I'm an experiment?"

Colin couldn't think of how to respond. She was right. She was an experiment.

"What happened to the first person?"

"That was a long time ago—"

"They died?"

"Lily, all that matters is that the cure saved your life."

He looked down at his hands. They were trembling. He hoped he was right.

Chapter 44: Anniversary

Lily looked at the date on her phone, as if she needed to be sure it was really the day she had dreaded all year: the anniversary of her mother's death. She picked up the photograph she kept in the table beside her bed and held it above her. She wrapped her arms around the cold, hard frame. It only increased the pain instead of easing it. Her mother felt more distant than ever as Lily held her photograph in her arms. She squinted as the stinging pressure rose behind her eyes. Tears rolled down her cheeks and onto her pillow. She wiped the back of her hand against her nose when she heard a knock at the door.

"Come in!"

The door cracked open. "You awake?"

"Yeah." She caught Colin looking at the photo in her arms. "I keep it in my drawer so I can look at her when I miss her."

"I wondered where it went."

He moved toward her bed and sat in silence for a moment. Lily held on to the photograph, waiting for Colin to tell her she needed to get ready for school. It was already 7:14 a.m. Her bus would be pulling up in ten minutes.

"I called your school and told them you wouldn't be there today, because of—you know. Today, we can do whatever you want, as long as it doesn't involve jogging. You're playing hooky."

She gasped and threw her arms around him. "Really?"

"What do you want to do, munchkin?"

She tried to think for a moment about all the things she and her mother used to do together, but only one thing came to her mind.

* * *

Colin sat on the hard barstool and looked around the sports bar. Every TV was playing something different—boxing on one, football on another, news on yet another. It was overkill. He turned and looked at Rob after the silence had gone on just long enough to feel awkward. "Thanks for meeting me so late."

Rob nodded. "I was surprised you called."

"Yeah. I just needed to get out of the house. Today, it's been a year since the day my mom died."

"I'm sorry. I didn't realize—"

"It's okay."

"How's Lily handling it?"

Colin sighed. "The best she can. We went to the park today. It was her favorite place to go with our mom when she was alive. I'm not sure how much it helped, though."

"I remember." Rob laughed. "Where's Lily now?"

"Sleeping. My neighbor is keeping an eye on the house for me."

Rob laughed. "Crazy Robin?"

"You mean Red Robin? Yeah. That's the one."

The bartender slapped the edge of the counter. "All right, what can I get for you boys?"

Colin smiled at her. "Water for me."

She pouted. "You sure you don't want something stronger?"

"No, thanks."

"A beer for me," Rob said.

"Here's your water, sweetie." She winked at Rob. "And one beer coming up."

Rob looked at Colin. "Water? Why'd you want to meet at a bar?"

"It was the only place open this late."

The waitress slid a beer across the countertop. "There you go, love."

Rob sipped his beer.

Colin lifted his eyebrows at Rob. "She's flirting with you."

"She's just trying to get a good tip."

"Whatever you say."

"It doesn't matter. I'm taken anyway." Rob glanced at Colin. "Sorry I didn't tell you about Olivia. I meant to tell you before."

"It's okay. You don't owe me an explanation."

Rob looked at Colin. "How's your dad?"

"He's in rehab. Or so he said."

"Rehab? For what?"

"He's an alcoholic. I'd seen the signs for a long time, but I tried to ignore them. One day he just ... left."

Rob set down his beer. "I'm sorry. I wouldn't have ordered a beer if I'd known."

"No. You're good, man."

"This is just a lot to take in. When did he leave?"

"Right after I moved back in."

"Why didn't you tell me?"

"I don't know. I just didn't want to deal with it, I guess."

Rob rubbed his neck. "I'm glad you called. It's been a while."

"Yeah. It has."

Chapter 45: Cancer Girl

The rumors were still circulating on Wednesday when Lily got to school. She'd already overheard two girls gossiping about her in the bathroom, because they didn't know she was in one of the stalls. Lily couldn't get the words out of her head: "What teenager wears a wig?"

For once, she wished she could just fit in. She grabbed the number 3 brush and dipped it into the blue oil paint. At least she could enjoy art class, or so she thought. She sank lower into her chair as the boy behind her whispered loudly to his friend: "Did you hear about Cancer Girl's wig falling off in gym last week? That's her right there."

Heat rose to Lily's face. She tried to hide behind the curtain of hair so the boys talking about her couldn't see her face turning red.

Another boy started whispering: "No way, man."

"Yeah, Makayla told me all about it. Apparently, she passed out or something. Her hair just plopped on the ground behind her."

"Maybe it's a good thing she was wearing it. It probably broke her fall or something."

The other boy chuckled.

Lily tried to ignore them and stroked the brush against the

canvas. It sounded like the boy had said Makayla had told him, but he couldn't have meant her friend Makayla. She wouldn't have gossiped about Lily. It was probably some other girl with the same name. Lily tried not to think about it again and formed the blue blob into a perfect circle with her brush. Suddenly, Bryce's voice was in her ear.

"So you are an artist after all."

"What?"

Bryce smiled. "That looks great. Is it you?"

"No."

"It looks like you. Blue eyes, blonde hair."

"Well, it's not me."

"Then who is it?"

Lily started on the other eye. "My mom."

"Cool. Why'd you paint her?"

"Because I wanted to!" she snapped.

"Okay." He paused. "I won't bother you anymore. I'll go back to my own painting. Sorry."

She glanced at Bryce's painting. "What's that supposed to be?"

Bryce laughed. "A field. You can't tell?"

"Sorry. It's just green and brown strokes. It's abstract, right?"

"Exactly," he said sarcastically. "It's okay. I know I'm terrible at this."

"You'll get better. I used to be terrible too—not that I'm saying I'm good now."

"It's okay if you were saying that. You are really good." He smiled. "So how'd you get better?"

She thought about Dr. Reece having her paint during their sessions. "Uh, just ... practice."

Lily went back to her painting and added the tiny black circles for the pupils. She smiled as she leaned back. It was perfect. She squinted at the painting as it began to look blurry. It felt like the room was spinning. Not again, she thought. She tried to grab hold of the desk but instead knocked the tray of brushes onto the floor. Suddenly, an arm was holding her up before she could hit the ground.

"I got ya. Are you okay?" It was Bryce's voice.

"Everything's ... s-s-spinning."

Mrs. Bell said they could go to the nurse's office. Lily kept her eyes closed as they walked through the hall, his arm holding her up. She tried to open her eyes, but that made it worse. The hallway appeared to be spinning. She squeezed them shut again.

A moment later, Bryce stopped walking. "We're at the nurse's office, Lily."

"Sit her down right there, honey." Lily recognized the nurse's voice from the other day. "You can go back to class now. Thanks for helping her."

His voice sounded farther away. "I'll see you later, I guess."

She tried to say thanks, but instead she grunted.

"He already left, sweetie. Is that your boyfriend?"

Lily shook her head. Moving made it worse.

"That's a shame. He's a cute one." She sounded closer. "I need to check your temperature. Say *ah*."

The cold thermometer slid under her tongue.

"Your temperature is 98.6. You probably just need to eat a snack." She paused. Lily nodded.

"You're not a diabetic, are you?"

She shook her head.

"Well, I think you should keep a snack in your backpack. Just in case." She handed her an apple. "Here you go. Eat this, and you can go back to class."

Chapter 46: Hello, Stranger

L ily walked quietly to the peephole. Who would be knocking at their door at four in the afternoon? It was probably just Red Robin, asking for sugar or milk again. Lily pulled her phone out of her pocket. The police could be at her house in a matter of minutes. The second knock almost gave her a heart attack. Geesh. They were impatient, whoever they were. She pressed her eye against the peephole. A tall man was standing too close for her to make out his face. It seemed like he was facing the other direction. She watched patiently. He would probably turn around and knock again in a minute.

The tall man started to walk away from the door. Lily watched through the hole until he was out of range. She dashed toward the curtains and peeked. Her mouth dropped open when she saw the black Chevy in the driveway. What was he doing here?

He was getting in his car when she opened the door.

"Dad?"

Chapter 47: Breaking the Silence

L ily had invited him in, because what other choice did she have? It was strange to her that he'd knocked on the door to his own house, but it would've been even stranger if he hadn't. All in all, everything about his visit felt strange. To make matters worse, they hadn't spoken since they'd sat down. It was like sitting in the room with a stranger. She'd started to say something when her dad cleared his throat.

"The school called me."

"My school?"

"Yeah. They said you passed out."

"Why'd they call you?"

He stared at his brown leather shoes.

"I meant, why didn't they just call Colin?"

"I know what you meant. They still had me listed as the emergency contact."

"Oh."

Lily twirled her finger around one of the fringes hanging off her shirt. She glanced at him. He was still staring at his shoes.

"Well, I'm fine now."

"It doesn't sound like you're fine. They called me again today. I'm worried about you."

"Well, nothing happened today. I didn't feel good, that's all."

"They said you went to the nurse's office. Does Dr. Long know you've been passing out?"

"I'm not passing out. It was one time."

"So, that's a no?"

"No."

"No, she doesn't?"

"No, that's a yes, she does know."

He looked around. "I didn't see Colin's car outside. Where is he? You're not alone, are you?"

"He's at work."

"You're home alone?"

She yanked a fringe off her favorite shirt. "I'm thirteen, Dad."

"You're still a young girl. It's not safe for you to be here alone."

Tears came to Lily's eyes. "Then maybe you shouldn't have left," she mumbled.

Her dad's gaze broke away from his shoes finally.

"I didn't want to—I just—I—" He stared at his shoes. "I'm sorry."

Both of them were silent again. Then Lily told him that she was cancer-free. He got up and hugged her. She could feel his body shake like he was crying. It took everything in her not to cry in his arms.

Then they talked about school, about the wig incident. They even laughed. She wondered if he knew about the cure, too, but decided not to ask. One question remained unanswered.

Lily took a deep breath.

"Why did you leave? I know you were working, but why didn't you call?"

"Oh, umm, it's complicated, sweetie."

"I'm not twelve anymore. I can handle it."

Her dad chuckled. "You're right—you're not twelve anymore. I'm sorry. I just couldn't cope with losing her."

"Mom?"

He nodded. "Your mother was the love of my life. When she died, I just couldn't be here anymore. Everything reminded me of her. This house, this town, my job ..."

"And me?"

"No! Gosh. No." He stared at his shoes again. "I fell apart, Lily. I was barely able to take care of myself. I couldn't have taken care of you. I know it was wrong to leave you without saying goodbye, but I was afraid."

"Of what?"

The door swung open. Her dad stood up. Lily watched anxiously as Colin walked in. She hadn't realized how late it was. They'd been talking for hours.

"What are you doing here?" Colin asked.

"This is my home."

"You should've called first."

"Colin, let's talk outside. Not in front of your sister. Okay?"

Colin stormed outside. Lily watched through the window and tried to listen. They were too far away for her to make out anything they were saying. Colin was yelling about something, by the looks of it. His arms flew around in the air while he talked. Her dad started talking. He used his hands a lot while he talked too. Colin seemed to be calming down. After a while, they walked back toward the house. Lily slid back onto the couch and pretended she'd been reading a book.

The door opened. Her dad gave her a hug and left. Lily glared at Colin as he walked through the living room and sat where their dad had been sitting not ten minutes prior.

"Why did you do that?" she asked.

"What?"

"You made him leave."

"No, I didn't."

"We were talking, and you came in and messed it up."

"He was leaving anyway, Lily."

"Who knows when he'll come back now!"

She ran to her bedroom and buried herself under the blankets. Colin came in a moment later and sat by her feet.

"Why didn't you tell me you passed out?"

"It wasn't a big deal. And I didn't pass out. I was just dizzy."

"We don't know that. I asked you to tell me if you'd had any other symptoms."

"My blood sugar was low. That's all."

"Maybe. We need to make sure that's all it was."

Chapter 48: A Friendly Face

T he next morning, they sat in Dr. Long's office.

"Thank you so much, Dr. Long," Colin said. "I really appreciate you seeing her without an appointment ... again."

Dr. Long turned the small flashlight off. "It's no problem. You did the right thing, bringing her in. You said she wasn't doing any sort of physical activity when she got light-headed?"

Lily answered for him. "I was just sitting. The nurse thinks I had low blood sugar."

"Your blood glucose is fine. I'm going to take her back to do the MRI and CAT scan, just to be sure she doesn't have any new tumors. Hopefully, we won't find anything."

"Could you write me a note saying I can't go to school for a few days, either way?" Lily asked.

Dr. Long smiled. "School's that bad, huh?"

"You have no idea."

"I think I know something that might cheer you up." Dr. Long looked at Colin. "If you don't mind."

A moment later, they were following Dr. Long down the hall. She stopped in front of Parker's room. Colin told Lily he would wait outside. As she walked in, he heard Parker's voice: "Hey!"

Dr. Long smiled at Colin. "How's your dad doing?"

Colin shook his head. "He says he's doing better, and I want to believe him. I'm just having a hard time forgiving him."

"It's probably going to take some time. I'm glad to hear he's doing better."

They both looked at the doorway as the sound of laughter came from Parker's room. Dr. Long looked at her watch. "I hate to break up the fun, but I need to take Lily to get the MRI now."

"Thanks for doing this for her."

* * *

Lily stared at the strange pile of meat on her lunch tray. The vent above her blew cold air on her head. She took her beanie out of her backpack and pulled it down until it covered her ears. Lily smiled at the doctor's note in her bag. She'd hoped Dr. Long would excuse her from class for a few days, but at least she'd written one saying the beanie was a medical necessity. She'd hated having to go to school without it over the past few days. Lily looked up as someone set a tray down in front of her.

"I missed you this morning."

Lily looked at the owner of the tray. "Bryce, I don't mean to be rude, but you shouldn't sit there."

"Why not?"

He took a bite out of a pear.

"Wait, where did you get a pear? I didn't see any up there." Lily craned her neck toward the cafeteria line.

"Don't bother looking. I brought it from home."

"Oh." She started to zip her backpack shut. "I wasn't joking. You really shouldn't sit next to me."

"Again, why not?"

"Look around. Everyone's staring at us. Besides, if

Makay—never mind. You just shouldn't sit with me."

Bryce squinted. "So what?"

"Remember? I'm the cancer girl, the wig girl, the weirdo girl who passed out in gym. Nobody likes me. If you sit with me, they'll start talking about you too. You'll be Cancer Girl's friend."

"Too late, then. I already sat next to you. I might as well stay and finish my lunch."

He took another bite of his pear. Lily looked at her tray of soggy fries and something brown and unidentifiable. She frowned at her meal and looked back at the friendly face across from her.

"Fine. I guess you can sit here."

He laughed. "Thank you?"

She bit into one of the cold fries. It tasted like what she'd imagine soggy cardboard would taste like. She really needed to start packing her own lunches. She gave up trying to eat the mush and looked at Bryce. He was eating a sandwich that looked delicious. Her stomach growled.

"Thanks for helping me the other day. You'd already left when I tried to tell you that."

"No problem." He took another bite of his sandwich. "Hey, isn't your last name Durnin?"

"Yeah. What about it?"

"Is your dad's name Thomas Durnin?"

"You know him?"

"I know *of* him. He was a football star twenty years ago."

"So ... you're a jock?"

"I don't like labels. I would've thought that of all people, you'd get that." He raised his thick eyebrows. "Cancer Girl? Wig Gi—"

"Fine. You're right. I'm sorry."

Lily pushed her fork into the mystery meat. It made some sort of squishing sound that made her want to yak.

"Here, I have my other sandwich."

"Thanks." She dug into the ham and cheese sandwich like an animal. Suddenly she remembered her manners when Bryce chuckled.

"Hungry?"

She felt her face blush. "Why are you being so nice to me?"

Bryce laughed. "I'm sorry, but why are you tearing the sandwich apart like that?"

"I have sensitive teeth. The crust hurts them. What about my question?"

"I don't know." Bryce shrugged. "I like you."

Lily blushed.

"I mean, I think you're really cool, even though you can be kind of rude sometimes, but I get it."

"You do?"

"Yeah, you're friends with Makayla, and Makayla likes me. So you can't be my friend. Right? Isn't that girl code?" He smirked. "I have sisters."

Lily's mouth dropped open, until she remembered the chewed-up ham and cheese. She closed it, but not before Bryce could laugh.

"How'd you know she likes you? And who told you I was friends with her?" Lily squinted. "Are you stalking me or something?"

He looked uncomfortable. "She tells a lot of people a lot of things. Can I give you some advice about her?"

"Yeah."

"Don't get on her bad side. She hasn't always been the nicest person."

"What do you mean?"

The bell rang.

"See you in gym."

Bryce swung his backpack over his shoulder and disappeared into the crowd of students. Lily stood and walked over to where the trash cans were lined up along the wall. She scraped the pile of mush into the trash and put the tray in the tray slot. She walked through the swinging doors into the gym and headed for the locker room. Even though Dr. Long had told Lily not to do any physical activity until she could get the results back from the MRI, the coach said everyone was required to wear a uniform, whether they were participating or not.

Lily grabbed the balled-up pile of clothes. They were wrinkled and smelled of mildew from the constant moisture in the locker room. Lily pulled her shirt off. Some girls laughed and whispered loud enough for her to hear. For a moment, she thought they were laughing at her, until she realized they were standing on the other side of the lockers.

"I saw it with my own eyes. They were sitting together," the first girl said.

"Yeah, I saw it too. She was flirting for sure," said the second.

Lily held her breath as she slid her gym shirt over her head.

The third voice sounded like Makayla's: "I can't believe she'd do that. She knew I—"

Lily stumbled as she tried to put her foot into the leg hole of her gym shorts. Makayla's voice stopped. Footsteps approached. Makayla and two other girls looked at Lily. They looked like the Three Musketeers in their matching outfits.

"Hey," Lily said.

"Hey," Makayla said.

She and the two other girls left the locker room. Lily almost fell over as she tried to balance on one foot while tying the shoe

241

on her other foot. She sat down and finished tying her shoes and then headed for the gymnasium.

By the time Lily had gotten to the bleachers, the other kids were already throwing red balls across the gymnasium and attempting to dodge them. The coach blew his whistle at one of the kids when he got hit. He was out. Then another. Players were dropping like flies. Lily cringed as one girl got hit in the stomach. The coach whistled again. She was out. Only half the class remained.

Her attention was drawn to Bryce, who was looking her way and smiling. She could feel her skin turning bright red again, against her will. She tried to look to the other side of the room to avoid looking at Bryce any longer. Suddenly, Lily realized that Makayla was glaring at her. Out of nowhere, a ball slammed into Makayla's face and knocked her down. A few of the other kids laughed. Coach blew his whistle and helped Makayla up.

Lily jumped to her feet as Makayla walked toward the bleachers. "Are you okay? It looked like you got hit pretty hard out there."

"Probably not as hard as when you passed out, so I'll be fine."

She mumbled something; it sounded like she said Cancer Girl. Lily thought about what Bryce had said about not getting on her bad side.

"Are you mad at me or something?"

Makayla smirked. "What made you think that?"

"You just seem upset."

"Well, maybe that's because my head's throbbing and you're asking me a million questions."

Lily watched as Makayla got up and walked toward the locker room. Was she mad because she'd seen Bryce smiling at Lily? It all seemed very immature, even for middle school. Lily couldn't help it if Bryce wanted to be her friend.

Bryce slid into the bleacher beside her. "Is Makayla all right? It looked like she got hit pretty hard."

"Why would I know?" Lily sneered at him.

"Whoa, sorry for asking." He held his hands up playfully to plead innocence.

The coach blew his whistle.

Lily stood. "I shouldn't have snapped like that. Sorry."

"It's okay."

Bryce got up and followed the other students toward the locker rooms. Lily followed too. She couldn't wait to get back into her regular clothes.

When she reached the locker room, girls were running around, hectically trying to change and reapply their lip gloss. Lily walked to her locker and pulled the wrinkly gym shirt over her head and stuffed it back into her locker. The red shirt she'd picked out that morning went back on in its place. With a quick tug her beanie and wig were snug against her head again. She bent over and tied the laces of her shoes while sitting down, instead of trying to balance on one foot again. Footsteps approached, and three sets of shoes appeared in front of her. She recognized them from earlier. What did they want? Lily was starting to glance up when suddenly a hand grabbed her head and yanked. Lily stood up so fast the blood rushed to her head. The Three Musketeers were standing in front of her again, one with her beanie in her hand. Makayla stood in the middle of the group, smirking again. Lily reached up and pulled her wig down.

"What's your problem? Give it back to me." Lily tried to get it back, but missed.

Makayla stepped forward. "Why were you smiling at Bryce earlier?"

"What are you talking about?"

The other girl dangled the beanie. "Maybe we should take her wig too."

Lily tried to grab it again.

The tall brunette girl laughed. "She has terrible aim. She was like a foot away that time. No wonder Coach lets her sit the entire class."

"Bryce came up to me. Not the other way around."

"Sure he did. You knew I liked him. Why would you stab me in the back like that?"

"He came up to my table."

The girl holding her beanie laughed. "Why would a guy like Bryce want anything to do with you, Wig Girl?"

Lily could feel the heat rising in her eyes. She couldn't cry, not now, not in front of them. How did Makayla even know about lunch? Suddenly, Lily remembered the conversation she'd overheard before. The two minions standing next to Makayla must've seen her eating with Bryce.

"I don't know what they told you, Makayla, but I told Bryce to go—"

"Hey, I don't think she's getting how this works, Makayla. She hasn't even apologized yet."

Lily looked at Makayla. "Look, I'm sorry you're upset. But I swear I didn't backstab you."

"That was a pathetic apology." The tall girl pulled out a pair of scissors from her backpack. "I say we do some arts and crafts with this old thing. That'll teach her not to backstab."

"That's too far, Ashley," Makayla said.

Ashley scowled at her. "She went after the guy you specifically told her you liked. Isn't that what you said? So, I think it's just far enough."

Lily knew what was going to happen next, but she couldn't do anything to stop Ashley. Makayla and the other girl stood and watched with their mouths hanging open. Tears filled Lily's eyes as she watched the pieces of the beanie her mother had given her fall to the floor.

"Aah, look, she's crying now," Ashley said with a smirk. "It'll be your wig next time, if you hurt our girl Makayla again."

"Let's go before someone catches us in here," the third girl said.

The bell rang. Suddenly the locker room was empty, other than Lily and what was left of her beanie.

* * *

The fork clanked as Colin set it down against his plate. He'd watched Lily twirl her fork around a piece of pasta for five minutes. He hadn't seen her eat one bite since they'd sat down at the table, and she hadn't said a word about school. Something was wrong. She ran to her room before Colin could ask where she was going, then reappeared a moment later without her wig on.

"Was your wig bothering you?"

"It was itchy."

She nodded and twirled her fork some more.

"I haven't heard back from Dr. Long yet, but I'm sure I'll hear from her soon. You're not worried, are you? You seem kind of quiet."

"Nope."

"So, how was your day?"

"Fine."

Lily shivered.

245

"Are you cold?" Colin reached up and tugged on the chain to turn off the overhead fan. "Where's your beanie?"

"In the laundry. Can we eat something besides Italian food tomorrow? I'm kind of burnt out on pasta."

Colin squinted. "I just folded the laundry. It wasn't in there."

"Oh. I must've misplaced it. Can we eat Chinese food or pizza tomorrow?"

"Pizza is Italian. You misplaced your favorite beanie? That's odd. You never take that thing off."

"Yeah. I don't care if pizza is Italian. Just something besides pasta."

There was no way she could be this calm about misplacing the beanie their mother had given her. She loved that thing.

"I'll pick up something from Sal's Pizza tomorrow. Is something the matter?"

"Nope. Can you get it from that place Mom always ordered from instead of Sal's?"

"Pizzeria Extreme?" Colin laughed. "Do you remember that delivery kid that Mom almost killed last time?"

Lily looked up, like she was surprised. "Mom told you about that?"

"Yeah." Colin chuckled. "She was ready to drag that kid back in and make him apologize to you if she had to."

She didn't crack a smile. Her eyes returned to her plate. "What is this?" She pointed her fork at the food on her plate as if she was afraid to get too close.

"Stuffed zucchini blossoms. They're the flower that blooms before the zucchini grows."

Her face contorted. "Why would anyone want to eat a flower?"

"Because it's good. Try it."

Lily jabbed her fork at the blossom. She was in a strange mood.

Something was obviously bothering her, but Colin couldn't figure out what. It didn't seem like she was in the mood to talk about it, whatever it was. Colin carried his plate to the sink and rinsed it. He looked back at Lily, who was still jabbing at the food on her plate.

"Don't you know it's impolite to play with your food?" he asked teasingly.

Lily sighed.

"Lily, seriously, what's up with you today?"

"Nothing." She set her fork down on the plate. "Have you heard from Dad since that day?"

Colin hesitated to answer. "Yes."

"Do you think he'll visit again?"

"Not right now. He's trying to ... overcome some stuff."

"What stuff?"

Colin rubbed the two-day-old scruff on his chin. "He's sick, but he's getting help."

"What do you mean, he's sick?"

"I didn't want to worry you, but I think you should know why he left."

"Oh, you mean he wasn't on a business trip for a thousand years? Shocker." Her eyebrows pinched together. "Are you finally going to tell me where he really was?"

Colin sighed. "He was in a rehab center recovering from alcoholism."

"Dad's an alcoholic?"

"When Mom died, Dad just—well, he broke inside. But he's getting help."

"Is that why he looked the way he did the other night? I almost didn't recognize him."

"Yeah."

247

"So, all of those business trips he went on … were those rehab too?"

"I don't know." He reached for her plate. "I'm gonna put this in the fridge. How about you go finish your homework. If you get hungry, just heat it up."

She walked over to the couch and cracked open a book she'd wrapped with a paper bag book cover. Colin couldn't tell what the book was, but he knew it was a school book by its size. She never did her homework without being asked. Something was definitely on her mind. Colin watched her stare at the pages with a blank look on her face. He wondered if he'd done the right thing by telling her about their dad. She was bound to find out eventually, now that he was coming back around. She'd asked him a hundred times before why their dad hadn't come home yet, and so far Colin had found excuses for him, but lately he'd been running out. Then Lily had stopped asking, almost like she knew their dad had left. It seemed better that she knew why he'd been gone than to let her think he'd left for no reason.

Colin walked over to the couch, where Lily was concentrating on her book.

"What subject is that?"

"Math."

"Oh. Need help?"

"No."

"How was school today?"

"I don't want to talk about school."

Colin thought for a second. She was being impossible. "Did something happen at school?"

"School's just stupid. That's all. I have a lot of homework to do tonight."

"Okay. I'll be in my room if you need me."

Colin walked to his door and looked back. Lily was wiping her eyes as if she was wiping a tear away. He wished she would tell him what was going on. It was probably just teenage girl drama.

* * *

Colin turned off the TV when he saw the incoming call on his phone. He was surprised to see Dr. Long calling so soon. It had only been twelve hours since the MRI. She never called that soon. He answered it after the first ring. They got the greetings out of the way quickly. He knew they both wanted to get to the reason she was calling: the results. He was expecting the worst. In addition to Lily's coordination getting worse again, he could tell that talking had been getting harder for her recently. Colin's chest was tight as he waited to hear the words he'd been dreading—Lily's cancer was back.

"Colin, I'm afraid I have some bad news ..."

Chapter 49: The Visit

Lily cried for an hour straight when Colin told her about Dr. Long's phone call. He'd asked her if there was anything she wanted to do the next morning, after she'd had time to process everything. She said there was one place she wanted to go before they went to the hospital. Her answer surprised him, but there was no way he was going to tell her no.

He sat on the couch and waited for her to come out of her room. Despite being on his third cup of coffee, he was still tired from not sleeping the night before. He didn't want her to see him worrying, even though he was worried sick. The combination of worrying, too much caffeine, and exhaustion had mixed into a sickening cocktail. He wanted to throw up all the nauseating emotions spinning around in his stomach. He wanted to scream or punch something. The cure had been his only chance of saving her. Now how was he going to save her?

He tried not to think about any of that as Lily's bedroom door opened. She appeared in the hallway, wearing the same outfit she'd worn the first day of eighth grade. He tried to capture the moment in his mind, since a part of him knew it might be the last time she would look that nice for a while. Neither of them said a word. They both seemed to be frozen, as if they could stop time if neither of them moved. Finally, Colin stood up and walked to the door. Lily followed behind him.

Fifteen minutes later, they were sitting in the car, staring at the depressing white building. Colin looked over at Lily, in the passenger seat. She'd been unusually quiet on the drive over.

"We don't have to do this. I didn't tell him we were coming, in case you changed your mind."

"I just need a minute."

"Take your time." Colin stepped out of the car. Another five minutes went by. Finally, the passenger-side door opened. Lily stepped out.

"Do you think he'll know I'm sick by looking at me, though?"

"You look beautiful, but we need to tell him you're sick." He walked around the car. "Here, take my arm for balance, just in case."

"I'm fine."

"Lily, don't be stubborn."

"I'd like to walk on my own while I still can." She walked forward. "My balance is fine."

Colin interlocked his arm around hers, despite her protests, as they walked to the building. The glass doors slid open. Lily said she was surprised at the lack of colors on the walls, couches, chairs, and desks. It was depressing. She was right. Everything was either white, gray, or black. They sat on one of the gray sofas and waited for the woman at the reception desk to call them back. A large nurse appeared in front of them a few minutes later and told them to follow her.

Colin looked straight ahead as they walked by a tall guard, which was saying something, since he was usually the tallest person in the room, other than his dad. In the corner of his eye, he could see Lily's head lift up to get a look at the tall man.

The hallway was just as depressing as the waiting room: hues of gray and white everywhere. The nurse stopped in front of room 8. A small placard beside the door read THOMAS DURNIN.

Colin walked in first. For a moment, he wondered if Lily was about to pass out again. Then she followed him into the room. Their dad called out to the nurse as she closed the door behind her. "Thanks, Doris." His attention turned back to Lily. "Hey, sweetie!"

Lily glanced at Colin as if she was asking for permission. Colin nodded and watched as Lily ran into their father's arms.

"Hi, Dad," Colin said after a moment.

"Hey, son, come here."

Lily was staring at him—waiting, watching, hoping. Colin wrapped his arms around his dad.

"I would've cleaned if I'd known you were coming."

"Sorry about that. I wasn't sure if this one allowed visitors. They seem nicer here than the last one you stayed at."

Lily gave Colin a look that said, *This isn't the first rehab Dad's stayed at?*

"It's more lenient, but in my opinion it's more effective. But enough about that. Take a seat, you guys."

They looked around the small room. There weren't many choices. Colin let Lily take the chair. The only other place to sit was his dad's bed, so he stood beside her.

"Do either of you need anything? Something to drink, maybe?"

They both shook their heads. Lily smiled. "Colin let me get a vanilla bean Frappuccino on the way here!" Her words slurred so much it seemed to take their dad by surprise, but he quickly recovered.

"Oh, really?"

Colin smiled. "It's caffeine-free."

"Take a seat, Colin. I know it's kind of cramped in here, but I don't mind being close to my two favorite people in the world."

Their dad was in a particularly good mood. Colin sat on the end of his small bed.

Lily craned her neck to look at the bars on the outside of the only window in the room. "Why are there bars on the window?"

"To stop contraband."

"Contraband?"

"Yeah. You know, like mocaccino and stuff."

Lily chuckled. After another moment of awkward silence, their dad asked what was new. Colin caught him up on work—the new help Al had hired was driving him crazy. He'd only been talking for two minutes before he ran out of things to say. Lily decided to help him by adding the small detail he'd purposely left out about his ex-girlfriend getting engaged to his best friend. His dad looked at him wide-eyed. "Wow. How'd you forget to mention that one?"

"I didn't forget."

They laughed at Colin's expense. Colin joined them after pretending he was upset at first. As long as Lily was laughing, he was happy. Besides, this was the first time his dad had seemed like himself in a long time.

When it was Lily's turn to say what was new with her, she got quiet suddenly. Colin couldn't tell if it was because of how difficult speaking was for her, or if she just didn't want to talk about school. Lily watched her Converse as she swung them under the hard plastic chair, the kind they used in schools. Then she started to talk as if she were telling her shoes a story.

"I like art class, I guess. It's not as bad as the other classes."

"You're a bright girl," their dad said softly, as if she were a butterfly that might fly away if he spoke too loudly. "Why don't

253

you like your other classes? You've always loved school."

She bent her neck even more, making her wig cover her face. She looked like Cousin Itt. She didn't need the wig anymore— her hair had grown into what she'd informed Colin was a "pixie cut"—but she said she preferred to wear it anyway. It made her feel safe. It was her safety blanket.

"That was because Mom helped me."

Colin felt guilty suddenly. "Sorry, Lily. I didn't realize you needed help. You could've told me, you know."

"It's okay. It's just not the same without her. School is ... I don't know. Different. The kids are meaner too."

Their dad's eyes narrowed. "What do you mean? Is someone bullying you?"

Lily inhaled and exhaled sharply. Almost like she was crying. "I just thought Makayla was my friend, and then ... I guess she wasn't. Bryce was right."

"Who are Makayla and Bryce?" their dad asked. Colin wondered the same thing.

"Makayla is just a girl I met in seventh grade. She had a crush on this boy, Bryce. He sat with me at lunch, and ..."

She continued to recount the story of the three girls in the locker room who threatened her and cut the beanie her mom had given her into little pieces. Colin had a flashback of that night, when he'd asked her where her beanie had gone. So she'd lied about the beanie after all. His stomach twisted into a pretzel. How could those girls have done that to her?

To Colin's surprise, their dad listened calmly through the entire story about Cinderella's three wicked stepsisters. To the untrained eye, he seemed cool as a cucumber. But Colin knew better. In his head, he was arresting those girls and their parents. Then again, to the untrained eye, Colin must have looked quite serene as well. And he didn't want to admit that he was imagining those girls getting their due justice in the form of terrible haircuts. They deserved to know what it felt like to be humiliated—the way they'd made Lily feel.

Colin realized Lily was no longer talking when their dad stood up and walked across the small room to hug her. She continued staring at her shoes while his arms enveloped her like a big blanket.

Once he'd come back over to the bed and sat again, his eyes narrowed. "So, this Bryce kid. You like him?"

She lifted her head and gave him a face that said she was appalled by the idea that she, Lily Durnin, could ever like a boy. Cousin Itt was gone. Lily was back.

Their dad laughed heartily. "I'm going to take that as a yes."

Lily's face shimmered from the thin film of sweat that had suddenly appeared. The room was cool. Why was she sweating?

"Lily, are you okay?" Colin asked.

"It is a little hot in here. Could we turn on the AC?"

Colin went to her, reached his hand out, and pressed the back of it against her cheek.

She glared at him suspiciously. "What are you doing?"

"You're burning up, Lily."

Their dad walked over and placed his hand against her cheek, then her forehead. He pinched his eyebrows together and looked at Colin. "She has a fever. You should take her to the hospital."

"I don't want to go yet."

"Yet? Were you planning on going to the hospital?"

"Dad, I was going to tell you." Their dad looked at him. "Lily's cancer is back."

His eyes opened wide. "How could it be back?"

Colin shook his head. "I don't know. I'm checking Lily into

the hospital today to start treatment."

"I don't want to go yet."

"You're burning up, sweetie."

"Lily, Dad's right. We need to go."

Lily looked like she was on the verge of crying.

"Sweetie, we're just trying to do what's best for you."

"How would you know what's best for me? You left!" She was sobbing, her voice cracking. She turned to Colin. "Why'd you have to give me that stupid cure?"

His dad gave him a look. "Cure?"

Colin tried to think, and quick. "That lead I told you about, it was a doctor. He ... gave me some to give to Lily. It worked at first."

"Wait, what doctor?"

"His name is Dr. Lloyd. I found him on the internet." Colin looked at Lily. "We need to go. Can we talk more about this later?"

Before Colin could hug Lily, their dad's arms were wrapping around her. She tried to push him away, but he held her tighter. The sounds of sobbing were muffled by their dad's large body, holding Lily close. Colin watched but said nothing. After a moment, she seemed to stop struggling to get away. He kissed the top of her head and promised he would see her again soon.

Chapter 50: Decisions

C olin checked the time on his phone. It'd been twenty minutes since the nurse had last checked on Lily. He was starting to get worried. Lily had already been admitted to a room, and she looked snug as a bug in her hospital bed. She'd been calm ever since they'd pulled into the parking lot of the hospital. Colin figured she'd worn herself out from crying. Her room wasn't the same one she'd stayed in before, but the layout was exactly the same — the same ridiculously happy wallpaper, the same yellow lamp, the same depressingly happy decorations.

Dr. Long rushed into the room. "I came as quickly as I could after your call. Let's check that fever."

"I feel fine."

Dr. Long looked at the pale girl, whom Colin knew was far from fine.

"Looks like you've got a fever of a hundred and two."

Colin sat in the recliner quietly. Dr. Long asked him to step into the hallway for a moment, like she always did when she had bad news.

"You look worried."

Colin let out more of a sigh than a laugh. She had no idea how right she was.

"It's happening all over again."

"I know. This came as just as much of a surprise to me as it did to you. I never understood how she made that kind of recovery—I mean, it's unheard of—but this is just as much of a mystery. Her cancer seems to have come back more aggressively than ever. She's in the best place now. I'll take care of her as if she were my own child. How about you go home and rest."

"I can't leave her."

"You won't be doing her any good if you're tired. You have to keep your spirits up."

Dr. Long and Colin stood in the hallway. Nurses and patients passed by busily. The world moved on around them, but Colin felt stuck.

"I'll sleep here."

"Would you like me to get you something to help you sleep?"

Colin shook his head. He was exhausted, but he needed to stay alert. It was not even eight o'clock yet, but worrying had a way of draining his energy. Dr. Long pushed her glasses through her red hair and rubbed her eyes.

"Colin, do you remember what I said back in May about putting her in hospice?"

He nodded and stared into her tired-looking green eyes.

"I know it doesn't seem like it yet, but the cancer has spread throughout her brain. Fortunately, for lack of a better word, it's mostly grown around her cerebellum, the area of her brain that affects her balance and coordination. That's why she's still very cognizant, for now. I can't explain why she's done so well over the past five months, or how her cancer disappeared in the first place, but I must warn you that I don't see how she's going to make another miraculous recovery like she did last time. I can offer the same treatment as last time—chemo and radiation—but they'll only prolong her life; they won't save it."

She touched his arm. "Don't make your decision now. Sleep on it."

When Colin returned to the room a few minutes later, Lily had already fallen asleep. He stretched across the couch. He knew better than to try to sleep in the recliner. The couch wasn't much better, though. It was as hard as a slab of concrete, and the pillow was nothing more than a flimsy sack of cotton. His legs curled under him so they would fit on the five-foot-long couch. Being a six-foot-two guy, the math was obvious: this would be a miserable night. Meanwhile, Lily snored softly from her bed. She seemed to be able to fall asleep just as easily at the hospital as she could at home. He thought about what Dr. Long had said. How was he supposed to make a decision like that?

Chapter 51: An Unexpected Visitor

The next morning, sunlight filled the room, making it impossible for Colin to sleep. He stretched his legs out so they hung over the couch by at least a foot. His back ached from being cramped up the entire night on the concrete slab pretending to be a couch. Lily was watching him.

Colin grunted. "Morning."

"Did you sleep okay?"

Colin laughed. He rubbed his eyes and sat up. The full effect of sleeping on a couch was sinking in. His entire body ached.

"Thanks for staying."

"Of course."

Colin stretched his arms over his head. He ran his hands through his thick blonde hair. He'd let it grow down his forehead over the past few months. He hadn't found the time to go to a barber. He pulled his bangs back, away from his eyes, and smiled. "I'm going to get some coffee. Want anything from the cafeteria?"

There was a knock at the door before Lily could answer. He told the person knocking to come in. To Colin's surprise, it wasn't a nurse. The young man stood in the entrance of the room looking sheepish. Colin stared at the unexpected visitor.

"Is this a good time?" the stranger asked.

"I'm sorry, who are you looking for?"

"Lily."

Colin glanced at Lily, who was blushing.

"I'm Bryce. I go to school with Lily."

"What are you doing here, Bryce?" Lily asked.

"When you weren't at school yesterday, I got worried and asked the nurse if she'd seen you. She hadn't, so I asked Coach where you were, and he said he'd heard you were in the hospital." He held up a small bag and pulled out a painting. "Since it's Saturday, I thought I'd stop by and bring you your painting, now that it's dry."

"So, you're stalking me?" Suddenly, Lily's face turned the color of a clown's nose. She reached up. Oh no, Colin thought. Lily seemed to read his thoughts. "Oh no—I don't have my wig on. Look away!"

Bryce smiled. "You don't need the wig. I think you look great without it."

"Urr," Colin said. He stood up and rubbed his neck. "Lily, I'm going to go to the cafeteria, if you're okay here? Want something?"

Lily nodded. "Blueberry muffin, please."

"Okay. I'll be right back." Colin waved. "Nice to meet you, Bryce."

He left the door open as he walked out of the room. He may not have had the stomach to sit there and watch his little sister blush over that jock kid, Bryce, or whatever his name was, but he sure wasn't going to give them complete privacy. What was that, anyway: "So, you're stalking me?" Had he just witnessed Lily flirting with that boy? Colin's shoulders shivered. Bryce. What kind of name was Bryce? It sounded like "rice" and "Bryan" mixed together.

A nurse gave Colin a funny look. He realized he'd been mumbling to himself as he walked to the elevator. He smiled at the nurse and walked faster.

He waited for the elevator to reach his floor. Lily had looked so happy to see that kid—Bryce, or whatever his name was. Maybe it wasn't all bad. Still, Colin couldn't be in that room one more second while they batted their eyelashes at each other.

* * *

The cafeteria was busy. People in hospital gowns were eating with people in normal clothes. Family members who had stayed the night like Colin stood out as a group of their own. Their clothes were wrinkled, their hair was messy, and their hands rubbed the cricks in their necks. That was the real giveaway. Everyone had come to the cafeteria for the same reason: caffeine.

Colin grabbed a tray and started down the line of packaged sandwiches, overpriced fruits, and day-old pasta salads until he got to the breakfast foods. He reached for the last blueberry muffin. Another hand beat him to it.

"Excuse me."

The hand grabbed the last muffin before Colin realized what had happened. He glanced at the woman standing beside him—the owner of the hand. Her hair was on top of her head in a messy bun that reminded him of a bird's nest. Her dark-blue eyes were worn and tired. There didn't appear to be a drop of makeup on her weary face. Still, Colin was struck by how beautiful she was.

"Uh. Hi," he said.

The woman looked up from her tray, which now had the

addition of the last blueberry muffin, and glared at Colin. She apparently wasn't in the mood to make friends. "Hi." Her voice sounded flatter than the paper-thin pancakes Colin added to his tray.

She walked around him. Colin followed her with his eyes. The farther she got, the more of her he could see. She was tall for a girl, maybe five eight or five nine. Her clothes were wrinkled, like she'd slept in them. She was obviously here visiting someone.

Colin slid his tray along the metal railing. She was in front of him, but her messy bun was all he could see. Suddenly he noticed the muffin on her tray. Shoot. He couldn't go back to Lily empty-handed.

The woman stopped walking so abruptly that Colin almost walked into her. She turned around and grabbed a bowl of fruit. Colin smiled at her.

"You visiting somebody here?" he asked.

"No, I just like visiting hospitals."

Colin laughed. "Right. Stupid question."

"No, it wasn't a stupid question at all. I'm just tired. These hospital couches are terrible."

"Believe me, I know. I'm pretty sure the couch I slept on gave me scoliosis."

She smiled and started walking down the line again. He swore she almost laughed.

"My theory is that they don't want us guests to get too comfortable. Next thing you know, we'll be trying to get ourselves admitted."

"That's how they make money. Wouldn't that be a little counterintuitive?"

Colin laughed again. "You make a good point."

She continued to slide her tray down the metal bars. They were almost at the register.

"I'm here with my little sister," he said. "I haven't seen you before. Is this your first time staying here?"

"Yeah. My nephew was admitted last night. I came to support his mom. She's a mess. He just got diagnosed with leukemia. Is your sister going to be okay?"

Her voice had softened.

"Hopefully. I'm sorry, my name's Colin."

"Emma. Emilia."

"Nice to meet you, Emma. I hope your nephew gets better. You must be a pretty cool aunt to stay here with him."

She glanced back at him enough for him to see that she was smiling.

"Thanks. You must be a pretty cool brother. Well, I guess I should be getting back to my nephew."

"Yeah, me too. My sister, I mean. Nice to meet you, Emma."

She turned around. "Nice to meet you too, Colin."

* * *

Colin was humming a made-up tune as he walked into Lily's room with a brown cup in his hand. He couldn't carry a tune in a bucket, but he didn't care if he embarrassed himself. He was on cloud nine. Four eyes were staring back at him. Oh, right ... Bryce was still here. Lily lifted one eyebrow.

"Where's the muffin?"

"Huh?"

"The blueberry muffin. You only have a cup of coffee in your hand."

"Oh. Emma took the last one."

"Emma?"

"Do you want something else?"

"If *Emma* won't take it first."

"Ha ha."

"Did they have any chocolate muffins?"

"Yep. Coming right up."

Colin ran back down to the cafeteria. Hopefully, this time he'd come back with a muffin.

* * *

She was starving. Lily looked back to her visitor. Bryce reached into his bag and pulled out a plastic bag.

"This is for you. It's a gift."

"You brought my painting, and a gift? Wow. What is it?"

"Open the bag."

Lily opened the bag. She looked back at Bryce. There were no words to express how she felt. He smiled. "Put it on. I want to see how it looks on you."

Lily slid the red beanie over her short hair.

"Why did you—"

"Rumors spread around school about what Makayla and her friends did. Who does something like that?" He paused. "So, I went out and got that one, because it looked like your other one."

Lily shook her head. She was speechless.

"What? You don't like it?"

"It's—my mom bought me that beanie when I first lost all my hair ..." Her voice started to break.

"Oh, I didn't know—"

"It's the perfect gift."

Bryce smiled. "The perfect gift for the perfect girl."

Lily could feel her cheeks turn red again. "That is so cheesy!" She threw a pillow at him. Bryce caught it and wound his arm back as if he were about to throw a football.

A moment later, Colin gave them a funny look as he walked into her room. He handed her a chocolate muffin without saying anything. Before Lily could take a bite, Dr. Long walked into the room behind him.

"Lily, I'm sorry to interrupt. We need to do some tests. I'm sorry, Lily. I can't let you eat that muffin yet."

Bryce stood up. "I'll get going."

"Thanks for the beanie. I really like it."

"Welcome." He smiled and looked at Colin. "Can I come by tomorrow and check on her, sir?"

Colin laughed. "I'm her brother. Colin. You don't have to call me 'sir.' If she doesn't mind you coming by, neither do I."

Chapter 52: Shuffle

L ily stopped laughing when she noticed someone in a wheelchair in the doorway of her hospital room. "Parker!" Parker didn't say anything; his gaze seemed to be fixed on Bryce. "This is my friend from school, Bryce. Bryce, this is my friend from here, Parker."

Bryce waved. "Hey, Parker."

Parker nodded.

Lily laughed. "What's wrong with you, Parker? Come in. I would've come to your room, but I'm on strict bed rest."

Bryce jumped up and walked over to Parker. "Here, let me help you."

"No. I've got it."

Lily smiled at Bryce for trying. "Parker, when did you get the new ride?"

"A few days ago." He appeared to be struggling with one of the wheels. "I'm still figuring out how to use it, though."

"You'll probably love it once you get used to it." She smiled as a memory popped into her head. "You remember when we used to steal random wheelchairs around the hallway, and we'd take turns pushing each other around?" She looked at Bryce. "We had so much fun watching the nurses dodge us as we flew around the hallway. Dr. Long told us not to, but it was the only fun thing to do around here."

Parker smiled. "Yeah. Except for poker."

"You know how to play poker?" Bryce asked.

Parker stopped fighting with the wheel and pushed himself forward without answering Bryce. Lily looked at Bryce and shrugged her shoulders.

"Well, we tried to play, but we weren't very good," Lily answered.

Bryce stood up. "I guess I'm going to get going. I have to study."

"Study? On a Saturday?" Lily asked.

"My mom said if I don't get my grades up, no more football for me. So ..."

"Okay. Happy studies, I guess."

Parker nodded as Bryce walked past him.

"So, he's your boyfriend?"

Lily laughed. "No. I wish everyone would stop asking me that."

Parker suddenly seemed happy again. "Oh. Well, I'm sorry you're back, but I'm kind of happy you are."

"Aah. You missed me?"

He blushed. "I'm just happy to have someone to hang with again. It's been boring here since you left."

"Did you bring any cards?"

Parker held up the deck.

"I only have a few minutes, but we can play one game." She smirked. "Get ready to read 'em and weep. And don't expect me to hold back anymore. You're nine years old now. I can't keep babying you."

Parker rolled his eyes. "Stop trash talking and shuffle."

Chapter 53: Code Blue

Colin hugged Rob. "Thanks for coming."

Rob whispered, "Yeah. Of course. How's she holding up?"

"Pretty well for being held hostage in a hospital bed for the last three weeks."

They walked into the room together and looked at Lily. Olivia leaned over and hugged his sister.

"That's a cute hat."

"Her boyfriend got it for her." Colin couldn't help but laugh as Lily's face turned a soft shade of pink. "Oh, sorry, not her boyfriend. Just her friend that visits every day after school and on the weekends."

Rob smiled. "Sounds like a boyfriend to me."

"Okay, enough embarrassing her," Olivia said. "Why don't you two go get something from the cafeteria. Lily and I need to do some girl talk."

Colin could hear Olivia ask his sister about her "friend" as he left the room. Rob looked at him and smiled. Without saying anything, Colin knew what Rob was thinking.

Colin nudged Rob with his elbow. "You getting cold feet yet? The wedding's only two weeks away. You're going to be a married man."

Rob smiled. "No cold feet. I'm so lucky, man. I still can't believe she said yes."

"Yeah, me either. You're no me or anything."

Rob pretended to punch him like Rocky.

"Hey, you know you would've been my best man. Right?"

"Of course. You asked me, remember? I just can't leave Lily that long."

Rob stopped talking as they turned the corner. A nurse asked who Colin's handsome friend was. Colin told her he was taken already, and she pretended to pout and asked why all the good ones were taken. Colin pretended to be hurt at her insinuation. Rob was quiet. He didn't seem to notice that they were talking about him.

"Hey, you okay?"

"Oh, yeah." Rob suddenly looked like he had come back to earth after a trip to the moon. "So, do you like this kid? ' Cause if you don't, my dad knows a guy."

Colin smiled. Rob loved making corny Mafia-style jokes.

"He's nice. I'm just worried about him getting so attached to Lily."

"Why?"

Colin stopped walking. "Rob, she's not going to make it."

"You can't actually believe that. Didn't you say that the doctor said that last time? They were wrong then; maybe they're wrong now."

Colin nodded. "I've tried to tell myself that, but I know they're right."

"No, you don't—"

"Yes, I do. Rob, I know you're trying to help, but I need to accept this." He sighed. "She's dying, and I need to accept it, or I'll go crazy trying to save her."

"Maybe—"

"No 'maybe.' I can't save her. I've already tried. I've done everything. Now I need to be prepared for what comes next. Please don't try to give me hope. It's easier this way."

"Okay. If that's what you want."

Colin nodded. "It is. Thank you."

"So ... how long, then?"

"A couple months, at best. The less she suffers, the better."

"I'm so sorry, Colin."

Rob's arms wrapped around Colin's shaking shoulders. Suddenly, a woman's voice was coming from the intercom overhead. "Code blue in room 14 ... code blue ..."

"That's Lily's room."

Colin sprinted in the same direction as the nurses. He felt like he was caught in the tide, being drawn in the direction he wanted to go, yet not allowed to swim faster by the pull of some invisible force. As he turned the corner, he could see Olivia pacing outside Lily's room. She intercepted him before he could go in.

"They said we can't be in there."

"I have to—"

Olivia held his arm. "You'll only get in the way."

"What happened?"

"She was laughing, then suddenly her eyes just kind of started to roll backward and her head started to shake. I ran into the hallway and yelled for help, and when I looked back, she looked like she was having a seizure."

A nurse ran out.

"Nurse, is she okay?"

"I don't know yet. I need to get Dr. Long."

Rob ran up. "What happened?"

Colin could hear his heart beating as he watched Dr. Long

run toward Lily's room. It was as if everything was happening in slow motion. Sounds sounded farther away than they really were. As if he were suddenly underwater. His head felt foggy as he stood in the doorway and watched the nurses try to stop Lily's body from shaking.

"This is it," he whispered. "I didn't get to say goodbye."

A tear rolled down his cheek.

Chapter 54: Flower Girl

L ily begged him. "Please let me be the flower girl, Colin."
"Lily, you're not in any condition to leave the hospital."

"Colin, please."

"You just had a seizure." His throat tightened. "I was so scared that I'd lost you."

"But you didn't. I'm still alive."

"Going to a wedding isn't worth risking your life."

"Colin, I'm dying anyway. Can't I do this one last thing?"

"No. I'm sorry."

* * *

Olivia adjusted the wreath on Lily's head. "You look perfect. I'm so glad that dress fits you."

Lily smiled. "No, you look perfect. Rob's going to die when he sees you! It's so romantic. I wish I could ..." Her voice trailed off. She'd started to say she wished she could get married someday, but she stopped herself because this was Olivia's day.

Olivia admired her reflection for a moment. "Thanks. I'm so nervous, but I'm so happy you and Colin could make it."

"He's not happy that I'm not tied down in my hospital bed."

Olivia smiled. "He's just worried about you. He loves you a lot, Lily."

"I know."

"I'm so nervous. Are you ready?"

Lily nodded. "If you are."

"Okay." She pushed the air out of her mouth. "Let's go."

* * *

The music started. One of the bridesmaids walked behind Lily's wheelchair and pushed. Heads turned as the two large doors opened. They went through them slowly enough for Lily to throw the petals as she was pushed forward. The little white petals sprinkled the aisle like snow. Lily smiled as she approached the groom and b est man. In the end, Colin had caved and agreed to be Rob's best man after all. Colin's eyes looked watery, as if he was about to cry. She stuck her tongue out quickly so only he would see, then returned her expression to its previous angelic disposition.

The bridesmaid who had helped Lily stood on the opposite side of the groom's party. Olivia had said she didn't mind breaking tradition for Lily by allowing her to possibly be the oldest flower girl ever. The audience got quiet as the bride entered the room. All eyes watched as Olivia moved down the aisle. Lily glanced at Rob, who was smiling from ear to ear, then at Colin, who glanced back at her and smiled.

Thirty minutes later, the ceremony was over. The newly married couple ran through the showers of flower petals being thrown at them from every direction. Colin approached Lily.

"Have fun?"

"Oh my gosh. Wasn't that so romantic?"

"Yeah, it was."

"I wish I could have a wedding this beautiful."

"Please don't say things like that."

"Sorry."

He exhaled. "Well, I held up my end of the deal. Time for you to hold up yours."

"Colin, do we have to go now? Couldn't we just stay an hour longer?"

"Lily." He sounded serious.

"Fine."

"Hey, aren't you glad you got to come? You made a great flower girl."

"Yeah, I am. Thanks for letting me come."

She felt him push the brake in with his foot. The wheelchair moved forward. "It was worth it to see you look so happy."

"Do you like the wreath Olivia made me?"

"Yeah. You look like an angel." He winked. "Hey, I think your boyfriend is anxious to talk to you. He probably wants to tell you how beautiful you are." Colin changed his voice to a mocking tone. "Lily, you're the most beautiful thirteen-year-old flower girl I've ever seen."

Lily pinched him weakly. He pretended to flinch. She glanced over at Bryce, who was sitting in a chair covered by a yellow silk ribbon, tied like a bow. He did look a little like a lost puppy. Lily waved at Bryce from her wheelchair. He accepted her invitation and made his way over to her. Colin cleared his throat and said he was going to go congratulate Rob.

"Hi," Lily said.

"Hi."

Was he blushing?

"You, uh, you looked beautiful."

275

"It was the makeup. Olivia did it."

"It wasn't the makeup."

Now it was Lily's turn to blush. She said, "Did it look awkward, the flower girl being pushed down the aisle in a wheelchair?"

"Not at all. It was pretty cool, actually."

"Thanks. This was the only wedding I've ever been to, but it's more beautiful than anything I ever imagined. If I ever have a wedding, this is exactly what I would want it to look like." Lily looked around the white tent, covered by thousands of twinkle lights and yellow roses. "Are you okay? You look, I don't know, sad or something. Am I getting too sappy for you?"

He looked at his shoes. "Not at all. I was just thinking—I don't know. You're just such a good person. It's not fair."

"What's not fair?"

"That you are possibly the coolest girl I've ever known, and if anyone ever deserved to have the wedding of their dreams, it's you."

"Thanks. But who said I won't still get to have one?"

"I was just thinking, if we were older—never mind."

"No. Tell me! What were you going to say? You have to tell me now. Bryce. Come on. Tell me."

Bryce laughed. "Fine, but it's going to sound stupid. Do you remember that old movie we watched in Mr. Ward's class about the girl who had cancer? I think Mandy Moore played the girl."

"*A Walk to Remember*?"

"Yeah. I was just thinking … I wish I could do what the boy did in that movie."

Lily's heart stopped and then started again. "You wanna marry me?"

The words came out too loud. Colin glanced over suspiciously. Lily blushed and looked at Bryce, who was bright red too.

276

"Great, now your brother's going to kill me for real."

"Yeah. Rob knows the Mafia."

"He told me."

Lily smiled. "So, you were saying?"

"I'm starting to regret saying anything." He laughed. "Wow, I'm super nervous now. And sweaty."

"That was really sweet of you, but you know, if I live to be twenty, you can't take it back. You're stuck with me now."

"Then I'm even luckier than Rob."

Bryce leaned closer to her and kissed her cheek before she realized what was happening. She could feel her heart run, do a double somersault, a triple backflip, and finally land in a split—a routine that could've won a gold medal in the Olympics.

"What was that?" she asked, still half stunned.

"I don't know. I just wanted you to know I like you."

"I kind of figured that out when you proposed to me."

"You're not going to let me live this down, are you? Well, your brother's staring at me like he's going to murder me and bury my body somewhere in the woods, so I should get going. I'll see you tomorrow after school." He turned to leave.

"Hey, Bryce." He turned back. "I like you too."

Chapter 55: Cards and Flowers

Lily had been asleep more than she'd been awake. Colin hadn't left her side for a week. Dr. Long had said chemo would only drag out the pain Lily was in. The cancer was coming back more aggressively than ever, and this time her body couldn't fight it. It would be any day now.

Visitors had come and gone. Bryce continued to visit after school most days. Even Lily's friend Makayla had stopped by to apologize for the way she'd treated Lily. Before their shifts started every day, Rob and Olivia came to offer their support.

Half the visits Lily couldn't remember, and the other half she'd slept through. Colin showed her the cards and flowers that people had brought. Gifts filled the room from wall to wall. Lily told Colin that her favorite gift was the teddy bear with the message "We hope you feel better" on its belly. He didn't tell her that he was the one who'd gotten it.

Colin stretched and looked at his phone. It was nine in the morning. He stood up and looked at Lily. She looked sound asleep and would probably still be by the time he got back with her muffin.

He had timed how long it took him to get to the cafeteria every morning. His average time was four minutes, sometimes five if more people were in the elevator. He needed to know, in case Lily had an emergency again. Dr. Long had told him that seizures were not uncommon and that he should expect to see more of them as it got closer to the end. Conversations like that felt unreal when they were happening. Usually, the pain would hit in waves, days after the conversation had happened.

Colin realized he was on the elevator as it suddenly stopped, making him hold on to the railing for balance. The doors opened.

"Hey, stranger."

"Emma, how are you?" he asked.

She laughed softly. "Tired. Frustrated. Worried. You?"

"Same. So, your nephew is still here, then?"

She sighed and nodded. The elevator doors closed. He noticed that she didn't press a button. "Are you going to the cafeteria too?"

"Yeah. I needed to get some air."

"Do you want to talk? I was about to get some coffee and could use some air too."

She smiled. "That'd be really nice. Thanks."

He could feel his heart flutter.

A few minutes later, he joined her at one of the tables. She was wiping the crumbs off.

"They probably never wash these."

Colin grabbed a napkin. "Here, let me help."

His hand bumped into hers. "Sorry."

"It's okay. I think it's clean enough now." She smiled and sat down. "How's your sister?"

He shook his head. "Not good."

"Are they giving her anything? My nephew's doing better now that he's getting chemo every week."

"I'm glad he's doing better." He tried to smile. "Umm, to answer your question, there's nothing they can do for her now.

279

So, every day I just wait to get the news that ..." His voice trailed off.

She reached for him and held his hand. "It's okay. You don't have to say it. I'm really sorry."

He stood up. "I'm sorry to leave so soon, but I need to—"

"I know. Go be with her."

He heard her voice as he walked away.

"Colin, wait." She was running after him with something in her hand. A note. "Text or call me, anytime."

"Thanks." He looked at the note she'd handed him. "I will."

Colin stared at the ten numbers scribbled onto a sheet of paper. A number! That was it! He couldn't go back to Dr. Lloyd, but maybe there was someone who could. He'd all but given up hope. And here it was—a sign.

Colin threw his tray into the dirty tray slot and sprinted toward the elevator. The doors were just opening. He broke out into a full sprint. To his surprise, Emma was just now stepping into the same one he was trying to catch. The elevators had probably never been renovated since the hospital had been built, so they were slow and clunky. Emma turned around and looked surprised to see Colin sprinting after her.

"Hold it!"

Emma threw her hand between the closing doors. His momentum was only stopped when he crashed into the back of the elevator. The only other person with them was a terrified-looking woman.

"Sorry, ma'am."

The terrified woman looked at the wallpaper close to her without responding.

"You miss me already?" Emma asked with a mocking tone.

Colin normally would've tried to come up with something

clever to say, but he was distracted from thinking about how to save Lily, again. So instead he said, "No. I just need to talk to Dr. Long." Emma's expression brought him back. "Oh, I didn't mean that I didn't—"

The ding of the elevator, followed by the doors opening, interrupted Colin's thoughts. He'd probably just blown it with the most beautiful girl he'd ever seen, but he couldn't think about that now. He broke into a sprint. "I'll call you, I promise!" he called back without looking to see if she was smiling or giving him the universal sign for "Drop dead, jerk."

Dr. Long was at the nurses' station up ahead. Colin slowed down as he approached the counter. Nurses stared at him. The younger one smiled. The older ones scowled and shook their heads. One of them mumbled something under her breath. It sounded like she'd called him a meathead. She couldn't have been more wrong, if she had.

"Dr. Long. I know how to save Lily."

Dr. Long opened her mouth. She was probably about to say something about there not being a way to save Lily again. It was impossible to know, because Colin cut her off. "Dr. Lloyd," Colin panted between sentences. "He's a cancer researcher." Deep breath. "He made a cure, and it works. I know his number. Don't ask me how. Can you call him? Doctor to doctor?"

Dr. Long batted her black eyelashes, which were probably red underneath the layers of caked-on mascara. She glanced at the nurses watching with wide eyes and dropped jaws. Colin followed her as she walked away from the station.

"Colin, what are you talking about? I'm sorry, but I just don't understand what you're suggesting."

"Dr. Lloyd has the cure. It works. Trust me. We just need to get it. It hasn't been clinically tested yet—that's why I've never asked you before—but maybe Dr. Lloyd will let you give it to Lily as some sort of clinical trial. I'll sign whatever paperwork you need me to sign."

Dr. Long looked stunned, but she quickly recovered. "Colin, I'm very familiar with Dr. Lloyd's work. I've been a fan of his for years. He's the reason I became an oncologist." She seemed to have forgotten what her point was. She slid her glasses into her curls. "Before she passed away, your mother and I talked about putting Lily on the waiting list. I've already placed Lily and Parker, and half the kids here, on a waiting list for Dr. Lloyd's cure. I didn't tell you, because I didn't want to get your hopes up."

"Forget the waiting list. I-I kind of know Dr. Lloyd."

Her eyes popped open, exposing half an inch of white above the green. "You do? But Dr. Lloyd is—"

Colin hardly heard her speaking. "Well, 'know' is the wrong word. I've met him, and I think he would give you the cure if you explained—"

"Colin, Dr. Lloyd is dead."

* * *

Lily was awake when he returned to her room. She smiled when she saw the brown bag in his hand.

"Is that what I think it is?" she asked with slurred speech.

Colin nodded as he handed her the brown paper bag. Her hands trembled as she pulled the blueberry muffin out. It felt like tiny needles were poking his eyes as he fought back the tears. His last chance of saving her was gone. Why hadn't he gone back sooner?

She struggled as she took a bite out of the muffin, stealing

Colin's attention back.

"Do you need help breaking it up into small enough pieces?"

"No thanks," she said, with a small piece of muffin stuffed in her cheek. "Hey, Colin?"

"Yeah." His voice was weak.

"I was thinking about those dandelions Mom used to pick out of our yard. When I was little, I used to cry whenever the little fluffy seeds blew away in the wind. Then one day, to make me feel better, she told me that one dandelion could make four hundred other dandelions. So I didn't need to be sad about the one."

"Yeah. She hated those dandelions." He smiled as he remembered fondly. "What made you think of that?"

She licked her cracked lips. They were testament to how hard her body was fighting to go on. Colin spoke before she could answer. "I think you wore yourself out trying to talk. Just rest. You can answer me later."

She shook her head, determined to answer him. When she opened her mouth, her lips peeled away from each other like they were being unzipped. Colin's stomach twisted tighter. It looked painful.

"I was just thinking about how I might be kind of like a dandelion too." She licked her bottom lip again. "You know, because of the cure you gave me, and ..."

Colin's phone started to ring before she could finish. "Hold on, Lily. It's Dad." He answered the incoming call. "Hello?"

He smiled at Lily while their dad talked on the other end of the line. "Yeah, she's right here. Let me ask her."

Colin cupped his hand over the phone and whispered to her. "It's Dad. He wants to say something to you. Are you up to talking?"

She nodded. "Can you give me some water?"

Colin helped support the back of her head with his hand as she took a sip of water. He swiped his finger over the screen to put it on speakerphone so Lily could hear too.

"Go ahead, Dad. You're on speakerphone. She can hear you."

"Hi, Dad," Lily managed to say.

"Hey, sweetie."

Colin let her head rest on the pillow again.

"I'm planning on visiting you this afternoon, after I make a quick stop somewhere. So you get plenty of rest before I come. Okay?"

She grunted.

"She's nodding, Dad," Colin said for her.

"I love you, sweetie."

Lily smiled as if to say, *Love you too*.

"She loves you too."

"If your mom was alive, she would say the same."

Lily smiled.

Colin pulled the phone away from her ear. She closed her eyes. Colin watched her drift back to sleep. He pulled the covers over her bony shoulders. Her skin felt cold.

"Lily?"

The monitor beside the bed showed her heart rate slowing down. It dropped steadily until the alarm on the monitor started to go off. Colin yelled for help. Nurses flooded the room. His heart raced as they pushed him out of the room. A nurse pushed a crash cart with paddles on it into her room. One nurse yelled: "Clear!"

Chapter 56: An Unwelcome Guest

Thomas looked around again. There was only one car in the long driveway, a well-cared-for Monte Carlo. The lawn was well manicured. Somebody had to still live here, but the house was silent. Maybe the doctor wasn't home. He needed to be back at the rehab within an hour if he didn't want to be kicked out of the program. He pushed the doorbell in for the fourth time. The bells chimed melodically. If someone didn't answer, he'd give up.

He'd turned to leave when he heard someone yell through the solid oak door. The voice sounded like it belonged to an older woman.

"What do you want?" she asked.

"I'm looking for a Dr. Lloyd. Does he live here?"

"I've already called the police. They'll be here any minute."

"I'm not breaking any laws by standing on your porch. I just wanted to ask Dr. Lloyd a few questions."

"I know my rights. You and the rest of those reporters can go to—"

"Reporters? I'm not a reporter. My name is Thomas Durnin. You can call the police if you want, but my daughter is dying because of a medicine that Dr. Lloyd gave her before it'd been FDA approved. So either Dr. Lloyd can come out here and talk to me, or I'll call the cops myself and have him arrested for a felony."

He couldn't hear anything through the door. Suddenly, the door opened. An old woman stood in the doorway glaring at him. "How dare you. How dare you accuse my late husband—wait. You're that punk from that night! How dare you come back here after what you did?"

Thomas stepped back. "I'm sorry, you must have me confused with someone else. I have no idea what you're talking about."

"You have some nerve showing up here, you know that?"

"Ma'am, I'm sure you have me confused with someone else."

She stepped toward him so that one of her feet was in the house and the other was on the porch. "I told Harold we needed better security, but did he listen to me? Nooo. Then you show up, waving your gun at my husband, threatening to shoot him if he didn't give you the cure." She pointed her finger at Tom's chest. "Now you have the nerve to show up here and threaten to call the police on me? How dare you!"

Thomas was speechless. This woman was crazier than a bag of cats. "I'm very sorry about what happened to you. But you have me mistaken for—"

"I saw you with my own eyes, pointing that gun at my husband. Did you come back to kill me too? Go ahead! I have nothing to lose anymore."

"Ma'am, slow down. Did someone kill your husband? Did you tell the police?"

"Don't play dumb with me. First you rob my husband at gunpoint; then my husband goes missing a week later, and they find him dead in his car on the side of the road. Now you're here to finish the job. Go ahead and kill me. I have nothing to lose anymore."

Thomas looked into her sad eyes. "I'm sorry about what happened to your husband. I hope whoever did that to him gets what they deserve. I wouldn't have come here if I'd known it was going to upset you. I was just trying to save my daughter."

She studied him. Suddenly she gasped and covered her mouth with her wrinkled hand. "I don't have my glasses on—forgive me. You look just like the man who robbed my husband, only he was much younger than you."

A horrible thought crossed Thomas's mind. He dismissed it. There was no way his son could've ...

"It's okay. You're just upset, and you have every right to be. I'm sorry my appearance brought back such bad memories for you."

"Did you say that my husband gave your daughter the medicine?"

"Don't worry about what I said earlier. I'm sorry for upsetting you."

"Harold said that the cure wasn't ready to be tested on humans. I can't imagine he would've given it to your daughter before ..." She sighed. "Was your daughter one of my husband's patients?"

"No, ma'am. I'm not sure exactly how my daughter came in contact with the cure. I was ... on a trip when she received it."

"What symptoms is she experiencing?"

Thomas told her about Lily's condition, her symptoms. He couldn't understand why she looked so calm suddenly.

"The research was stopped when my husband passed, but his apprentice has been trying to continue his legacy ever since. It would be a stretch, but maybe he could look at her. Where is your daughter staying?"

"The HGCH, the oncology division. Her name is Lily Durnin."

After he gave Mrs. Lloyd his contact information to give to

Dr. Lloyd's old apprentice, he thanked her and said goodbye. Thomas got back in his truck and put it in reverse. He'd be at the hospital in twenty or so minutes and would tell Colin and Lily the good news in person.

Chapter 57: Late

D r. Long looked tired. "Colin—"

Tears flooded his eyes. "No. I'm not ready. I'm not ready to hear it. She can't—please tell me she's okay. Please ... don't say it."

"Colin, she didn't make it. I'm sorry."

He fell to his knees. "No, no, no, no, no," he sobbed. "I didn't get to say goodbye. This is all my fault."

"This is nobody's fault. I'm sorry I couldn't save your sister."

Colin could feel the words creeping up his throat. "Dr. Long, I-I," he said, his throat croaking. "I gave her the cure. And it worked! But I didn't go back. I-I didn't go—"

Dr. Long pressed her eyebrows together, but she couldn't say anything before Colin began to sob again.

"Colin, would you like to say goodbye to her before they move her body downstairs?"

She'd asked it as if she hadn't heard what he'd just told her. His heart stopped. Her "body." She was no longer a person. Only a body. He stood up despite his legs trembling underneath him. They walked to her room together.

Before they'd made it to the door, he stopped. He held on to the wall to stop himself from collapsing again. Dr. Long came over and wrapped her arm around him to help him stand.

"I can't do this. I can't see her like ... like this. I can't."

"It's okay. You don't have to."

He nodded. "Yes, I do. I need to say goodbye. I just ... can't."

"Honey, take all the time you need. I'm not going anywhere."

"Dr. Long, I—she was—"

Dr. Long pulled him to her. "Come here, sweetie. You don't have to say anything. Just cry ... that's it. You'll be okay. I promise the pain will not always feel like this."

"It hurts ... so bad," he sobbed.

* * *

His eyes were puffy and sore from crying for the last ten minutes. He walked into the room. Her body was covered with a sheet. Dr. Long walked over to her bed and pulled the sheet down so he could see only Lily's face.

"She looks cold."

Dr. Long nodded and smiled sympathetically.

"Did she suffer?"

"No."

"How do you know?"

"She had already passed away when we tried to resuscitate her. She didn't feel anything."

"So, I was with her when it happened?"

"Yes. You were the last face she saw." She paused. "And I believe she died in peace because of that."

Colin approached the bed slowly. He placed his hand on her beanie. It was still warm. His heart ached.

"I'm going to give you some privacy, but I'll be right outside the door if you need me."

Colin heard the door close as Dr. Long left the room. He stared at his little sister's face. It looked like she was dreaming. He watched to see if she was breathing. He exhaled.

"Lily, I don't know …" He sniffled and added, "We didn't get to say goodbye, but I'm glad …" He inhaled. "I'm glad you didn't suffer."

He rubbed his finger over her cold face. "You were the best little sister I could've asked for." His voice trembled. "I'm sorry that I couldn't protect you from everything. I'm sorry you lost Mom. I'm sorry that Dad left you here. I'm sorry that the cure didn't work." His knees felt like they would buckle. "I tried to save you. I hope you knew that."

He leaned over and kissed her forehead. "I love you, Lily."

He could hear someone's footsteps walking up behind him. He turned around to see if it was the people there to take Lily's body. It was his dad, standing frozen in the doorway. He was too late.

Chapter 58: The Donation

L ike their mother's funeral, Lily's was small. They'd only invited seven people to the house to remember her. After a few hours, everyone had shared their memories of Lily and had given their condolences. Rob and Olivia hugged Colin and said goodbye. Al followed behind them. Even their crazy neighbor, Red Robin, had managed to not overstay her welcome. One by one they'd left until only Dr. Long and Bryce were remaining. Dr. Long told Colin to rest while she cleaned up everything. Colin sat on the couch and looked at the small picture of Lily on the front of the double-sided card that summed up Lily's life in less than two hundred words. The picture had been taken the day at the park, when it had all started. She was smiling at the top of the slide. She had two perfect dimples on both cheeks. His mother had taken the picture right before she'd slid down. How could that perfect little girl in the picture be gone now?

"I'm really sorry about your sister."

Colin wiped his eyes and looked up. It was Bryce.

"I'm going to miss her a lot. She was really special, you know."

"Yeah, I know she was." Colin smiled.

Bryce held out the small bag in his hand. It looked familiar. "I wanted to give you something. It's a painting Lily made. She said I could keep it, but I think you should have it."

Colin looked at the painting, of his mother. "It's beautiful."

"Yeah. That's what I told her, but she didn't believe me."

Colin smiled. "Sounds like Lily."

He studied the painting. It was hard to believe his mother and now Lily were gone.

"My parents are outside waiting for me. Thanks for inviting me."

"Hey, Bryce." Bryce looked back. "Your friendship meant a lot to Lily."

Bryce smiled and turned again.

After Bryce had left, Dr. Long came over and said goodbye to Colin too. His dad sat down on the couch and put his hand on Colin's shoulder. They were the only ones left. The house looked the same as it always had, when his mother was alive, when Lily was alive. It was only quieter now.

"How you holding up?"

"Not too well."

"Me either. It's too quiet now ... Colin, listen, I know I wasn't there for you like I should've been when your mom died. But I'm here for you this time, and I'm not going anywhere." He squeezed Colin's shoulder. "And I'm sorry. For everything."

"Lily already forgave you, and so did I."

"I meant for not being there to say goodbye to her."

"That wasn't your fault. You got to the hospital as fast as you could."

His dad followed him as he walked to the kitchen to get some water.

"Well, I would've been to the hospital sooner if I hadn't stopped at Dr. Lloyd's house." Colin's heart stopped. "I put the pieces together after you and Lily visited me at the rehab that day. It was obvious that your lead was Dr. Lloyd. What I couldn't understand is why a doctor would just hand over a medication that hadn't been approved by the FDA."

Colin turned off the faucet and looked at his dad, wide-eyed. "You went to Dr. Lloyd's house? Was he there?"

"No, but his wife was, and she told me that Dr. Lloyd passed away."

"When?"

"Not long after you robbed him at gunpoint."

Colin almost dropped his glass of water. "Dad—I—"

"You could've gotten hurt. What if they'd shot you? This is the South, where everyone and their uncles have guns. What were you thinking, trying to rob someone?"

"I know. I was stupid."

"Yes. You were stupid, but I know you were just trying to save your sister. Love will make you do stupid things. Don't misunderstand what I'm trying to say, though—I don't condone what you did, but I understand why you did it." He patted Colin's shoulder. "At least tell me you didn't use a loaded gun."

"I didn't. It was a bluff." Colin could picture that night like he was there again, holding the gun to that old man's chest. How could he have done something like that? And why hadn't he just gotten more medicine while he was already there? He'd already committed the crime. The tears started to sting his eyes like needles. "It's my fault she died. I didn't know how to give her the medicine, or how much—and I didn't go back in time. I was just too afraid."

His dad pulled him in and held him like he was a child again. "Colin, listen to me. Lily's death was not your fault. You were trying to save her. Only love could make a nice kid like you do something so out of character. And you didn't go back because

294

you had a conscience—that's a good thing. You'll have to forgive yourself. It's not going to be easy, trust me, but you have to remember that you did what you thought was best for her. You have to let go of that guilt, or it'll eat away at you until there's nothing left."

Colin sobbed into his dad's shoulder. His dad was right, but it wasn't going to be easy.

Chapter 59: The Trial

P arker knew it was Dr. Long by her footsteps. She walked around the bed and smiled at him. Parker's mom sat up on the couch.

"Hi, Dr. Long." His mom rubbed her eyes. "I was just closing my eyes for a moment."

"Mrs. Bryan, I'm sorry to wake you up, but I have very good news." Dr. Long smiled. "Parker, don't try to lift your head."

Parker rested his head obediently and smiled at her.

"I was just informed—" She looked up and blinked. "I'm sorry for being so emotional. I was just informed that there's a—"

She sniffled and wiped her eyes. Parker watched her closely. He'd never seen her cry before.

"I'm sorry." She sniffled. "There's a cure, Parker. They found a cure for cancer."

Parker felt a spark of hope inside.

His mom held her hand over her mouth. "Wh-when can we get it? Is it available now?"

"They've started clinical trials, and as of now, the cure has worked on five patients."

His mom shook her head. "So, wait, it's not available yet?"

"When I heard about the trial, I submitted an application for Parker. I didn't want to tell you unless he was approved."

"Was he?"

Dr. Long nodded. "Parker has been approved to join the clinical trial ... if you're okay with it, Mrs. Bryan."

"Can I take some time to think about it?"

"Of course."

Chapter 60: Full Circle

The park hadn't changed a bit over the last eight years—except for a new merry-go-round. Colin closed his eyes and felt the cool breeze across his skin. He crossed his arms over his broad chest and smiled. The March sun disappeared behind a cloud for a moment, making it feel cold suddenly. He shivered. Then it reappeared. He let his mind travel back in time and imagined Lily laughing as she slid down the slide. He could see his mother's face smiling at him as she tried to extract details about his life. She looked young and beautiful with her wavy blonde hair, blue eyes, larger-than-life smile. Then he saw Lily's face, a younger version of their mother's. She hadn't lost her hair yet. It was long and hung straight down her back.

Footsteps approached. He wished he could open his eyes and see Lily and his mom walking up, but he knew if he opened them the memory would disappear.

"Colin? Are you okay?" his wife asked.

He opened his eyes, the memory gone. Emma was standing in front of him with a concerned look. He patted his hand on the cold bench, inviting her to sit next to him, which she did. Emma stared at him with the sweetest look. He uncrossed his arms and held her hand.

"I was just remembering the last time I was at this park. I was so upset, for one stupid reason or another. It was cold, if I remember right. Lily was so stinking excited to go down the slide. I just thought to myself, 'Why is she still enjoying slides when she's almost twelve years old?' I was being such a jerk. We found out she was sick that day, you know?" Colin laughed and shook his head. "God, I felt so guilty at the hospital that night."

Emma rubbed her hands over his to warm them and listened.

"She looked so scared—so did my mom, which really freaked me out. It was the scariest moment of my life up to that point."

"Yeah, I bet."

"You've heard this story a million times, probably. I'm sorry."

"Don't be. I enjoy hearing stories about her. I wish I could've gotten to know her."

"You would've loved her."

She kissed his cheek. "Of course I would've."

"I still don't know if I'll ever be able to forgive myself for what happened."

"You were trying to save her! What you did gave her more than five months."

"I know."

"The cure has saved my nephew's life already, and it's going to save millions of other people's lives when they finish the clinical trials." Colin nodded. He knew Emma was right, but it didn't change the fact that Lily was gone. Emma nudged his arm. "Here comes trouble."

"Dad, come on!" their daughter demanded. She dragged Colin's dad behind her. "Grandpa said he's tired and needs a break."

His dad winked. "I'm an old man now, Colin. This outdoor stuff is for the birds."

Colin stood up. "Here, take my seat, Dad."

His phone buzzed in his pocket. He looked at the number on his phone screen. "Give me one second, Lillian." Colin answered it. "Hello? Yes, this is. Can I help you? ... Yeah, of course I remember you. How are you? ... That's awesome; I'm happy for you ... What'd you say it's called? ... You mean Dr. Lloyd? ... When did you see that on the news? ... Thank you for calling. It was good to hear from you, Parker."

Lillian stared up at him with her big blue eyes as he hung up the phone. "Who's Parker?"

Colin kissed his daughter. "Your aunt Lily's old friend. You ready for the big slide?"

Emma winked at Colin. "Have fun."

She turned back and started talking to Colin's dad again. Their voices faded as they walked toward the slides.

"Mommy said I was ready to go on the big slide today."

"Really? That was your aunt Lily's favorite slide, you know."

"Was she scared when she went on it?"

"Of course she was scared, but she tried it and found out she loved it. After that, we couldn't get her to stop going on it."

"I'm going to be like Aunt Lily, then." Lillian dashed up to the top of the slide. "You ready, Dad?"

He looked at the small girl with blonde hair and blue eyes. She looked just like Lily did at that age. It was as if he'd stepped into a time machine and gone back to eight years ago. Lillian squealed at the top of the slide and clapped her hands. He smiled and held his arms out at the bottom of the slide. Lillian pushed off the sides and slid down into his arms. He picked her up and twirled her around.

"Good job, sweetie!"

They walked back to the bench where Emma and his father

were sitting and watching. They clapped and cheered for Lillian as she ran toward them, showing off her two missing teeth as she laughed giddily.

Colin sat on the bench on the other side of his wife while Lillian told her grandfather about the big slide. Emma looked at him and smiled.

"You look happier. What was that phone call about?"

Colin smiled and felt tears come to his eyes. "One of Lily's old friends just called to tell me that the clinical trials are over. He said they were talking about it on the news this morning. They predict that it's going to eliminate cancer completely."

Emma's eyes lit up. "That's amazing, baby! Oh my gosh, I need to call my sister and tell her the good news!"

Colin spoke quietly, more to himself than to his wife. "They named it Lily's Cure."

She reached for his hand and held it. "That's the perfect name."

Lillian tugged at her mom's hand. "Come on, Mommy!"

Emma laughed. "I'm being summoned."

Colin slid down the bench to be next to his dad once Emma and Lillian were gone. As he relayed the news, his dad placed his face in his hands and began to cry. Colin wrapped his arm around his dad like he had with his mom eight years prior. "Thank you," was all his dad said. Then they sat together silently and watched Lillian. Colin knew what his dad was thinking, because he was thinking the same thing.

Colin spotted a lone dandelion in the grass below him. He picked it and wrapped it gently in his palm to protect it from the wind.

"You know, Dad, I think Lily somehow knew this was going to happen." His dad looked surprised and listened. "Right before she passed away, she said something about a dandelion. I didn't know what she was talking about then, but I think she was talking about this. I think she knew her death was going to save lives. She told me this story about how she used to be sad when the dandelions died, until she found out they made more dandelions. I think she was trying to tell me not to be sad."

His dad smiled and looked at the dandelion in Colin's hand.

Colin opened his hand and watched the wind carry the fluffy white seeds on its wings.

"Goodbye, Lily."

Deleted Chapters

The cure The doctor squinted into the small hole the microscope provided.

"Come look at this Greg."

"What it is Dr. Loyd?"

"My old eyes can't see a thing. It's the sample from subject RT440."

"You mean Mickey?"

The doctor shook his head. "What have I told you about naming the mice?"

"Not to." Greg leaned in closer to the microscope. "That's interesting."

"What is interesting? Speak up. My old ears can't hear a thing."

"There are no abnormal cells."

"Are you sure?" He squinted. "I'm...sure."

Dr. Loyd removed his glasses and looked at Greg. He shook his assistant's shoulder. "It worked! By golly. It worked."

"Congratulations doc you did it." He paused. "Does this mean we can move on to clinical trials?" "We need to check the other subjects first. But it'll be very soon now."

"What about the lawsuit?"

Dr. Loyd picked up RT441 from the cage. The needle drew blood as he held the squirming creature still. "Let's hope we don't lose. Those hippies really believe a they are saving the world by saving a few rats. We are on the verge of curing a disease that wipes out billions of human lives. I'm sure the judge will see which is more important."

Greg walked over to the window and peeked out thru the blinds. "They're growing in numbers." "Our security can handle a few picketers."

Greg frowned. "I received a death threat yesterday."

Dr. Loyd laughed. "Your first death threat. Welcome to the club."

Greg sighed. "Doctors are rats. Let's experiment on you."

"What?"

"It's what the sign says. Kind of clever."

"Come help with this. And buck up. We just cured cancer."

Dr. Loyd lowered RT441, Minnie, back into the cage. Greg took the syringe from his boss. Dr. Loyd watched as his assistant carefully pressed and smeared the blood to stop it from coagulating. Greg was finally getting the hang of it. He walked to the window and bent one of the blinds. He scoffed and walked back to the cages.

"You guys don't mind being here do you? It's a lot better than having to survive in the real world. You have it good."

"You're an exceptionally nice captor Dr. Loyd. If I do say so myself."

Dr. Loyd ignored his assistant's comment. He reached for RT460. He started the recorder, and spoke into it.

"The immune cell could not recognize the intrusion of the malignant cell due to the process in which the cancer cell disguised itself as harmless. In addition to the cancer cell escaping the immune cell's detection, they also rendered the immune cell useless. While the ultimate goal was to rewrite the cell's 'escape phase' of a potentially malignant cell, a more immediate solution would be to re-active the immune cell, and alert it to the mutant cancer cell. The cure, or APX247, was designed to pervade the cancer cell with cytokine antibodies, giving them a shuttle in a sense to be immediately absorbed by all mutant cells, and alert the immune cell to its existence. The immune cell will theoretically alert the body to the intrusion and attack the cancer cell. The host's body would release hormones such as cortisol, HGH, as well as a number of other defenses. Subject RT460 received the first application of APX247 on Tuesday, 15:03, 17th of May, 2028." His thoughts were interrupted by something loud outside. He scowled at Greg. "Who gave those lunatics a megaphone?"

"At least my tombstone will read, 'He died for a good cause.'"

"Stop being dramatic Greg. Those people wouldn't hurt a fly. Their protesters. It's the silent ones you've got to worry about."

"Sir?"

"The corporations. The ones with the money. They can off you and make it look like an accident. If you're going to worry about something, worry about them bugging our homes or rigging an IED to your car."

Greg let out a chuckle. "How do you know the word IED?"

"Like I said, welcome to the club."

Interview With the Author

1. A short summary of the whole story in 10 sentences max. We will be reading the book when you send it to us however this will enable us to understand what is really important for the Author herself.

Lily Durnin is a shy pre-teen who is (in her brother, Colin's, opinion) too naive for her age. The story begins one weekend at the park, where all is well, until Lily ends up being carted off by an ambulance. When her family receives news that Lily is sick, they find out quickly that Lily isn't the only one affected by her illness. When Lily needs her parents most, they can't seem to get on the same page. After tragedy strikes the family once again, they find themselves picking up the pieces of their lives. Only, not everyone seems to be able to get it together. At school, things aren't any better for Lily than they are at home though. However, not all hope is lost for the Durnins. The story is about hope, love, and forgiveness. Along a bumpy road, the Durnins find friendship, romance, and maybe even a cure.

2. Write 3 keywords that you want readers to remember when they finish reading the book.

   Forgiveness. Love. Family.

3. Write 3 key events from the book that you want readers to remember when they finish reading the book.

I want them to remember the way Parker and Bryce treated Lily when she was alone and afraid. People sometimes see that someone needs a friend, but they're too afraid to step up and be that friend. I also want readers to remember the forgiveness Colin and Lily showed throughout the book. So many times, we hold on to grudges, thinking that it hurts the person that hurt us. But it doesn't. Grudges are like putting poison in your cup, and thinking it'll kill the other person. And lastly, I want readers to remember the way Lily was affected by Makayla. Bullying can make us feel powerful, but it doesn't actually make us powerful. It makes us weak. Putting ourselves in someone else's shoes is sometimes enough to make us stop and rethink our actions.

4. Please write a short brief about yourself because we also would like to publish some information about you.

When I was fourteen, my parents decided we were going to move from California to Virginia. I was terrified and upset. When I first started going to a new school, I didn't understand people's accents, and I felt out of place. People made fun of me because I was from California, and made a lot of assumptions about me—like that I would enjoy surfing and know famous people. Neither of those assumptions were true. Then, at sixteen my mother was diagnosed with carcinoid cancer. The doctor's said she would die in six months. Instead of spending quality time with her, I rebelled and fought with her constantly. Looking back, I realize why I did it. I was afraid of losing her, and figured it would be easier if I was too mad at her to care. But I was wrong. Meanwhile, my father struggled with addictions, and I wasn't sure what would happen to me if my mom did die. However, my mother is still alive and well, thankfully. Those experiences taught me a lot though.

Interview by LionClaw Book Club

About the Author

About the Author

   Laurinda Ruby lives in Georgia with her husband and two German shepherds. She enjoys outdoors activities, reading good books, and any form of art that she can find. She works part-time as a personal trainer as well as a dog-sitter. She found that she enjoyed writing as a way to express herself after her father passed away. *Lily's Cure* is her first novel. She is currently working on her next one.

You can connect with me on:

🌐 https://laurindaruby.com
🅕 https://www.facebook.com/booksbylaurinda

Also by Laurinda Ruby

In addition to a couple of children's books, my most recent work has focused around thrillers and rom coms. Here are two of my favorites!

The Descendants: Book One of Thriller Series
Julie thought found her prince charming when she met Peter. This prince is a little too charming. Will Julie discover the dark secret about her family before it's too late?

Out Of The Woods: Thriller Anthology
Three stories. Three girls desperate to survive.

Vanishing Minds. Face To Face. The Descendants. Just when you think it's over, it's just starting.